THE
WATCHER
GIRL

OTHER TITLES BY MINKA KENT

THE WATCHER GIRL

MINKA KENT

Published by Thomas & Mercer, Seattle

www.apub.com

Amazon, the Amazon logo, and Thomas & Mercer are trademarks of Amazon.com, Inc., or its affiliates.

ISBN-13: 9781542026789
ISBN-10: 1542026784

Cover design by Shasti O'Leary Soudant

Printed in the United States of America

In memory of Jennifer Jaynes

CHAPTER 1

I shouldn't be here.

The swell of nausea in my middle intensifies with every step toward the front door of my childhood home. When the taxi disappears from view, I tell myself there's no turning back. And then I remind myself this isn't about me.

I park my suitcase at the welcome mat, clear my throat, and wait for my father to answer the door.

A moment later, heavy footsteps are followed by the rasp of a deadbolt and the swing of the heavy door I used to run through a lifetime ago.

"Grace?" His tortoiseshell glasses are crooked on his nose, and his salt-and-pepper hair is tousled on one side. Safe to bet I woke him from a nap. Judging by his white cotton-poly pants and olive-green golf polo, it's also safe to bet he played a round this morning. "What are you doing here?"

My mother's peonies bow in the early June breeze, their frilly heads blooming with resilience despite my mother's twenty-years-and-counting prison sabbatical. The lush Kentucky bluegrass is edged to meticulous perfection along the double-wide sidewalk. The elms are taller than I remember, naturally, but their canopy of shade still extends across the driveway, painting my father's vintage Porsche a darker shade of platinum.

I should have called—but I talked myself out of it a dozen times, knowing he'd have questions I wouldn't be able to answer without changing my mind about coming here. Buying a nonrefundable airline ticket and shoving my things into a suitcase seemed like the path of least resistance in this scenario.

"Surprise . . ." I force a smile and splay my hands, a cheap attempt to make this exchange as lighthearted as possible.

His narrowed gaze eases, and the lines on his tanned forehead fade as the corners of his mouth curl one by one.

My father has an impressive knack for acting like nothing happened. It's an art form, really. The man is bulletproof. Scandal and misfortune have a tendency to ricochet off him and hit the innocent bystanders instead.

And he just . . . carries on.

He *always* carries on.

Sometimes I wonder how the man views himself when he looks in the mirror—truly views himself. What does he see when he strips back that perfect, persevering outer layer? Does he see a man who failed his wife and family by chasing after a younger woman? A man whose infidelity ultimately cost that young woman her life? A man whose ex-wife rots away in a prison cell an hour from here all because he couldn't keep his dick in his pants?

Something tells me he sees none of that.

His ego won't let him.

"Was hoping it'd be okay if I crashed here for a bit?" My palm dampens against the purse strap digging into my shoulder. I relax my gaze, tamping down the disgust that always forces its way to the surface anytime I hear his voice or find myself unavoidably in his presence.

"I just . . . you never . . . this is . . ." His expression morphs from wrinkled to relaxed and back. Despite everything we've been through, his softness for me has never wavered. I both love and hate him for this, but now is not the time to litigate old memories. "Of course you can stay here. Forgive me, Grace. It's been so long . . . You're the last person I was expecting . . . but yes, please stay. We'd love to have you."

We.

He and his girlfriend, *Bliss.*

I know all about her despite our never having met—what I didn't know, however, was that she'd moved in.

My father reaches across the threshold to take my luggage, and I follow him in.

The house no longer smells of my mother's ostentatious floral arrangements. Nor does it retain a hint of her French perfume that used to leave invisible trails from room to room, since she could never sit still for more than thirty seconds.

My lungs fill with a cocktail of scents that represent someone else's life.

Lemon dusting cleaner.

A hint of lavender.

An unexpected trace of sandalwood.

Leather dress shoes.

Stale air.

Vintage rugs.

Time.

I think of my mother now, confined to a cinder block cell with a roommate named Angel. There are no flowers to arrange. No windows to open when she craves fragrant petrichor after a hard rain. There are no children to chase after. No mile-long grocery lists or elaborate dinners to make. No company to entertain. No designer-filled closets to organize or dry cleaning to grab between school runs. No coffee shop stops. No neighborhood gossip to secretly enjoy. No summer afternoons lazing by the backyard pool, hardback bestseller in hand.

No handsome, philandering husband to kiss her good night . . .

I imagine her lying on the bottom bunk, reading one of the many used books my sister, Rose, sends to her, her silky blonde strands now gray streaked and straw-like. Her skin paper thin. Her eyebrows finger plucked to nothing. At least that's how she appeared the last time I saw her, ten years ago. The only reason I visited was to confront her about a true crime novel called *Domestic Illusions: The Daphne McMullen Story*.

While my mother's murder conviction legally prohibited her from profiting off her crime or the death of Marnie Gotlieb in any way, it didn't stop *Chicago Post* bestselling author Dianna Hilliard from taking a stab at it. She even had the audacity to dedicate it to my brother, my sister, and me.

We'd never met the woman a day in our lives.

The finished product painted my mother as a saint—a slave to her beautiful, privileged life. And it smeared my father as a sex-addicted narcissist. After tearing through paragraph after paragraph of family details only my mother could have provided, I was forced to pause our estrangement so I could share my disgust with her in person.

She sold us out.

My father may be a self-serving man with severe codependency issues—but he's no murderer. Graham McMullen's hardly a saint, but he'd never throw us under the bus.

Not like that.

"So . . . what brings you here?" His tone is pleasant, but his eyes squint as he studies me in the blue-green twilight of early evening.

The truth is complicated.

"Been gone long enough," I say on a long exhale. "Thought maybe it was time to come home."

Home.

I use the word for his sake. It makes him smile.

While I resided at 372 Magnolia Drive the first ten years of my life, calling it "home" would be a stretch at this point.

His dark eyes turn glassy, and his fingertips twitch at his sides. He wants to hug me, I'm sure, but he knows me too well. At least that part of me.

"Your room's exactly how you left it," he says instead of asking more questions. I imagine he'll space them out, fishing casually for tidbits until he has the whole picture. An investigational paint-by-numbers. "Good to have you back, Grace. I mean that. Stay as long as you need. We'll catch up whenever you're ready."

I thank him before grabbing my roller bag and climbing the winding staircase in the sweeping foyer. Every step rustles an unsettled sensation in my center, but I force it down with tight swallows.

I'm here on a mission, and as soon as it's over, I'm leaving again.

Stopping at the top of the stairs, I'm greeted by an outdated family portrait—the original McMullens dressed in coordinating navy-blue outfits, the children hand in hand, grinning against the autumnal backdrop of some local state park.

There we are.

Frozen in time.

Blissfully unaware of fate's cruel plans for us.

We were beautiful together—enviably happy from the outside.

Hashtag blessed.

My attention homes in on my parents, the way my mother gazes up into my father's handsome face, her golden hair shining in the early evening sunset, his hand cupping the side of her cheek. If I didn't know better, I'd think their love for one another was equal and balanced.

I trace my fingertips against the burnished-gold frame before pressing it just enough that it tilts, off-center. Noticeable only if you stare too long.

I have no desire to rewrite history, and I have little patience for those who feel the need to do so.

When I reach my old room, I flick on the light and plant myself in the doorway.

My father's right. It's exactly how I left it: Dark furniture. Blue walls. Pile of stuffed animals in the corner. Perfectly made bed complete with an ironed coverlet and a million pillows.

Aside from the fresh vacuum tracks in the carpet, no one's set foot in this room since the last time I was home my senior year of college.

I lock the door and collapse on the bed, digging my phone from my bag and pulling up the Instaface account for my ex from college and staring at his profile picture for the tenth time today—the hundredth time this week. Same coffee-brown hair trimmed neatly into a timeless crew cut. Same hooded eyes the earthy color of New England in autumn. Same dimples flanking his boyish smile like parentheses. He's exactly how I remember him, only with a decade of life tacked onto his face. Shallow creases spread across his forehead. A deep line separates his eyebrows. Maybe there's a little more hollowing beneath his jovial gaze. But other than that, he's the same as I remember.

I could describe Sutton Whitlock fifty thousand ways, but at the end of the day, I can sum him up in five words: he was a good man.

Eight years ago, I broke his heart—and not because I wanted to.

I had to save him from a lifetime of disappointment.

I had to save him from me.

But a handful of things have come up online recently—things that indicate he's not okay.

I need to rectify what I've done. I need to apologize for hurting him. Explain my reasons. Give him permission to move on, to be happy.

And then I'll disappear . . . again.

CHAPTER 2

So this is how we meet.

I amble into the kitchen at a quarter past six the next morning to find my father's girlfriend frying eggs, her back to me as she tends to the skillet. I wanted to grab a cup of coffee before my shower, but that requires riffling through cupboards to locate mugs and coffee pods. And now that *she's* here, I'm reminded of my guest status, and rummaging feels wrong.

Cracked brown shells rest in the sink. Unsanitary. My mother never would have done that. They'd have gone straight to the garbage.

I clear my throat and plant myself behind the island, fingertips curled around the marble edge.

Nothing.

Maybe she can't hear me over the sizzle of eggs?

My father shuffles from room to room above us. I guess he doesn't sleep in on the weekends anymore.

I clear my throat—louder this time—as Bliss turns from the stove to grab a plate from the cupboard to her right. She's lanky but in a feminine sort of way, the fabric of her Bandhani-print robe clinging equally from the protrusion of her bony shoulders to the nipping of her waist to the subtle rounding of her hips.

Her eyes widen, her lips curl, and she clutches her paper-thin lapels. "My goodness. Didn't see you there."

Bliss pops two white earbuds from her ears and approaches me without a hint of reluctance.

"I'm Bliss." She extends a manicured hand and offers a disarming smile. Her eyes are small but pretty, the darkest ocean blue and set deep behind a fringe of thick lashes. Her features are angled, German perhaps, a contrast against the silky-soft blonde hair piled on the top of her oblong head. Dare I say, she'd give my mother a run for her money in the looks department. But knowing my father, that's exactly why he's with her. He's always loved pretty, shiny things. "It's so wonderful to finally meet you."

"Your eggs are burning." I don't mean to be rude, but I know how my dad is when it comes to his food. Spoiled by years of my mother's perfectionistic ways in this very kitchen, the man has standards.

Without wasting a second, Bliss spins on her bare feet and pulls their breakfast from the fiery depths of burned-food hell before flicking off the gas burner.

"Oops." She laughs a humbled laugh, brushing a pale tendril from her forehead. "That's what I get for trying to multitask."

The human brain isn't capable of multitasking. It's a proven fact. She—a Princeton-educated-psychotherapist-turned-life-coach-slash-meditation-guru—should know this.

"Join us?" Bliss points to the unset table in the nook. "I know your father's anxious to catch up with you—and me . . . I've heard so much about you, I feel like I know you already . . . but I have so many questions. Just dying to pick your brain."

She's rambling, saying the kinds of things a person doesn't normally say to another upon first meeting. Is she nervous? I've been told some people find me intimidating, that my presence has a heaviness to it. It's quite the contrast from Bliss's lighter-than-air exuberance.

"Hope that's okay," she continues. Her movements are easy and relaxed. She's a sunny day of a human being. Clear and bright-eyed. Tepid, soothing voice. "I'm a curious person. Drives your father crazy sometimes, but I find everyone so . . . interesting."

Well, look at that.

We have something in common already.

Years ago, when this woman walked into my father's life, I scraped the internet in search of everything I could find. And with a name like Bliss Diamond, it wasn't that hard.

At first I assumed she was a retired adult film star, and given my father's past dalliances, I didn't think I was that far off.

But I assumed wrong.

Bliss Diamond—at least the internet version of Bliss Diamond—was a neohippie, self-made, meditation-guru influencer with a social media following that numbered close to a million. She's the antithesis of my father's usual bimbo Barbie, young-enough-to-be-his-daughter fare. Though with the help of fillers, Botox, and her natural lit-from-within vibe, she appears years younger than her legal age of forty-six. Five years ago, she successfully self-published a book on "aging from within."

Now that I've seen her in person, I'm thinking I should give it a read.

"Maybe another time?" I'm lacking the energy to be social this morning. I force a smile as I search for a coffee mug in the cupboard where my mother once kept them . . . only to be met with bottles of ibuprofen, jars of manuka honey and elderberry syrups, and various herbal tinctures. "Could you point me to the mugs?"

Bliss retrieves a ceramic teacup from a stainless steel carousel next to the sink, one that was hiding in plain sight this entire time. None of the mugs match, and their kitschy, exotic patterns suggest they've been collected from all over the world. My mother would gasp at the clash of color against her muted, neutral, classic kitchen.

Handing it to me, she lifts a natural brow. "At least join us for coffee?"

Her eyes are tender as they hold my gaze, and her lips relax into a hopeful smile.

I've never liked any of my father's girlfriends, and I don't intend to start now, but she's making this the tiniest bit challenging. It's next to impossible to be cruel to someone who has shown you nothing but kindness.

"Good morning, good morning." My father appears out of nowhere, his hair damp from his shower. "Bliss." He rests a hand on her hip and leans in to deposit a peck on her cheek before facing me. "Grace, how'd you sleep?"

I can't help but wonder what he's told her about me. Does he point out the fact that I'm adopted? Unlike Sebastian and Rose? Does he tell her why they adopted me? That my mother convinced him she was infertile because she wasn't ready to have kids? Or does he simply state that I'm his oldest child and then shrug off any questions about why we look nothing alike or why I'm so different from my well-adjusted younger brother and sister?

I roll the empty teacup in my hand as the two of them study me.

I loathe being on the spot, examined under an amateur microscope. The average person has no idea how to look beneath the surface, how to peel back layers upon layers of body language, how to read between the lines of the spoken word.

And even if I'm to believe everything the internet says about Bliss Diamond—and I don't—I doubt she's versed enough to take one look at me and think she has a snowball's chance in hell of figuring me out.

"Slept well. Thank you." I point to the mirrored gold espresso machine. "Don't want to be in your way. Was just going to grab a coffee and a shower and get to work."

It's the truth.

"Sure you don't want something to eat?" Bliss motions toward her half-burned eggs.

"You know, it's a gorgeous morning already. Why don't we take this outside? The three of us?" my father interjects before I have a chance to decline Bliss's invite again. "Surely you've got a few minutes to spare? Haven't seen you in years, Gracie . . ."

He's using my nickname to mollify my resistance. Only I don't feel soft—I'm entrapped by the guilt wafting off him and the way his expensive aftershave makes me think of different times. Not happier times. *Different.* I don't know that we were ever truly happy. Happy-ish? In an ignorant, unaware sort of way?

I pour my coffee and leave it black. "All right. I've got a few minutes."

He exhales, shoulders relaxing, and then he bustles about the kitchen with new life in his step as Bliss plates their food. My father pours two coffees, one for him and one for her, and we head out back like none of this is awkward.

The weather gauge by the pool house reads seventy-eight degrees, and the breeze is just light enough to tousle a few loose waves around Bliss's face.

She smiles and chews, smiles and chews.

Always smiling, this one.

Maybe it goes with the territory when your name is *Bliss.*

If I weren't crashing here, about to ask for favors, I'd ask her what her name used to be—before it was "Bliss Diamond."

The internet has no record of her until eighteen years ago.

But I keep my mouth shut.

I'm not here for her. Or for my father.

I'm here because of Sutton.

One sip of my coffee tells me it's expensive, but not the good kind of expensive—the kind where you're paying for the brand and the marketing. The bitterness lingers on my tongue after the first drink, making me long for the Turkish coffee place down the street from my apartment in Portland. The powder-soft grounds. The cinnamon and cardamom. The electric jolt of caffeine that wastes zero time hitting my bloodstream.

Soon, I remind myself, I'll be back there again.

This is temporary.

My father devours his eggs with his stick-straight posture, occasionally reaching over to pat the top of his girlfriend's hand.

I don't remember him being this affectionate with my mother. Then again, I'm sure there are a lot of things I don't remember. They say a child's memory can be grossly inaccurate and distorted. Some things I recall as though I'm viewing them through ripples of murky water. Other things I recall with terrifying clarity.

"So . . . Grace . . . what've you been up to these last couple of years? Rose said you were in Vegas? Phoenix? Colorado Springs? And then Billings for a bit?" My father pushes his eggs around on his plate, picking out bits of black. "Where's home these days?"

Rose has always been the information hub of this family, so it doesn't surprise me that he knows these things. It does, however, surprise me that he's been keeping tabs. I figured he'd have more important things to do.

"Portland. But not for much longer. I don't like to stay in one place for too long," I say.

"Where to next?" He brings his fork to his lips, pausing as if he has to will himself to take a bite.

Poor Bliss.

I shrug. "Was thinking Charleston, maybe? Or Charlotte. Kind of want to experience a different coast this time."

"Now that'll be quite a change of scenery," he says with the misplaced confidence of a man who was raised in New York and has spent his entire adult life in New Jersey.

I try not to judge him for never stepping out of his bubble because I know that deep down—beneath the McMullen family money, beyond the debonair features that have aged well, past the flashy car and the merry-go-round of stunning girlfriends and the country club social circle—he's afraid. Though of what, I'm not sure. All I know is that we all have our fears, and oftentimes those fears dictate exactly how we live our lives—whether we realize it or not.

My biggest fear was becoming my mother—a woman so desperate to hang on to her sham of a life, her carefully crafted illusion of happiness, that she was willing to kill for it. Or in her case—hire someone to do the killing for her. God forbid she got her manicure dirty. But in the end, fear got the best of her. It commandeered her decisions and drove her to do the unthinkable.

If I'd stayed with Sutton, he'd have given me a perfect life. That much I know. And he'd have loved me more than a person deserves to be loved. With each passing year, I'd have clung to him—to our beautiful marriage and family—like lifeblood. And if anything so much as threatened to step in our path, I'd have snapped. Like my mother.

Maybe it's not in my blood, per se. But it's there. A learned unsteadiness simmering in my veins.

It's in all of us.

Some people simply control it better than others.

"Charleston is breathtaking. So charming. You'll adore it." Bliss's eyes light, and she splays a hand across her chest. "Oh, to be young and untethered again." She points her fork at no one in particular. "I remember those days. Cherish them. Once you settle down and have kids, you have to bloom where you plant them."

My father chuckles like he *gets it*, and I recall that in my quest to unearth the dirt on Bliss Diamond, I came across her website bio, which described her as a California-native-turned-entrepreneur living in New Jersey. No mention of kids.

"Do you have children?" I ask.

She looks at my father first, whose lips flatten, and then she shakes her head. "Wasn't in the cards for me."

He pats her hand again, as if this is a sore subject for her.

"Grace, your father says you do a lot of freelance work." Bliss frames her question as a statement. "Something online? Background checks or something?"

"My employer prefers I keep details to a minimum," I say. "But essentially I'm an internet sanitizer. People pay me to remove things they don't want online. Unflattering articles. Revenge porn. Harsh reviews. Outdated photos. Stuff like that."

I leave out the worst of the worst of the things I'm sometimes tasked with removing—things that require eye bleach, things that reaffirm my deep disappointment with society. Like the woman whose ex kept posing as her to post rape-fantasy requests on a dark web version of Craigslist, hoping a sick bastard would assault her. Or the husband who secretly attacked his wife's successful, homegrown bakery business with accusatory online reviews involving race and gender and religion so she'd be forced to close her doors and once again be financially dependent on him. There was also the mother-in-law who hired us to dig up dirt on her new son-in-law, who she was convinced was an ex-con living under a stolen identity, only in the process of digging up dirt on the man, I stumbled across the mother-in-law's secret involvement in a human trafficking ring. The son-in-law? Undercover agent. The worst part was that the woman got off on some technicality. I'm not sure she spent a day behind bars. I'm also not sure where she scampered off to, but I'm willing to bet my life savings that wherever she is, she's up to no good.

If people like Bliss and my father knew how many truly sick and sociopathic individuals lurked among us, they'd sleep with guns in their nightstands, keep knives under their mattresses, and second-guess every word that comes out of another person's mouth.

Sometimes I find myself envious of that level of ignorance. Being able to turn a blind eye to all life's misfortunes. To go about my day like the sickest of souls don't walk among us.

But there's no going back now.

I've seen too much.

"That's fascinating." Bliss is finished with breakfast—apparently she has the appetite of a bird. It must be how she keeps her yoga-thin figure. She rests her chin on her hand and leans closer. "I've never met someone who does that before. How'd you get into that line of work anyway?"

My father smiles, and despite our finicky relationship, I still know him: he loves that things feel normal in this sliver-sized moment.

"It started as a part-time job in college. I worked for a major search engine, mostly removing things that violated copyrights, adding adult filters, recategorizing improperly indexed search items . . ." After graduation, I was approached by someone in senior management, who offered me double my salary and told me I could work anywhere in the world doing private assignments. I leave that part out. People always want to know how much this line of work pays, and it does nothing more than make for awkward conversation. Whenever it does come up, I typically say it pays enough to compensate for the dinners I've flushed down the toilet after digesting some of the more disturbing things I've seen. That tends to add a period to the conversation. "Made some connections, and it took off from there."

I peer across the picturesque backyard, over a thicket of manicured boxwoods, to the house behind us: a story-and-a-half bungalow that was once an agreeable robin's-egg blue. It's blanketed in a sunny yellow now, with white trim and a wooden butterfly wind chime dangling outside the back door. The new owners have added a cedar pergola out back, and a stainless steel grill rests uncovered, exposed to the elements. Lazy or carefree? It's anyone's guess.

Twenty years ago, it was home to a man and his girlfriend—a deranged and obsessed woman who stalked our family online and infiltrated her way into our lives. We would later discover she wasn't our neighbor by coincidence, though we couldn't have known that at first.

She had a plan, and when she began working as my family's nanny, she put that plan into action.

She claimed her name was Autumn Carpenter, which I later discovered was the actual name of my biological mother. Her real name was Sarah Thomas. And while she didn't give birth to me, she knew the woman who did—a woman who also happened to go missing a few years after the McMullens adopted me.

But while Sarah was sick, it wasn't a kill-your-husband's-lover kind of sick. She was more along the lines of an unmedicated-and-delusional kind of sick. She was sweet and gentle and especially fond of me. There were times, even as a ten-year-old girl, that I fantasized about Sarah being my mother. Sometimes I prayed for it. Made wishes on dandelions and shooting stars. I was convinced that if I believed anything hard enough, it would come true.

And it almost did.

At least according to a chapter in that *Domestic Illusions* book, where a police report claimed Sarah intended to kidnap me from school and drive me across the border to Mexico.

I'll admit there were years I wished it would've happened.

Sometimes I think I'd have been better off.

Even though Sarah wasn't my mother, she loved me in a way Daphne never could—another factoid outlined in great detail in that unauthorized tell-all. Daphne couldn't connect with me, it said. The bond felt forced. It was complicated. I was a handful, and while she gave me all she could, it wasn't enough.

I don't blame Sarah for what happened to us—or for the self-serving choices my parents made. She happened to waltz into our life during a familial cataclysm of the inevitable. Life as we knew it ceased to exist the moment that woman stepped into our world.

Pure coincidence, I'm certain.

She just happened to be in the picture.

If it hadn't been my parents destroying this family, it would've been me.

I was born with a darkness inside.

"Eyes like two empty black holes," as my mother described me in *Domestic Illusions.* I was a *"precocious child. Destructive. Hard to love."*

Hard to love.

I dig my thumbnail into the painted enamel of the perfect little teacup in my hand, leaving a noticeable scratch.

The urge to ruin all that is perfect is a sickness I've known my entire life, one I've yet to understand in my thirty years. And this sickness isn't simply relegated to things—people fall into this category as well.

The more perfect they are, the more I want to destroy them.

Sutton was perfect.

I left before I could ruin him.

Rising from the patio table, I palm the damaged ceramic. "I'm sorry—can we catch up later? I've got a few deadlines I'm up against . . ."

"Of course," Bliss answers for my father, waving her hand like she understands.

She couldn't possibly.

He gives a tight-lipped nod. "You let me know if there's anything you need. Just glad to have you home."

"Actually . . . there's one thing," I say.

I hate asking favors. *Hate.* Needing other people for any reason is a third-degree burn to my ego. But this request is minor enough, so the sting shouldn't last too long.

"Anything." My father perks up, happy to help. It's a desperate look for a man of his stature, but I appreciate it nonetheless.

"Can you give me a ride to the Enterprise in Valeria in a couple of hours?" I bite my lip. I should've grabbed a rental at the airport yesterday, but the never-ending lines wrapped and zigzagged, and I didn't feel like waiting two hours. On top of that, another minute of being shoulder to shoulder with smelly, grouchy, traveling humans would've had me coming out of my skin.

He checks his diamond-and-sapphire-rimmed timepiece—an antique that once belonged to my grandfather, whom I never met as he passed when my father was a teenager. Supposedly this is why my father pushed so hard to start a family when he was fresh out of college, before my mother was ready.

"Well, shoot," he says under his breath. That's my father—the most helpful man on earth but only at his convenience.

Bliss pats his arm. "Sweetheart, I'll do it. I'd be happy to."

Sweetheart.

They're like an old married couple, which is ironic given that my father doesn't know the first thing about long-term commitment. Bliss doesn't know it yet, but he'll be trading her in a year from now.

Maybe sooner.

None of his coquetries have ever lasted more than a small handful of years.

I give Bliss a showy couple of thank-yous—mostly to spite my father but also to illustrate my gratitude—before heading upstairs to start my day. She didn't hesitate to offer her assistance, unlike my father, who hemmed and hawed as he tried to come up with an excuse. I imagine he didn't want to have to move a tee time or cancel a lunch reservation. And I get it. I showed up unannounced after years of radio silence. I can't expect him to rearrange his schedule at the drop of a hat.

As soon as I wrap up a work email, I'll shower and catch a ride to the Enterprise downtown, grab myself a car, and start scoping out Sutton's life.

His *real* life.

His home, his work, his comings and goings. The things he does when he thinks no one's looking. Mundane or not, these are the things that tell you everything you need to know about someone.

I'm not interested in the version of his life curated across the front page of his Instaface account, nor am I interested in the version of his life summarized by a handful of internet searches.

If I were to take those at face value, then that would mean he's lost his mind. It would mean he actually moved to my hometown, married a woman with my uncanny likeness, and named his firstborn child after me.

I hope I'm wrong.

I pray to anyone who'll listen that it's all a freak misunderstanding, a handful of eerie coincidences with laughably logical explanations.

I lock my bathroom door, strip to nothing, and climb under the hot spray of a pristine shower that likely hasn't been used since the last time I was home years ago.

My heart hammers beneath searing skin, the surrealness of this fading away as reality sets in.

Yesterday, I was three thousand miles away from the life I'd walked away from.

Now I'm back, elbow deep in Sutton's world, and he hasn't the slightest idea.

It would've been easier to call the man, to send him a letter or a message on social media as most people tend to do with ancient lovers.

But phone calls are easy to ignore, and messages are easy to miss, and the written word is easy to misconstrue.

I want him to know that I'm sorry, that he mattered to me—that he was the *only* one who ever mattered to me. And I want to see this with my own eyes—what I've done to him.

And then I'm going to make it right.

Whatever that entails.

CHAPTER 3

It's an ideal day for watching. Clear skies. Sunny. Not a soul in sight.

I cruise past Sutton's office building shortly after one in the afternoon. I'm here not to find him (yet) but to get my bearings, to paint an observant picture of his day-to-day life.

The parking lot is mostly empty, save for a handful of imported sedans and a red SUV parked beneath a shade tree. No sign of Sutton, not that I'm surprised. He's a family man. He's clearly enjoying his weekend with his wife and daughter beyond the confines of this steel-beamed, glass-walled fortress.

I attempt to envision what they might be doing in this moment—only to draw blanks.

It's strange . . . this feeling of knowing someone so well but also wrestling with the reality that I don't know him at all anymore. Not the man he's become. I can only make educated assumptions based on a shared history.

Time changes people.

And people change all the time.

I'd like to believe he kept his gentle demeanor, his jovial spirit, and his easygoing affinity for life, but I won't know for sure until I find out.

Parking beside an expired meter, I pull up my phone and log on to the central app for Watchers and Guardians—my longtime employer.

It's linked directly to the dark web, where I can retrieve any kind of information on almost anyone in the world . . . aliases, social security numbers, passwords . . . and then store it in encrypted files easily accessible by my company. Odds are if I can't find that information myself, I can pay someone to find it for me. Fortunately, I've uncovered the best internet hiding places over the years, and I've established virtual friendships with the most resourceful of souls.

My file on Sutton is small given the fact that it was created a little over a week ago. But I have enough for now. Addresses, mostly. Public voting records. License plate numbers. Seedlings of intel. Jigsaw pieces of data. Sometimes they come together to create a big picture; most of the time they don't.

If I were here on a weekday, I'd likely find his silver hybrid Toyota SUV parked in the back row—he always liked to get those extra steps in. It's a sensible car for a sensible man. Environmentally conscious. Reliable. Family-friendly. It gives me hope that he's still the same old Sutton. Then again, I don't know what a heartbroken, secretly-obsessed-with-his-ex kind of man would drive.

I imagine him exiting the double glass doors in the front of the limestone building, heading for his car, and running home for lunch at noon to steal a kiss from his wife, maybe even partake in a quick playdate with his young daughter before her nap.

If his life turned out anything like the way he wanted, it's a Technicolor fantasyland of pressed khakis; ironed button-downs; meticulous-yet-flexible schedules; organic, home-cooked meals; tropical cruise vacations; and a family-focused center.

He once told me his goal in life was to be the perfect husband and the perfect father. Nothing more, nothing less. It was all that mattered to him. His father was *perfect*. His father's father was *perfect*. Whitlock men were family men, born and bred. Traditional. Loyal. All-American.

Perfect.

It made me nauseous to think about all that perfection . . . because I knew what I would do to it if it were mine. All the buttons I would push. All the levers I would pull. All the testing and watching and waiting and suspecting. All the problems I'd invent.

No one deserves that.

My mother, Daphne, got the worst of it. As a child, I pushed every last one of her buttons and frayed every nerve that woman had down to the wire. I would steal. Break. Hide. Scream. Lie. Her patience and tenderness only acted as an accelerant to the fire deep within me. The more she tried to coddle and hold me, the more I kicked and name called. I was never satisfied until her eyes filled with tears. But it was never about making her cry. It was about what would come afterward, after she'd send me to my room for hours of alone time. I lived to see the look on her face when the maelstrom was over, hoping that once . . . just *once* I'd see love in her eyes.

But I never did.

I retrieve Sutton's home address online, punch it into my phone's GPS, and make my way toward 72 Lakemont Street with sweat-prickled armpits and my air conditioner blasting. For years, I pretended this place—this city—didn't exist. And 90 percent of the time it was easy to forget about the people who live here (my family). But now that I'm here, the air is thick with reality. Every breath anchors me into this moment, where I can't escape my past because it suffocates me with every familiar street sign.

I'm halfway to Lakemont when I realize it's all of three blocks from my childhood home—a detail that sends a spray of tingles down the back of my neck.

Intentional?

Over twenty-two thousand residences pepper the winding, picturesque lanes of Monarch Falls. What are the odds he chose that one?

I end the GPS midsentence once I turn onto his street. I know what his house looks like thanks to the public listing on the county assessor's website. I also know what he paid for it and the exact date he and his wife signed the papers—two Augusts ago on a Wednesday at the Crawford Mills Credit Union.

I recall the summer before our junior year, when we moved into that brick duplex off College Row on the hottest day of the year. For hours, we hauled moving boxes inside. Just us two. My hair held steady in a messy ponytail, and the back of his gray T-shirt was spotted with sweat. We ordered pizza—pepperoni and mushroom for his half, cheese for mine. And we split a six-pack of Miller Lite. We devoured dinner picnic-style, seated on pillows next to our glass coffee table. Bellies full, we contemplated christening the place, but after a cold shower (water heater was busted) with no soap (it was packed away somewhere), the mood was lost. We ended up crashing early, plunking our mattress on the hardwood floor and passing out before the sun went down.

The memory plants a smile on my face—one I wipe away as Sutton's current home comes into view. It's better to leave the past where it is. Over the years, I've found that if I carry too many things with me, the load gets unbearably heavy.

My car crawls, my foot hovering over the brake pedal as I take in the view.

This neighborhood didn't exist twenty years ago, at least not like this. Once upon a time, it was a part of historic Monarch Falls. Its streets were lined with aging Victorians, regal Queen Annes, and pretentious Gothic Revivals, all of them leaning sideways or crumbling yet still unapologetically magnificent. According to an article I found online, a committee of local historians fought like hell to save it, but as the committee members aged out and died, so did their agenda.

A handful of years ago, a local builder persuaded the city council to let him raze the dilapidated properties to make way for highly sought-after new construction houses. The only stipulation was that the homes had to appear historic . . . which is why Sutton's place looks like an arts and crafts kit home straight out of a 1908 Sears catalog. Balanced and proportional, low roof, cozy front porch complete with chunky white columns and a swing.

The paint color is an interesting choice to me—brick brown bordering on bloodred in the right light—but my earlier research told me they're the second owners. They didn't choose that color. And I should've known—Sutton was always drawn to citrusy, jubilant colors or anything that conveyed lightness. Orange was his favorite, followed by clean, classic white. His house being brick-blood is jarring, but I get over it.

I park my car a few houses down and on the opposite side of the street, let the engine idle so the air can run, tuck my hair into a Dodgers cap, and adjust my sunglasses.

Then I watch for anything, for everything.

A middle-aged couple stroll by hand in hand, the husband smiling and nodding at me while the wife offers a suspecting glare. I've found that women tend to sniff out the bad in people easier than men, sometimes with nothing more than a passing glance.

That woman thinks I'm up to something, and she isn't wrong.

But I'm not the kind of *bad* she has to worry about.

The couple disappear around the corner by a four-way stop, where untrimmed hedges are far too tall to be safe—a covenant or city ordinance violation, I'm sure—and I return my attention to the red house down the street.

Popping a couple of earbuds in, I catch up on a podcast on Errol Flynn, never once removing my gaze from my target.

I settle back. Breathe. Convince myself this is what relaxed and natural feels like.

While I'm used to watching from behind a high-definition monitor, I take comfort in knowing that if Sutton were to walk out his front door and glance in this direction, he wouldn't be able to distinguish my features from several hundred feet away. In fact, I'm sure I'm the last person he'd expect to see on his street. If he did recognize me, I imagine his brain would refuse to make the connection at first—like spotting a polar bear in the Amazonian jungle.

It wouldn't make sense.

Not at first.

I finish my podcast and check the time, mentally calculating that it's been forty-two minutes now. The half-suspicious couple from earlier pass by, the woman giving me a lingering glare this time, as if to silently shoo me off her street.

I toss her one back as if to wish her a condescending "good luck with that."

I know the law, and I'm not breaking a single one.

Another podcast and a playlist later, I debate whether to stick around. I can't be obvious. I can't sit here all day. The longer I linger, the more neighbors will notice, and the less likely I'll be able to show my face (or my rental car) in this neighborhood again.

My empty stomach groans, and my head is light. I search my bag for a packet of almonds or a loose stick of gum, only to find a stale, unwrapped peppermint from a Thai restaurant down the street from my apartment in Portland. I take it as a sign to call it a day and press the "Engine Start" button, only the instant my dashboard blinks to life and the radio hums an overplayed pop song, the front door of Sutton's home swings open and out walks . . . me.

Only it isn't me.

It's *her*.

The one he married.

The consolation prize with whom he created this beautiful, perfect life.

The woman with an undeniable and head-scratching resemblance to myself.

Campbell is her name. Maiden name: Beckwith. Hometown: Blueberry Springs, Connecticut. *Adorable.* I don't know much else about her . . . yet. My focus the entirety of the past week has been on Sutton.

Their daughter—the one they named *Grace*—rests on her hip, clapping her chubby hands as the two of them make their way down the front steps and hook a left on the sidewalk—coming my way.

Shit, shit, shit.

I tug the brim of my cap and slump, a ridiculous and unnecessary move given the fact that she and I are complete strangers. She'd have no reason to recognize me, no reason to think twice upon seeing me parked here. She'd have every reason to glance over me and carry on about her day.

A cluster of mailboxes rests equidistant between us, and I spot a set of keys dangling from her hand as she walks. A few seconds later, she's unlocking a small receptacle, attempting to balance her daughter on her hip all the while.

An older man in a neon-green visor and bright-blue shorts strolls past them, stopping when he sees her struggling.

The two exchange laughs and words I can't make out from this far away. A moment later, he takes Grace off her hands so she can stack those mountains of junk mail and magazines under her arm for the journey back.

They visit for another minute before he hands the child over, and he leaves her with a wave as he continues on his way.

It hurts to blink, and I have no idea if I've done so in the past five minutes. My mind attempts to catalog every detail about her, from the logo on her pale-pink sneakers to the way her sandy ponytail bounces on her shoulders with each buoyant step.

I rub my eyes and force myself to focus on something else for a second. It's an old trick I learned after spending endless hour upon endless hour glued to a computer monitor. But the last thing I expect to see when I steal another glimpse across the street . . . is Campbell walking this way.

My throat constricts, and I reach for my phone, pulling up a random app in hopes of appearing preoccupied and nonchalant.

From behind the dash, I observe as Campbell walks closer, closer still. For a fraction of a moment, I manage to convince myself she's returning a neighbor's misdelivered mail, maybe strolling across the street to say hello to someone.

I close my eyes and brace, waiting for her to pass.

Stick me behind a computer screen and I'm fearless, unstoppable—a force to be reckoned with. But stalking people—*physically stalking people*—is outside my scope of expertise. It's creepy, and it brings with it the burn of acid bile in the back of my throat.

The sound of knuckles rapping on glass forces me to accept that I've completely lost control of this situation.

I roll the driver's side window down a few inches and ignore the heat inching up my neck despite the full-blast air-conditioning.

"Hi. Can I help you?" My voice is meek and mild. Pathetic. Not how I imagined meeting my doppelgänger—not that I ever imagined meeting her.

In all my scenarios involving Sutton, she was never a part of them. There was never any need. This isn't about her. Truthfully, I feel sorry for the poor thing because she hasn't the slightest inkling that she's anything more than a stand-in.

Second choice.

"Hi there," she says, her makeup-free lashes batting. She hoists the child on her hip again and almost loses a flyer tucked beneath her arm. My stare intersects with hers, causing my breath to hitch. We share the same oblong face, the same unremarkable plain-brown eyes. The same aquiline nose. Of course I've seen her in photos this past week, but nothing compares to up close and personal. "I'm so sorry to bother you."

She's apologizing to *me*?

"Just wanted to let you know you're parked in a no-parking zone," Campbell continues, nodding toward a red-and-white sign several yards ahead that clearly says **No Parking On Saturdays**.

Since when has that been a thing?

"Ah. Had no idea. I'm so sorry about that." I grip the steering wheel, foot pressed against the brake before I shift out of park. "I was just sending a few texts . . . didn't want to text and drive so I pulled over . . . wasn't paying attention . . ."

Since when have *I* been a nervous rambler?

Campbell manages a shrug, and her full mouth pulls into a smile. "*So* not a huge deal. It's just that it's trash day, and the truck should be coming through any minute. Those guys love doling out citations. They don't even give you a chance to move, they just take down your plate number and send it in. It's like the city gives them a cut of the profits or something."

She clucks her tongue and rolls her eyes as if this issue directly inconveniences her, too. An attempt to be personable, maybe? To get on my level? The scent of fruit snacks and the sweet tang of vanilla-clementine perfume trails from her to me—the very kind I'm all too familiar with, because it was my signature scent in college.

I conjure up a vision of Sutton breathing her in after a long day at the office, nuzzling his nose in the bend between her neck and shoulder, pretending she's me.

"Thanks. Appreciate it." I wave, roll up my window, and get the hell out of there.

In the rearview mirror I see Campbell and her daughter schlep home, mail in tow, and I can still smell her—no—*my* fragrance with every inhalation.

It clings to me the entire three blocks home, sticking to my lungs with each shallow breath.

Turning into our shady driveway, I park my rental behind the third stall of the garage in case our street, too, is suddenly a **No Parking On Saturdays** street.

Now that Campbell has seen my face—sunglasses and hat aside—this changes things.

I'm going to have to be careful about how I approach Sutton. I can't show up at one of his favorite restaurants and pretend to be back in town by chance—my original (if not lame) Plan A. I could show up at his office, but that'd be a jerk move regardless of my well-meaning intentions. Odds are, if I run into him outside work hours, he'll be with his family. With her. And she could recognize me. The idea of her mentioning to him that she saw me on their street sends me cringing.

Last thing I want is for him to think I'm the crazy one here.

I need to think about this some more.

I'm halfway to the front door, visions of researching Campbell in my head, when someone calls my name from the street, stopping me dead in my tracks.

From the corner of my eye, I spot my younger sister climbing out of her electric SUV in such a rush she almost forgets to shut the door. Her long legs break into a gazelle-like canter across the driveway. Before I have a chance to react, she wraps me in a hug that smells like gardenias—and our mother—and chokes every last bit of air from my lungs.

I haven't seen Rose in years. Haven't spoken to her since last Christmas, and that was only because she called me from a new number and I answered thinking it was someone else.

"I can't believe it's really you." Her cashmere voice is muffled against my hair, and she bounces on the toes of her ballet flats, towering over me an additional handful of inches. Still long and lanky, still a one-off Designer Imposter Daphne.

If we were a normal family, this might be a joyous moment. A cause for celebration. But we're McMullens, and we wouldn't know normal if it smacked us over the head with a prison sentence.

She peels herself off me. Baby-blue eyes lit from within. Flaxen hair shining in the afternoon sun. A knot tangles in my middle when I fixate on how much she looks like our mother, from her tender smile to the pointed tip of her nose. From the lithe shoulders that hoist spaghetti-strapped sundresses to the creamy complexion that's never known a blemish. From the lilt in her voice when she speaks to the long-legged strides that have carried her everywhere she's ever wanted to go in her twenty-seven years.

I have it on good authority that she and our mother have stayed in touch all these years. In fact, Rose's never explicitly stated this, but I'm certain she'll never leave the confines of New Jersey because she doesn't want to "abandon" our mother the way our father did after the trial.

The way I did.

"Dad didn't tell me you were coming," I say, taking a step back when I spot her boyfriend, Evan, making his way up the drive.

He stops at her side, towering over her by at least a foot, and hooks his Ivy League rowing-team arms over her narrow shoulders.

"Grace McMullen, what's up?" He greets me with my full name, and his awkwardness makes me wince, but only on the inside. The number of times we've met during the tenure of their relationship, I can count on one hand. But it's cool if he wants to pretend we have a thing, I guess.

"Hi . . ." I keep my attention on my sister, distracted by how much more she looks like our mom than the last time I saw her. Maybe it's this lighting. Or the angle. Or maybe my mind's playing tricks. I squeeze my eyes tight and reopen them. Nothing changes.

I'm silently grateful for the fact that I'll never have to look in the mirror and see my adopted mother's face staring back. For Rose, it's a blessing. For me, it'd serve as nothing more than a reminder that I've always been on the outskirts of this family.

"Dad texted and said you just showed up yesterday," Rose says. "Everything okay?"

I don't appreciate that they've been discussing me, but I don't let myself frown. "Why wouldn't it be?"

As a McMullen, I can deny with the best of them. We were practically raised on a steady diet of organic produce and denial.

Her mouth tugs at one side. "You haven't been home in years, and then you just show up one day? Without warning? That's not like you. Just want to make sure you're all right . . ."

"Something wrong with being homesick?" I deflect.

The truth doesn't matter. And it's none of her concern. Rose was hardly out of high school when I dated Sutton. I doubt she remembers him.

My sister's wide-eyed gaze amplifies. The corners of her lashes are fanned out with a double coat of volumizing mascara, the way our mother used to do hers. "You know you can tell me anything."

She peers toward the front door, as if to ensure we're not being watched.

"I won't say anything to Dad," she adds, her voice sweet and low.

Even if I were compelled to confide in Rose, I sure as hell wouldn't do it with Evan standing here like a statue. He may be gazing off into space, but his ears are at full attention, pointed toward us.

"What are you guys doing here anyway?" I change the subject and slide my hands into my back pockets, my best attempt at being casual.

"I wanted to see you." Rose shrugs, and for a second, I picture a seven-year-old version of her standing before me. Wispy blonde hair. Sugar-spun voice. My personal shadow.

The last time we were together was at our grandma's funeral in Boca Raton over two years ago. Sebastian made an appearance, too, though he'd looked so grown I hardly recognized him as he made his grand entrance through the main doors of the century-old First Presbyterian church, looking like he'd stepped off a Times Square billboard. And he brought not one but two distractingly attractive females—for moral support, I guess.

He is his father's son.

"It's so good to see you." She places a hand on my forearm, emphasizing each and every word. If I closed my eyes, Rose would sound exactly like our mother: proper, enunciated, regal, warm.

I wonder if she remembers the time I sheared off her hair. Or all the times I framed her for my wrongdoings or tasked her with my evil bidding, like teasing our little brother mercilessly.

She was seven years old when Mom was sent away and Nana Greta came to live with us and assist our father, who'd found himself a single parent virtually overnight.

Nana Greta was as cruel as she was obsessed with her only son. She'd pull my hair on purpose when she brushed it and count my calories when she thought I'd been snacking too much. Night by night, my bedtime came earlier and earlier. And if I couldn't sleep, she'd force me to read boring children's books she personally chose from the local library, spurring a lifelong aversion to leisure reading that I've yet to overcome.

It took only a few months of my obstinate, limit-testing antics before they shipped me to Florida to live with our mother's mother, where I stayed until I finished high school a semester early. Grandma Janet was no walk in the park, but she was Disney World compared to Greta.

"Shall we head in?" Rose points to the front door, and her nails are the palest, prettiest, glossiest pink I've ever seen. Not a chip in sight. I often wonder what it'd be like to make it more than twenty-four hours postmanicure without picking at my polish.

I follow Rose and Evan inside, ignore the acidic discontent bubbling in my center, and force myself to be cordial for the hour that follows.

It's a distraction at least: the small talk. Bliss serves homemade organic lemonade sweetened with agave nectar. We discuss Rose and Evan's new condo. We chat about Sebastian's law school progress, his latest "psycho girlfriend," and whether or not he's been using the guided meditations Bliss recorded for him. Dad shows us his new putter. Rose pulls out a funny video she took of Evan waxing poetic to his under-grads about the intricacies of paper wasps—probably the most I've ever heard him speak.

It's all strangely normal, while at the same time categorically unnatural.

But for a solid hour, I forget why I'm here. And I certainly don't think about Sutton's house three blocks away or his daughter with my name or his wife with my face who wears my perfume.

But at the end of the night, I remember.

In fact, it's all I can think about—and it almost kills me.

CHAPTER 4

I lace my sneakers and stretch my hamstrings by the front steps Sunday morning, grateful to have made it up and out the door unseen. It's been a week since my last run back in Portland, and I'm craving a clear head and that intoxicating flood of endorphins that always follows. That and it's less obvious than sitting outside someone's house in a parked car.

If and when I run into Sutton, it needs to happen naturally. I need to be able to tell him I'm *simply visiting my father* and I had *no idea he lived three blocks away.* From there we'll make small talk, and after that we'll set plans to catch up over coffee.

Over lattes and scones, I'll apologize for hurting him the way I did.

I'll explain all the reasons it was for the best.

I'll wish him nothing but love and happiness.

And I'll be on my way.

I stretch my arms over my head and do a handful of side bends before debating whether to sneak back inside to grab a bottle of water. I don't want to wake anyone, and I certainly don't want to run into someone who might mistake my mere presence as an invitation to socialize at this ungodly hour.

A shadow fills the glass behind the living room window, and when it moves closer, I realize it's Rose. She and Evan decided to stay last night after conversations stretched late into the evening. She offers a subtle, beauty-queen finger wave, and a few seconds later, the front door swings open.

"Since when have you been a runner?" She wraps her hands around her coffee mug, her petite frame drowning in one of our mother's old waffle-weave bathrobes.

"Since always."

I don't go into detail about being fifteen and starting a new high school in Boca Raton and having some asshole pizza-faced kid walk up to me in the hallway the second day and randomly tell me I needed to go on a diet. The joke's on that jerk, though, because while he was the catalyst that sparked this hobby, I stuck with it all these years because it's the only thing that quiets my mind. The joke's also on him because a few years ago, I found him online in all his pot-bellied glory. Add in his two baby mamas, one public urination, and a DUI, and I'd say life has settled our scores.

Rose takes a seat on one of the steps, adjusting the hem of the robe until it covers her striped pajama pants. "It's crazy to think that you're my sister and I barely even know you sometimes."

"You're not missing out on much."

"I doubt that." She offers a tender half smile. "Growing up, I always thought you were so cool."

"You saw me once a year." At Christmas, my father would fly down to Boca Raton with Rose and Sebastian to visit me. It started when I was eleven, too young to travel alone, and then it became tradition.

Our only tradition.

"Yeah, but you were so badass. You didn't care what anyone thought of you. You did what you wanted to do. You were fearless," she says, breathy and awestruck, like she's spent all these years idolizing me into what she needed me to be in her head. "And look at you now—jet setting all over the world. You've lived in more cities in the past eight years than most people will visit in their lifetimes."

"I promise it's not as glamorous as you're making it sound." I scan the empty sidewalks and give my legs an extra stretch. My shoes are in mint condition, fresh out of the box—I bought them before I planned this trip and haven't used them yet.

I scuff the side of one against the concrete step until it leaves a satisfying gray blemish.

Rose doesn't notice.

Instead, she clears her throat, running a flattened palm against her thigh. "So . . . I'm pregnant."

My sister gazes up, eyes round and expression unreadable while she assesses my reaction.

I laugh for a second, until I realize she's not kidding. "Oh. Cool. Congrats."

Rose peels her attention from me, chewing on her lower lip.

"Does Dad know?" I ask. "Evan?"

"Nope. And not yet. You're the first."

I'm confused. "Why me?"

"Because you're my sister."

I imagine she had an idea in her head about how she expected this to go. Happy tears, maybe. Hugs. The fusion of a bond long in the making.

I would give her those things if I could.

"How far along?" I ask, an attempt to keep things in neutral as opposed to emotional overdrive. Pregnant people, in my limited experience, can go from zero to tears in three seconds flat, and I don't do tears.

She lifts a shoulder, causing ripples to fan out across the surface of her untouched coffee. "I don't know. I just found out last week. And I keep forgetting. It's like every morning I pour myself a coffee, and then I remember . . ."

"It probably just hasn't sunk in yet. I'm sure it will."

She places her coffee on a concrete step, folding her hands over her face and breathing deep through her slender, graceful fingers.

It takes me longer than it should, but eventually I settle beside her, looping my arm around her shoulders. I'm tense, and everything about this is unnatural, but again, this is not about me.

"It's going to be fine," I tell her, wondering if she can feel the shake of my palm against her. Touching other people (and conversely, being touched by other people) isn't something I do every day. "It's not like you're fifteen." Like my birth mother was when she had me . . . "You're twenty-seven. And Evan seems . . . nice."

Weird. But nice.

My boss, Jonah, would call him an "odd duck," and I'd have to agree. The son of a retired Lebanese supermodel and a reclusive Silicon Valley genius, he's got both looks and brains, but zero personality.

"He just got that associate professor job," she says. "He said he didn't want to start a family until he was tenured, which could take years, maybe even a decade."

"You *do* know how babies are made, right?" I tease. "These things . . . they're preventable."

She cracks a smile like she catches my drift, like she's not as dense as I assumed.

"Ninety-nine percent of the time," she says.

I leave my arm around her and quietly mourn the relationship we could've had if only things had turned out differently. We were separated by three years and didn't share an ounce of DNA, but maybe we would've been close.

Guess we'll never know.

"When are you going to tell him?" I ask.

Rose sighs. "Soon."

"What are you waiting for?"

"I just . . . I know once I tell him, he'll want to get married. He's traditional like that."

"Then say no. He can't force you."

"I know," she says.

"Do you even love him?" I peel my arm off her and stand up again. I need space. And air. But mostly space. All this closeness is suffocating.

She shoots me a look. "Of course I do."

"Then what's the issue?"

Rose is quiet, but her brows are furrowed. "Everything is so perfect right now. What if . . . What if we get married, and he changes? Or I change? What if all of this goes away?"

"He will. And you will. And it will," I say. "Just be good to each other, and you should come out of it unscathed."

She smirks. "You make marriage sound like war."

"Isn't it, though?" I shrug. "I don't speak from experience, so my advice is probably shit."

"We didn't have the best example of what a healthy marriage looked like," she says, "did we?"

"History only repeats itself if you let it." Look at me, being all objective and rational.

It's always fascinated me how the mere presence of certain people brings out sides of us we didn't know existed, forcing us to be something we're not, if only for a temporary moment.

Rose runs her reedy fingers through her shiny, tousled hair. "You know, I've dumped every boyfriend I've ever had because I was paranoid that he was cheating on me. My biggest fear is that I'll marry Evan, and he'll turn out just like Dad."

I don't hesitate. "Evan is nothing like Dad. Not even close."

Dad has a personality, for starters.

"I'm sure when Mom married Dad, she never thought he'd . . ." She doesn't finish the sentence.

"If it makes you feel any better, I don't trust anyone either."

"And how's that working out for you?" She winks.

"Wonderfully." I rest my hands on my hips. "Thanks for asking."

Silence settles between us, as if we're quietly feeling out this new-found possibility of a connection that never existed before.

A silver SUV crawls by, and I hold my breath until I ascertain that it's not a Toyota, that it's not Sutton.

"What's it like not being afraid to be alone?" Rose asks.

"Like breathing air?" My answer comes out like a question because I don't know how else to answer something like that without using dramatic words akin to "survival."

Rose wouldn't know the first thing about surviving. After Mom was sentenced, Rose got to stay in the family home with Dad and Sebastian and Nana Greta, who thought her *Sweet Rose* hung the moon and could do no wrong.

Rose was the daughter Greta never had. Sebastian was the second coming of her beloved Graham. I was chopped liver. An afterthought living in a two-bedroom condo in a retirement community with our poker-loving, chain-smoking, gin-and-tonic-swigging Grandma Janet.

While Rose and Sebastian attended private schools, I attended a high school with a 68 percent graduation rate.

When Nana Greta took Rose and Sebastian on European summer vacations (my invite was clearly lost in the mail), I was sweating my ass off selling snow cones from a shack on Orange Avenue for minimum wage.

Rose was a cheerleader with a tight-knit circle of bubbly, popular, perfect-top-knot-wearing girlfriends who never had to scrounge around for a last-minute prom date.

I scuff my shoe against the concrete step again, leaving a bigger scrape than the last.

"Mom misses you. She asks me about you all the time." Rose avoids eye contact.

"I'm sorry I haven't been around for you." I'm not allergic to apologizing. I'm not afraid to acknowledge my weaknesses. I live with them every day, like a pack of obnoxious roommates. "But I stand by my decision regarding . . . her."

It's difficult to call her Mom, at least out loud. It's an unfamiliar word on my lips these days. I don't know that I could eke the word out if I tried.

Another car idles down our quiet street, and I'm jealous of its freedom, the fact that it never has to think or feel or wonder or worry or run away or numb itself into oblivion.

"She's going to die alone in that prison someday. Do you have any idea what it's like for her?"

A minute ago, I almost thought about confiding in my sister about the real reason I came home. I thought we were having a moment. And it would've been nice to open up to someone about all of this, to have someone else confirm that I'm not crazy or imagining these coincidences.

But our conversation has taken a sharp left turn, and we're gunning for a cliff.

I won't stand here and be guilt-tripped by my mother's avatar.

I lift my watch, press the "Run" setting, and take a deep breath. "Going to take my jog now."

And then I trot toward Sutton's house on Lakemont, leaving Rose—and all that noise—in the distance.

CHAPTER 5

I'm a block from 72 Lakemont, clipping along square after square of white sidewalk, sidestepping automatic sprinklers, and returning care-free waves from unsuspecting strangers on their Sunday drives.

Every stride puts me this much closer to becoming a regular neighborhood fixture.

An old-school hip-hop song plays in my ear, and a powder-faced elderly beagle on the other side of a picket fence tries to keep up with me for half a block.

We had a dog, once: a chocolate labradoodle the size of a small horse. Nana Greta ended up "rehoming" her shortly after she moved in because she was "too much to handle." But I knew the real reason—scooping the massive piles of crap that polluted the backyard was beneath her.

I think about that dog still, twenty years later. What became of her. If she had a good life. If she was loved. I'd have taken her with me to Florida, but Grandma Janet's apartment was strictly pet-free. When I was twelve, I captured an anole from the parking lot and fixed up a home for it in an old Nike shoebox from my closet. Grandma found it a week later and set it free while I was at school. At least that's what she told me. For all I know, she flushed it down the toilet. She could be heartless like that.

These days I much prefer animals over people, but I've never been able to bring myself to get one of my own. If something were to happen to me, who would take care of it?

More important than that . . . who could I trust to take care of it?

I spot the emerald-green-and-white street sign for Lakemont ahead, nestled above the untrimmed, sky-high hedges I noticed yesterday, and I pick up my pace.

My watch reads 7:16 AM, and I imagine Sutton and his little family are up for the day. Maybe Campbell is making buckwheat pancakes in the kitchen while he's discussing the yard work on the docket. *Sesame Street* plays on the TV in the living room, and a load of bleached towels is tumbling in the dryer. Campbell asks if they should open the windows today, and Sutton checks the weather. "Too humid," he tells her. "Tomorrow maybe." And if he squints hard enough when he looks at her, he sees me.

I round the corner by the overgrown shrubs, and my heart lurches in my chest with each bounce of my foot against pavement. But before my gaze so much as lands on 72 Lakemont, I find myself on a collision path with a woman pushing a stroller.

In an attempt to avoid pummeling into the innocent bystanders, I dodge to the right, only to stumble over my own feet and land against the concrete with a rigid smack that knocks the air from my lungs.

It all happens so fast.

My palms throb, like a hundred tiny fires.

I don't have to examine them to know they're pitted with pebbles of sidewalk and dirt. Pushing myself up, I spot a horizontal tear in my leggings, one that showcases a bleeding scrape.

It isn't profuse, but it stings with every pulsating second.

"Oh, my gosh. Are you okay?" The woman places her hand on my shoulder. "This corner is the worst. No one's lived in this house for months, and I've been trying to get the city to trim the hedges. They keep saying they will, but—"

Squinting in the direction of her voice, I find a familiar face partially obscured by the morning sun.

"Here. Let me help you." Campbell hooks her arm into mine. "You good to stand on your own?"

I brush bits of dirt and grass off my thighs once I'm on my feet. "Yeah."

"You're bleeding." She cups my scraped hand in hers, careful not to touch the damaged skin. "I live a few houses down. Why don't you come back, and I'll get you cleaned up?"

Jerking away, I give her a curt, "No."

Head angled, she examines me. "But you're hurt . . . I've got a first aid kit. I can get you some ice for your knee. I feel so awful. You fell because of us."

She points to the child, as if I could possibly not notice her in that bumblebee-striped stroller.

"I'm fine. I promise." I keep my head tucked and gaze lowered, wondering if she'll recognize me from yesterday and thinking of all the ways that could potentially complicate things.

"Seriously, I live right there." She points to the brick-blood house. A flash of inventive scenarios floods my imagination once more, this time settling on their first date. I bet he took her to an Italian place—his favorite fare—and I bet he asked if she wanted to walk around after. He always liked a long stroll after a big meal. It settles his stomach. "It'll take two seconds."

"I don't want to impose. I'm staying not far from here."

"So you're going to just . . . hobble home?" She half laughs, but not in an offensive, condescending way. "At least let me give you a ride."

There are a million ways to say no, and Campbell is having none of it.

Her daughter coos from the safety of her stroller and gives me a chubby-handed wave. Not that I ever fantasized about motherhood, but I used to wonder what our kids would look like.

She has Sutton's eyes. A stunning green-brown-gold cocktail topped with a fringe of silky chocolate lashes. I've never been one to fawn over adorable children, but I can't help staring longer than I should.

"Come on. Let's get you cleaned up." Campbell positions herself behind her stroller and waves for me to follow. "I'm Campbell, by the way."

I know.

Walking away now would be a jerk move. And while seeing Sutton like this (me sweaty, scraped up, and bleeding and him in the confines of his own home) wasn't part of the plan, it's an opportunity to get things moving in the right direction.

I follow Sutton's wife to 72 Lakemont.

This is happening.

My thoughts are gibberish and my legs are rubber with every step and the ground beneath me is unsteady, but we make it.

Campbell parks the stroller by the front porch, and a moment later, she slides a silver key fob from behind a terra-cotta planter by the door.

My stomach flips. This is insane. This is a bad idea. But this is exactly why I'm here.

I want to say something to make this less awkward, but clearly it's not awkward for her. She invited me. This was her idea. I didn't plan this—it fell into my lap. And I tried to say no . . .

I almost ask if her husband is home, but I think better of it. It's a strange question to ask if you don't know someone. Plus, she hasn't mentioned having a husband.

"This is so kind of you, really," I manage to say.

"Oh, gosh. Don't worry about it," she says with her back to me. There's a smile in her voice.

I run my dampening palms along my thighs and steady my breath when I deduce that the odds of Campbell locking up the house when her husband is home are probably nil. Most people won't do that unless they live in a sketchy neighborhood, and Monarch Falls has nothing of that sort.

Does Sutton know his wife is this willing to entertain a stranger? That she made no effort to disguise where the spare key is hidden? If I were a nefarious person or a woman desperate for a small child of my own, I could wreak havoc on their happy little nest. That Stone Wall Security Systems sign in their landscaping means zilch if someone knows where the spare fob is hidden.

My chest turns to steel, hard and aching with a longing to protect his family—the things he loves—from danger, from the sickos in this world.

Campbell presses the key fob against a black sensor. A second later, the lock pops, and with stinging, aching, elastic legs, I follow her into a house that smells like cinnamon, Cheerios, and newish construction.

She doesn't call out, doesn't announce her arrival.

I'm certain, at this point, he isn't here.

I release the breath I've been holding.

"Oh. If you don't mind." She points to my shoes as she slides off her own, and then offers an apologetic wince. "My husband is a freak when it comes to dirt in this house. One speck and I'll never hear the end of it."

Really? Sutton?

"Of course." I slide off my scuffed-yet-new running sneakers and swallow the disbelief lodged in my throat. When we lived together in college, I had to practically set up a sticker chart to remind him to load the dishwasher or pick his dirty clothes up off the floor. And don't get me started on the countless hours I spent scrubbing dried toothpaste from the bathroom sink because he was in such a hurry he'd forget to rinse it out.

"Kitchen's in the back." With baby Grace on her hip, Campbell takes me to the room where she prepares meals for Sutton and pulls out a chair at the head of the table, pointing for me to take a seat. Next she places her daughter in a high chair, gives her a handful of goldfish crackers, and retrieves a first aid kit from a cupboard by the fridge. "Oh. We need ice." She's talking to herself, mostly, buzzing about a tidy kitchen so clean I could eat off its polished tile floor.

She returns with her kit and an ice pack and settles into the seat beside me.

Her vanilla-clementine perfume—*my vanilla-clementine perfume*—blankets the air between us.

She slips a pair of latex gloves over her hands before laying out packets of antiseptic ointment, gauze, and bandages.

"This might sting for a sec," she says as she starts with my knee.

And it does. It stings like hell. But I focus on the happy baby in the corner. Then the silver coffee maker on the counter—the one Sutton uses every day. A built-in desk is next to the fridge, where a bulletin board hangs on the wall, scattered with cards and family photos.

This life he's built with her—it's real, but it isn't.

How many other heartbroken people in this world catapult an entire life off someone who merely qualifies as the next best thing? A knockoff of what they really want? How many children are born from these unions? How many lives are lived half-fulfilled? How many spouses know the truth? Do they ever learn to love, *really love*, the one they're with? How many people take these secrets to their grave?

There's an old song my grandma used to sing about loving the one you're with.

Is that what he's doing? Loving the one he's with because he can't have the one he loves?

"There you go. Good as new." Campbell gathers the waste, snaps off her gloves, and tosses them in a nearby trash can.

It's then that I spot a set of bruises on her left forearm—small and round. Fingerprint-sized. Though they could be anything.

"Thank you so much." I examine my bandages, the inner fabric brushing across my scrapes with each move, making them sting worse than before. But I appreciate the act of kindness. It's rare in this world. In my world.

"You know, I don't think I caught your name?"

I was hoping she wouldn't notice.

I clear my throat and avoid making eye contact with her child.

"Grace," I say.

Her eyes widen.

"No way." She grins. "That's our daughter's name. But we call her Gigi. I mean, we used to call her Grace, and then my husband started calling her Gigi, and it just stuck."

Did he stop calling her Grace because it got too weird for him?

Did it feel wrong?

Did it make him think of me?

"Are you from around here?" she asks.

"Sort of," I say. "My dad lives a few blocks from here. Just visiting. You?"

"Connecticut originally," she says. "A little town no one's ever heard of not too far from the Rhode Island border. You want something to drink? You'll have to forgive me. I don't get a lot of company these days." She pops up and heads to the fridge. "Bottled water? Coffee? Milk? Apple juice? I've got the good kind . . . Martinelli's."

She winks, and her humble show of kindness makes me forget for a moment what I'm doing here.

I don't want to be rude. "Water would be great. Thank you."

Campbell serves me an uncapped bottle along with a pale-pink tea glass filled with ice. I can't help but get the sense that she's trying to impress me. I also can't help but wonder if she's always going the extra mile with Sutton.

Acts of service—that was his love language. Mine was quality time. Words like "I love you" never came easily to me, so I gave him the only currency I had—my attention.

She fixes a glass of water for herself—careful to diligently wipe away a rogue splatter on the countertop—and sits down beside me once again, settling in like we're about to have some girl talk. Maybe she's lonely. Maybe she's stuck in the house all day with a toddler, and this moment right here is about to become the highlight of her week.

"So you're married?" I ask a silly, obvious question because the ring on her finger is quite noticeable, but I need to know where Sutton is, and it's the easiest way to steer the conversation in that direction. The thought of him blasting through the back door, grocery bags in tow, sends an anxious flush of ice through my veins. I've had enough surprises for one day.

"I am." Hopping up from her chair, she grabs a framed photo from the built-in desk and hands it to me. "That's Sutton."

My reality tilts sideways for a moment when I hear his name on her lips, as if I'm being told about a stranger. As if the years-long history we shared was nothing more than a figment of my imagination.

If she only knew.

"He's in Baltimore for work this week," she adds.

Thank. God.

I exhale, letting my shoulders fall with the relief that he won't be waltzing through the door anytime soon.

The pulsing sting in my palms subsides, and I hand the photo back. Does he know how vulnerable his wife and child are right now? Entertaining some random woman off the street? I think about the key fob in conjunction with this new tidbit of information, and I shudder.

"You have a beautiful little family," I say.

She presses the photo against her chest. "Thank you. These two are my whole world."

Her ordinary brown gaze turns luminescent, and she pauses to drink in the photograph as if she's trying to imagine it through someone else's eyes: how blissful they appear, how two perfectly ordinary-looking humans created a miniature version of themselves so adorable she could grace the labels of baby food jars all across the world. She places the picture back on the desk and returns to the table, chin resting on her hand as she studies me.

"This is going to sound weird, but you look so familiar," she says. "Why do I feel like I've seen you before?"

Because you did. Yesterday.

"I get that a lot," I lie.

"I do, too. Some people just have those kinds of faces." She takes a careful swig of water. "So you said you grew up here . . . where do you live now?"

"Kind of live all over the place," I say, "but for now, home base is Portland."

"Maine or Oregon?"

"Oregon." I always forget there's a different Portland tucked up into the northeast. Quiet. Minding its own business. Out of sight, out of mind. Much like I used to be . . .

She smiles. "Ah, yes. I've never been there, but I've heard good things."

It's what you say when you have no intentions of traveling somewhere, but I don't judge her. Portland's not for everyone—especially if her idea of nirvana is the kind of family-friendly bubble Monarch Falls encapsulates.

Little Grace—*Gigi*—smacks her hands on her high-chair tray table and babbles something incoherent. I get the impression she's not used to sharing her mother's attention with strangers.

"Are you done with your snack, sweet girl?" Campbell tends to her immediately, scooping her up and bringing her to the table to partake in our girl talk. Bouncing her daughter on her knee, she turns to me. "You have kids?"

I shake my head. "Not my thing. I mean, I love them, don't get me wrong. I've just never been bitten by the motherhood bug."

The motherhood bug . . .

I sound like an idiot, but I'm trying to be honest without going deep.

She twirls a wispy, three-inch strand of her daughter's hair. "It's definitely not for everyone, that's for sure. Hardest thing you'll ever do."

I'm not sure how I missed it before, but a hint of blue-purple settles beneath her eyes, like two subtle half moons. Is she sleep-deprived? I don't know much about babies, but I'm pretty sure they're sleeping through the night by this age.

"How old is she?" I ask, despite knowing her birth date. It's in Sutton's file in my Watchers and Guardians app. April 3. She's fourteen months.

These two don't sit still for more than three-second intervals. I've barely budged, and I'm exhausted just watching them. Constant squirming and readjusting. Always touching. And people willingly live like this?

This'll be Rose soon.

She'll make it look posh, though. Thousand-dollar stroller. Mommy-and-Me-and-Mozart classes. Designer onesies. Not that any of those things are bad—but if she's anything like our mother (and she is), she'll make motherhood look chic and fabulous, and she'll be the envy of her social circle and then some.

I've often wondered if all our mother's fanfare was to distract from the fact that she was in over her head with motherhood. With her marriage. With her life.

"Gigi's fourteen months . . . going on fourteen some days." Campbell snickers through her nose, and I do the same out of politeness. It's an overdone joke that parents always make when they want to humbly brag that their kid has sass and personality. I don't take Campbell as a humblebragger, though. I think she's simply naive. Maybe a tad unoriginal. But mostly naive.

"How long have you lived in Monarch Falls?" I need to get this conversation back on track. It has to be useful, otherwise I'm wasting both of our time.

Her forehead creases. "A couple of years now?"

"You like it so far?" I take a swig of water.

"It's okay. People aren't as friendly as I'd hoped. Or maybe it's just me." Her voice fades with each word, as if she's second-guessing whether or not she's the problem in real time. "I sit inside all day with this little one, and it's impossible to meet people. Guess it's lonelier than I expected. Thought about signing up for some Kindermusik or Baby Gym classes . . . Just haven't gotten around to it, I suppose . . ."

Her words fade, shaded with despondency like a murky, muted watercolor.

I imagine it's pretty hard to make new friends in a new town when you've got a baby glued to your side twenty-four seven.

"Have you made any friends in your neighborhood or anything?" I ask, thinking about the older gentleman who held her baby as she got the mail yesterday. They seemed friendly, and obviously she trusted him enough to hand over her firstborn child for a few seconds. Then again, she's not exactly the poster child of wariness.

"Not as many as I'd hoped by this point." She glances sideways as if she wants to add something. I stay quiet, an old psychological hack that gets people to talk more when they're having reservations. "There was this couple that moved in next door last year. We had a couple of cookouts with them. A few double dates before Gigi came along." Campbell pauses, lips pressed tight. "I guess after a while we didn't really hit it off?"

I don't mean to frown, but it makes no sense. Why would they spend all that time together and then decide they didn't like them anymore? Something had to have happened.

"They didn't have children," she adds. "Didn't plan to have any either. Maybe our interests just . . . naturally went in different directions."

It's almost as if she wants to make it clear that there was no falling-out.

"That's too bad." I place a compassionate inflection into my tone to overshadow my intrigue as my mind whirs with varying scenarios. When we were together, everyone who'd ever met Sutton loved him. I always teased him that he could walk into a room filled with strangers and walk out with five new best friends. The man was a people magnet in every sense of the word. He saw only the best in people—much to my dismay at times—and he never met a jerk he couldn't redeem.

Campbell nods. "My husband . . . he's choosy when it comes to who we associate with."

Really?

I stay mum again, trying to picture Sutton as some kind of judgmental asshole.

But I can't.

"He thought this other couple . . ." Her lips waver, forming a shy laugh as her cheeks tinge pink. This topic embarrasses her, I think? "He thought they were a bad influence. Or something."

A bad influence?

What, is she not capable of choosing the people she wants to associate with? He has to make that decision for her?

I scrape my jaw off the floor. None of this sounds like Sutton.

"This is going to sound silly." She leans closer. "But they liked to . . . smoke pot."

Sutton and I smoked together all the time in college. At least once a week. More if it was midterms or finals.

I remind myself people are allowed to change. And maybe it was a habit he outgrew as he grew into his family-man persona.

"Your husband," I say, "is he pretty . . . traditional?"

She smiles. "You could say that. He likes rules. And order. That kind of thing."

"Where'd you say you're from originally?" I ask, wondering if she has any friends from back home. Surely he wouldn't cut her off from them? Maybe when I get back, I'll do some poking around on her

Instaface account and see what I can find. Tagged photos. Comments. Anything that can point me in the direction of whether or not she's kept in touch with old friends. "I mean, where in Connecticut?"

"Blueberry Springs," she says. Her left front tooth overlaps the other in the slightest of ways, and I'm secretly satisfied to find a sliver of imperfection in this moment.

"How'd you two end up all the way out here?"

"Sutton found a job here, talked me into moving."

He *found* a job here. Interesting. So he wasn't *offered* a job here. A job here didn't just *fall into his lap*. He had to have been looking. I suppose it wouldn't be completely out of the realm of possibility that he'd find a job thirty miles from Rutgers, where we met as undergrads, but what are the odds that out of five hundred towns in this state, he'd search for a job in the only one I've ever called home?

Sutton knew what this town meant to me. He was aware of its significance. How much I associated it with some of the best years of my childhood—and the worst year of my life. He witnessed the panic attack building in my system the first time I brought him here to meet my father. And he understood when I decided to cut the visit short and head back to campus. The entire ride home I word vomited into his ear all the things I loathed about this city and its inhabitants and everything it represented. It was probably the most I'd ever opened up to him in the history of our relationship. When I was done ranting, I swiped my hand at an itch on my cheek . . . only to realize I was crying.

It was the first, last, and only time I ever cried in front of him.

A cold sweat blankets my neck when I realize that perhaps I got this all wrong. Maybe he didn't come here because of me . . . maybe he came here to get away from me because he knew I refused to set foot in this town?

"How'd you meet?" I ask, throat dry. I reach for another swig of water. "You and your husband?"

Her lips part, but before she has a chance to answer, her phone buzzes on the counter. "I bet that's him, actually. Will you excuse me for a second?"

She disappears, Gigi on her hip, into a room down the hall.

At least she has the good sense not to leave her daughter alone with a stranger.

The tick of the kitchen clock echoes off the walls, and her voice is nothing more than a murmur of words I can't distinguish from here. Do people normally take their spouse's phone calls in privacy, or is that a Campbell thing?

Or . . . is it a Sutton thing?

I take the opportunity to gaze around the room, cataloging details for my mental files. Nothing strikes me as out of the ordinary. It's a typical American household. Clean. Open. Neutral furniture in classic silhouettes like it was plucked from a warehouse showroom display. Baby accessories peppered around. A high chair. A playpen. A basket of toys. A neat pile of cardboard books. Aside from the family photos on the corkboard, this could be anyone's place.

Nothing around me is going to answer a single question I have.

"I'm so sorry about that." Campbell returns a minute later, bouncing Gigi in her arms. "Apparently he left an important file on his work computer, so now we get to run into the office and email it to him."

Before I can process her words, she's flitting about the kitchen, grabbing her purse and keys and shoving a bottle into a diaper bag, like a woman on a time-sensitive mission.

I rise. "No worries. I'll get out of your hair."

Campbell walks me to the door, stepping lightly, and when I turn to wave goodbye, I catch a sullen expression on her face—the same one I've seen on my father before when he's watched me walk away. Same one I've seen on the faces of men I've dated over the years. Unspoken longing.

Some people aren't good at being alone.

"Do you maybe want to get coffee sometime this week?" I'm not typically this friendly, and I know she's in a rush, but she's clearly starved for human contact, and Sutton's in Baltimore, so . . .

Besides, she still hasn't told me how they met.

I have questions. She has answers.

Was it a storybook meet-cute? Or did he spot a woman with my likeness and plant himself in her path so he could make his dashed dreams a reality? I don't want to believe he's capable of the latter, but given the evidence—it's not as far-fetched of a notion as I'd like it to be.

"Really?" Her straight lips curl at the sides, and her brows lift. "I'd love that."

I pull my phone from my leggings pocket, and she rattles off her digits so quickly I almost miss a number.

"I'll get ahold of you sometime this week," I say.

"Perfect." She lifts on her toes, gives me a quick wave, and closes the door behind me.

I'm halfway down the street when her garage door screeches open and she peels out of the driveway. When she passes, she gives me a wave and a two-second smile that fades the instant she thinks I've looked away.

And then she's gone.

Funny how quickly her demeanor changed the instant Sutton called. That intrinsic sweetness and desperate friendliness vanished, replaced with a frantic, frenzied excuse for a woman—almost as if she was afraid of what would happen if she didn't do exactly what he asked that instant.

I walk the three blocks home with a slight limp, making mental lists of all the questions I'm going to need to work into our next conversation. If she's always this much of an open book, I should be able to get all the information I could possibly need before I place myself in my ex-boyfriend's path.

At first I simply wanted to know how they met—but now? I want to know if she's fearful of him. Because if she is, then perhaps I should be, too . . . afraid of the man he's become.

The phone call in private. The social isolation. The complete control he has over her.

Is he . . . *abusing* her?

In a roundabout way, this is my fault.

He wasn't like this before. I did this to him. I broke him.

For the past week, I've been convinced that I need to help Sutton. I never could have anticipated that I'd be saving his wife instead.

CHAPTER 6

I've been thinking about Campbell a lot lately. More than I thought I would. More than I should. More than I've thought about Sutton.

I order a black coffee and find a booth in the back of the Riverton Café in downtown Monarch Falls Tuesday afternoon. I make sure there's plenty of room for her stroller or car seat or whatever contraption she'll be bringing for Gigi.

I also pilfer a coloring book and some broken crayons from the kiddie section of the shop, though I have no idea if she's old enough for that. Odds are Campbell will come prepared because she seems like a good, doting mother, but I don't want to risk this conversation being cut short because of a crabby, understimulated child.

Checking my watch, I attempt to quiet my mind. It's three minutes till. She'll be here soon.

It's been two days since our last chat, and every day with my father and Bliss feels like a bizarre eternity.

This morning I walked outside to take a phone call and interrupted their poolside meditation hour. Only a woman named Bliss Diamond could get my father to meditate—and for an entire hour. With Tibetan singing bowls, no less. I can only imagine how amused his neighbors must be every time he hooks a new girlfriend and enters into a new phase of life. The man sheds his old skin like a snake.

The bells on the shop door jangle, and I gaze across the coffee-scented space to find Campbell wrestling her stroller through. A blonde woman with an asymmetrical haircut steps out of line to help hold the door, and Campbell thanks her with blushing cheeks and a self-effacing smile.

She's endearing. Unpretentious. Sweet but not shy. Plain but not ignorable. Wonderfully average.

I can see why Sutton chose her.

She's the antithesis of me—which makes her safe.

I slide out of the booth and wave until she spots me.

She points to the coffee bar, implying that she's going to order a drink first, and I nod. It's like we have an unspoken language already. A connection. Literally.

I wait in patient silence, practicing my questions over the grind of coffee beans and the whirring of the cappuccino machine. A barista calls out for a "Robbie" and then a "Millie," followed by a "Patricia" and an "Antoine," before he gets to Campbell's order.

"Sorry I'm late," she says a few minutes later. Placing her coffee on the table, she turns back to unbuckle Gigi from her stroller before whipping out a baggie of Cheerios.

"You're fine," I assure her, watching as the two get settled. "How's your day so far?"

As much as I want to throw a grenade's worth of inquiries at her the instant she sits, I opt to ease into this conversation with small talk.

Gigi picks at her Cheerios, occasionally struggling to pinch them between her stubby fingers. I keep the crayons and coloring book out of sight on the seat beside me. She's clearly not there yet, and there's no need to illustrate how incompetent I am when it comes to kids.

"Nothing too crazy," she says to me, though her focus is on her daughter. "Yourself?"

"Worked for a couple of hours." I sip my coffee, wallowing in the awkwardness of this moment but determined to trudge forward anyway.

"What is it you do for work?"

"People hire me to remove things about them from the internet." I take another drink.

Her brows lift. "That's got to be interesting."

"It used to be. In the beginning. Now it's mostly boring or disturbing. Not much in between." I shrug and hope she doesn't ask for specifics. Over the years, I've trained my mind to compartmentalize the worst of the worst of the things I've seen. "Did you work? Before Gigi?"

Her face softens. "I did. I was an ER nurse."

I've never understood how people can spend all that time and money working toward a career—only to discard it all the second they bring a human life into the world. I mean, I get it. Raising children not to be assholes is important. It's the lord's work. But Campbell and Sutton are young. And it's not like they're raising a gaggle of kids. It's *one* baby. Surely they can afford the best childcare, right?

I try to recall if Sutton and I ever had that conversation. At times (mostly when he'd been drinking) he would wax poetic about what our ideal future would look like. Most of the time, he'd paint this *Leave It to Beaver* picture that would stir a swell of nausea in my middle, and I'd end up tuning him out. But I'm almost certain I mentioned hiring a nanny once, and he didn't balk.

"You think you'll ever go back to nursing?" I ask.

She shakes her head without pause and then grins at her daughter as she shoves a palmful of crushed cereal into her drool-covered mouth.

"My husband prefers that I stay home with her," she says before biting her lip. It's as if she didn't realize how archaic the notion sounded until the words touched her lips. "I mean, I've always wanted to be a stay-at-home mom." Campbell brushes hair from Gigi's forehead. "I can't imagine going back to work and leaving her with someone else all day." She sucks in a quick breath and leans in. "Not that there's anything wrong with that. It's just not something I could do. Personally."

All the excuses and the overexplaining—it's as if she feels the need to qualify her opinions. Another sign of abuse, or is she simply insecure in her opinions? Desperate to be liked? It's hard to be sure without getting to know her better. And I fully intend to do that.

"I'm sure if you looked hard enough you could find someone amazing," I say, just to test her reaction.

She doesn't strike me as someone with trust issues—especially given her hospitality the other morning—but maybe it's a new mom thing?

Daphne stayed home with us until . . . she went to prison. But we always had summer nannies and a rotation of babysitters. She had no qualms about leaving us in the care of other people so she could run errands and get manicures in peace.

"I'm sure." She sips her coffee, leaving it at that. Like the topic isn't up for debate. Like the issue has already been decided.

"You think you'll have more?" My question is invasive, and I wouldn't normally say something like this to someone I hardly know, but I'm trying to establish a dialogue here. And I want her to feel like she can open up to me.

"God willing." She doesn't look up from her daughter. "My husband wants four."

I know. I remember.

My insides cinch at the thought of bringing life into this world. They cinch tighter at the thought of four. My thighs fasten together.

"What about you? How many do you want?" I ask.

Her delicate fingertips graze the side of her coffee cup, and she draws in a long breath, as if she has to think about the answer. "I don't know . . ."

She doesn't know? She's "always wanted to be a stay-at-home mom," but she doesn't know how many kids she wants?

"I'm an only child, so I've always liked the idea of a big family," she says. "I just don't know how big. Gigi keeps me on my toes. Can't imagine having three more of her. Maybe when she's a little older?"

I think of Campbell and Sutton five years from now, then ten years from now. Flecks of gray at his temple (his father went gray quite early). Maybe an extra ten or fifteen pounds because . . . life. Coaching Little League on the weekends. I picture Campbell's cute little car replaced with a glossy red minivan, fully embracing the Whitlock family lifestyle.

Campbell runs her fingers through Gigi's hair. From the moment they sat down, I don't think she's stopped doting on her for two seconds.

She's a good mom. Loving and attentive. Sutton chose well in that department. She's a hell of a lot better than I'd have been.

The neckline of her blouse shifts as she moves, and I spot a faded green bruise along her collarbone.

I swallow. Hard. For a second, I wonder if I imagined it.

And then I spot it again.

"So how did you meet your husband?" I blurt out my next question, the one that's been lingering like an earworm since the other day.

"It's kind of embarrassing, if only because it's so not romantic or anything." Campbell stifles a smile and rolls her eyes before exhaling. "We actually met online."

Her cheeks tinge with pink warmth. This is a fact that embarrasses her.

"I know. It's so cliché," she adds, waving a hand in front of her face and glancing away.

"Not at all," I lie. My mind spins, conjuring up images of Sutton so desperate to move on from me that he completes an online dating profile, uploads a handful of flattering images, and puts himself out there in hopes of finding someone to fill my void.

My heart aches for this heartbroken image of the man I once knew.

"How long have you been together?" I fire out my next question slowly, to tamp down my anticipation. So far I've yet to locate this information online. They purchased their home two summers ago, and a year before that, they cosigned on an apartment in Hoboken, but everything before that is a question mark. Addresses and work history

I can find with a few clicks of a mouse. But a detailed timeline of their relationship and its intricacies isn't exactly the sort of thing I can scrape off the deep web.

"Seven . . . eight years?" Her face twists as she glances up and to the left. "I have to do the math sometimes. It all kind of blurs together after a while."

Eight years ago last month is when I ended our relationship.

He must have found her shortly afterward.

"You met online," I say, "so was that with a dating app?"

"Kind of." She winces, and I get the sense that she doesn't want to get into it. "It's a long story, a little boring actually. There were some emails exchanged, and then we met and it turned into . . . this."

She kisses her daughter's forehead.

"Do you have someone?" Campbell changes the subject. "A boy-friend, partner, whatever?"

Do I *have* someone? Interesting choice of words.

No, I don't *have* anyone . . . because I don't *want* anyone.

I shake my head. "Can't even keep a houseplant alive. Imagine what I'd do to a relationship."

Campbell laughs through her nose. "You travel for work?"

"No. For fun." And for sanity. "I can work anywhere in the world. I don't like to stay in one place too long."

"Must be nice." She sips her coffee. I don't believe her. She doesn't strike me as the type of person who's filled with wanderlust, craving adventure at every turn. "What's been your favorite city so far?"

"San Diego. Best weather, hands down. Not too cold, not too hot."

Her lips tug at the side. "I should visit someday."

Visit . . . me?

Or visit in general?

I wonder what Sutton would think if he knew I was sitting here hav-ing a lovely chat with his wife? That his daughter was sitting across from me? That I knew all about this life he'd engineered in my hometown?

Would he be embarrassed if he knew that I'm on to him?

It occurs to me like a shock of ice through my veins that perhaps he already knows. He's an intelligent man. If Campbell mentioned in passing that she's meeting a new friend named Grace who happens to be in town visiting her father . . . he'd put it together in a heartbeat.

"I love the idea of moving somewhere warm, but I don't think I could get my husband to step away from the East Coast," she says with a hopeless sigh. "He loves it here."

My fist clenches around my coffee cup. He doesn't care what she wants? She doesn't get a say in where they live?

I need to lighten the mood.

I also need more information.

"So . . . what do you do for fun around here?" I force some more small talk, trying to get an idea of where I might find (or avoid) the Whitlocks in their spare time.

Campbell digs into her back pocket and pulls out her vibrating phone. I briefly spot Sutton's name on the screen. I hadn't noticed it going off. I swear some people have a sixth sense about their electronics.

"I'm so sorry." She clutches it against her chest. "I'll be right back."

Before I have a chance to tell her she doesn't have to run off, she scoops Gigi into her arms and carries her outside to take her phone call, leaving behind her purse, her stroller, her coffee, and a mountain of cereal crumbs.

Again, so trusting. *Too* trusting.

Five minutes later, they're back.

"Everything okay?" I ask.

"What?" She places Gigi back into the booth and slides in beside her. "Of course. It was just my husband checking in."

I think back to the other day in her kitchen, when Sutton called and she took the call down the hall and behind a closed door.

"You don't have to do that, you know," I say.

"Do what?"

"If you ever need to take a phone call, I mean . . ." I glance out the window and back. "If you're trying to be polite or whatever. Don't inconvenience yourself for my sake."

Campbell waves a hand. "Oh, no. It's not that. Sutton is really big on privacy. I hope you don't think *I'm* being rude?"

"God, no," I assure her.

Sutton . . . big on privacy? Since when? Back in college, he'd take all his calls on speakerphone or over the Bluetooth in the car. He never demanded privacy of me, never required it of himself.

"So what's he like? Your husband?" Clearly he's a changed man. I need to know what I'm dealing with.

A vision of him playing air harmonica to "Mary Jane's Last Dance" comes to mind. He was always trying to put a smile on my face, always reminding me to lighten up. The man had no qualms about making a fool of himself to pull me out of my darkest moods, if only for a moment.

My mind refuses to conjure up a vision of a man demanding private, secret phone calls.

"Sutton?" She gazes up at the ceiling, contemplating. "Hmm. He's an amazing father. Old-fashioned. Driven. Though he can be a bit particular at times . . ."

"Particular?" Tell me more . . .

"He knows what he wants," she says, her voice matter-of-fact. She shrugs like it's a quirk of his she's come to accept and respect. "He's been that way since the beginning. He likes to run the show, I guess. And that's fine. It's nice not having to worry about things, you know? He's always taking care of us."

She's submissive and subservient—again, the antithesis of me.

But my mind refuses to picture Sutton as a control freak.

Eight years ago, had someone asked me to describe him, I'd have used words like agreeable, sentimental, tender, selfless, and soft-hearted. Movies made him cry, even the happy ones. He loved stargazing. And he was always asking what *I* wanted to do. Where *I* wanted to go for lunch. Where *I* wanted to live someday. He never tried to sway me one way or the other—he simply wanted to be with me . . . wherever that was.

Campbell picks at a hangnail.

Is she nervous? Is there something else she's not saying?

"You're one of the lucky ones," I say to feel her out.

"What do you mean?"

"You landed yourself a real family man. Aren't too many of those left these days." I think of my brother, Sebastian, who knows he's got it all—sharp looks, cunning wit, the promise of success as soon as he finishes law school. The guy's got a waiting list of beautiful women all desperate to lock him down. He lives for the moment. Words like "marriage" and "family" don't exist in his extensive vocabulary. Men like him are more the rule than the exception these days, especially for our generation.

She sniffs. "Yeah."

Yeah? That's all she's going to give me?

"So what do you guys do for fun around here?" I ask again. "Have you checked out the Marietto Running Trail or the Summerfield Aquarium downtown?" I cross my fingers under the table, hoping those places still exist.

"Not yet," she says. "Now that Gigi's getting older . . . I'm sure we'll do more of that. We don't even have a sitter yet."

No sitter? So they haven't had a date night in over a year? Surely Sutton has a colleague with a cash-hungry teenage daughter? Why wouldn't he put out the feelers? Take his poor wife on a date to get her out of the house? Let her put on a dress and heels and lipstick and feel like a woman again?

It's almost barbaric to keep her sheltered away like that. No wonder she was so desperate to clean me up after our run-in the other morning. This is a woman *starved* for attention. Socially and emotionally emaciated. Dying on the inside from loneliness—even if she doesn't know it yet.

One day she'll snap . . . the way my mother did twenty years ago . . . and Sutton will have no one to blame but himself.

"I think there's a children's museum on the east side of town," I add. I recall spotting it on the traffic-heavy trek from the airport to my father's house. "Or there used to be. Have you seen that park that looks like a medieval castle? Has a moat and everything."

My phone buzzes inside my bag. Without looking at it, I already know it's Jonah. I'm under a tight deadline with the Redwood project, which means I shouldn't be here, tending to personal business.

I check the caller ID and confirm my suspicions.

"I'm so sorry—it's my boss." I hate to take the call outside after our conversation a few minutes back, but it's best he doesn't hear the tinkle of coffee mugs and soft jazz playing in the background. "Will you excuse me for a sec? I'll be right back."

A week ago, I was tasked with a revenge porn project—my least favorite kind of gig, if only because as soon as one copy comes down, ten more pop up in its place. Virtual Whac-A-Mole. This particular case, however, involves the underage former stepdaughter of an Indiana senator, and his opponents would love nothing more than to manufacture a scandal so they can see him go down in flames. Or so his camp says. I was hired to do a job, not to ask questions.

"Watcher Girl." Jonah always calls me by my online handle when I answer.

"Jonah." I always call him by his name. Though once I made the mistake of referring to him as *Guardian Boy*—his handle—and he thought I was flirting.

"How's it going? You in, uh, New York?" he asks.

"Jersey." Close enough.

"You got a minute?"

"Yeah. What's up?"

"Think I finally got a hot lead for you on that Sarah Thomas case."

My heart hiccups, and for a moment, I forget the situation happening on the other side of the café door.

I've been searching for our former nanny for years, hoping she could shed some light on the possible whereabouts of my biological mother, Autumn Carpenter. Allegedly Sarah was the last person to see her alive. And given the fact that Sarah spent almost a decade living as her, she's the only person who can answer the origin questions that have plagued me my entire adult life.

"You think it's really her?" I ask. I've been burned before. There are thousands of Sarah Thomases in the United States. Even more if I expand my search abroad. With a name that common, hiding in plain sight is a breeze. And she'd have every reason to want to hide after everything that happened twenty years ago . . . working for our family, believing and acting as though I were her daughter.

I have it on good authority that they almost charged her with murder of my biological mother, but in the end, there was no dead body, which meant there could be no homicide case. Also, due to Sarah's extensive mental health history and personality disorders, her memories would have never been enough to comprise a confession the courts could take seriously.

All I want is a few minutes of her time—a phone call and some answers.

Mostly I want to know what my mother was like . . .

. . . if she had a darkness inside, like me.

If she pushed people away. If things like love made her skin crawl. If staying in one place for too long made her stir-crazy. If we shared the same brown eyes and lifeless, mousy hair. If she stared into the mirror only to find an abyss of emptiness staring back at her.

I also want to know why she chose the McMullens.

But more than any of that, I want to know if there's a chance she's still alive.

Not holding my breath on that last one, but I'm going to ask nevertheless.

"I'll shoot the file your way," Jonah says. "How's the Redwood project coming? Told 'em I'd have an update in the morning."

"Should have it all done by the end of the week." I underpromise so I can overdeliver. I should have it done in two days. "I'll keep you posted."

"Good, good." Jonah ends the call the way he always ends the call. It's never "Goodbye" or "Talk to you later." It's always "Good, good."

I tuck my phone into my pocket and head back to the booth, only the second I push through the jangling front door I realize something's amiss.

Our booth is vacant.

The stroller is gone.

Nothing but my coffee cup remains.

It's as if they were never there at all.

Sliding into my seat, I sit in stunned silence—until I get a text.

Campbell: So sorry . . . Gigi was fussy and felt feverish. Wasn't sure how much longer you'd be and didn't want to interrupt.

Me: No worries! Rain check?

Three dots fill the screen before disappearing completely. A second later, I glance outside just in time to catch her white sedan backing out of a parking spot so hurriedly she nearly collides with a truck backing out at the same time.

What just happened?

CHAPTER 7

Crickets chirp, and the moon reflects off the surface of the pool tonight. On the other side of the yard is the yellow house with the wind chimes, glowing from within. A family lives there now, I've deduced. Children's laughter floats from their open windows, trailing across our backyard. It's strange to think of the house being purchased and sold, painted and decorated, to think of babies being born and nurseries being set up—all the ways that life is constantly moving on.

It never stops.

That summer with the delusional Sarah Thomas as our nanny was a lifetime ago, and yet in this moment, despite everything having evaporated into ancient memories, I could reach out and touch it, it's so tangible.

Sometimes I used to stare out my window, gazing toward the glow of her house at night, trying to sneak a glimpse of her taking her dog out or washing dishes in her little kitchen, her handsome boyfriend kissing her neck from behind.

I wanted more than anything to be hers—before I knew who she really was.

Logging on to my Watchers and Guardians app, I pull up the file Jonah sent me earlier and dial the number on the screen.

An automated voice mail greeting answers in the middle of the third ring, and I silently mourn the fact that I won't get to hear her voice—not that I'd remember it after all these years.

I clear my throat and wait for the tone. "Hi. My name is Grace McMullen, and I'm searching for someone by the name of Sarah Thomas. I think you might be her. You worked for our family twenty years ago as a nanny. I have a few questions for you . . . about my mother. My biological mother. If you could call me back . . . I'd appreciate it. I won't take up too much of your time."

I rattle off my number, end the call, and don't hold my breath.

I've left messages exactly like that to hundreds of Sarah Thomases over the years, and never once have I received a call back—not even to tell me I have the wrong person or to eff-off. Not that I blame any of them. We live in a day and age where anyone can pretend to be anyone else, and people are constantly trying to take advantage of the kindness or naivete of others.

Long-standing disappointment aside, there's comfort in knowing my trust issues don't make me a special snowflake.

The patio door slides open and closed behind me.

"Grace? What are you doing sitting out here in the dark?" Bliss weaves through lounge chairs to get to me, her vibrant sarong glowing under the stars. Sleepwear aside, I've yet to see her in anything other than a sari, sarong, or caftan, always accessorized with a faux tan and a bold lip. She is radiant, always. Maybe it's all that inner peace. They say yoga and meditation are good for that, but I wouldn't know. I've tried to shut my mind off, but it doesn't work that way. Only when I'm running. And I can't run forever. "Could I interest you in a glass of pinot?"

A cut-crystal chalice with some ornamental design along the rim rests in her hand, filled to the brim with dark wine.

"You can have mine," she says. "I haven't touched it."

Before I have a chance to decline, Bliss hands me the glass and dashes inside. A moment later, she returns with another and settles into the lounger beside me.

"It's so peaceful out here in the evenings," she says in one long exhalation. Draping her sarong over her legs, she takes a sip. "Suburban paradise."

I never thought of it that way before.

"I hope you don't mind me joining you," she adds, though it'd be too late if I did.

"Not at all," I lie. Sort of. I don't dislike Bliss. Not yet. The worst thing about her, so far, is that she's dating my father, which means she's naive as hell. But her yoga-meditation-Mother-Earth-Gaia-herbal-tea-optimism doesn't bother me. People like her outnumber the palm trees on the West Coast, and they're not so bad. They could be doing a lot worse things than smoking a joint on their apartment balconies in West Hollywood while strumming their ukuleles and planning their next South American ayahuasca retreat.

"Do you smoke, Bliss?" I ask.

"Cigarettes?"

"No."

"Oh. Then yes. Sometimes . . ." Her gaze glints in the dark. "Haven't in a while . . . why?"

I reach into my bag beside me and retrieve a joint and a lighter. I press it between my lips while I light up, and then I take an exaggerated drag before handing it over.

Bliss pinches it carefully in her fingers, holding it over the empty space that separates our chairs so as not to spill any ash on herself. A moment later, she slowly brings it to her lips, inhales, closes her eyes, and hands it back.

I don't smoke often, but after my weird exchange with Campbell at the coffee shop earlier and after leaving yet another message for yet another Sarah Thomas a few minutes ago, I need this escape. Plus, it's too late for a jog. I don't like to run after the sun's gone down, not even in the safest of neighborhoods. People get killed and kidnapped that way. Cars. Serial killers. Freak heart attacks. Human traffickers. I'd be remiss to believe the dark underbelly of humanity doesn't lurk in a pretty little city like this.

"Does my father know you do this?" I ask out of pure curiosity. He's always been conservative—socially and otherwise.

Except that time he dated a girl almost half his age who had a secret drug problem . . .

If there's anything I've learned in the past thirty years, it's that Graham McMullen is full of all kinds of surprises. And in the end, none of it surprises me.

Bliss nods, reaching for my joint and then taking another drag, the red tip glowing in the dark.

"You have no idea how happy your dad is now that you're home," she says after an exhalation. Fanning the smoke from her watering eyes, she adds, "I hope you'll be staying awhile. At least for his sake. He's missed you. Talks about you all the time. Worries about you."

She chokes back a cough, fanning the skunky smoke away from her airspace.

I take the joint back, letting it burn short between my fingers.

In all my years away, not once did the idea of my father *worrying* about me ever cross my mind. I figured he was too busy chasing skirts and polishing golf clubs and bragging about Rose and Sebastian to fret about little old me.

"Why'd you stop talking to him? If you don't mind my asking?" The whites of Bliss's eyes glimmer in the dark, and the weight of her stare presses into me. "I don't mean to pry. It's just, I know what it's like to cut your parents out of your life. I also know what it's like to bury them six feet in the ground without ever having forgiven them. You're young. You've got too much life ahead of you to live with that kind of anger."

"What makes you think I'm angry?"

"A person doesn't disappear and cut off all communication with the ones who love them unless they're upset about something. At least in my experience. I used to be a therapist back in the day."

She says "back in the day" as if the fifteen-or-so years that separate us are some kind of generational divide. It's not like she's my grand-mother. She's barely old enough to be my mother.

"Why'd you stop?"

Her mouth inches up at one corner. "Nice deflection. Why don't you answer my question first, and then I'll answer yours?"

I take a hit of the joint, stare at the moonlit pool, and exhale. "Because I'm tired."

Besides, I don't know Bliss well enough to go over the intricacies of my intimacy issues, the difficulties I've had with maintaining relation-ships, my tendency to destroy things once I deem them too "perfect."

Plus, if she diagnoses me, she might feel inclined to help me—and I don't need help.

I stub the joint out on the concrete pavers and tuck it back into a baggie in my purse before rising from the lounge chair.

"Going to take this to go." I swipe my wineglass from a side table and give her a wink, though it's dark so I don't know if she can tell I'm being playful.

"Sleep well, Grace," she calls after me, her voice soft the way my mother's once was when she'd tuck us in at the end of an exhausting day.

As I trudge upstairs to my room, I think about what she said—about my father worrying about me, about how thrilled he is to have me home—and then I think about Sutton.

The mere notion of someone being elated to see me is farcical.

I don't bring joy to people's lives—quite the opposite.

I'm a rain cloud. I bring thunder, lightning, dusk, and gloom.

I see the worst in people. I prefer my own company to anyone else's. And things like love and togetherness make me physically ill.

Everyone—and I mean everyone—is better off with a little less of that shit in their lives . . . even if they don't know it. And most of them don't.

The average person has no idea what's good for them. In fact, my family should be happy I've made the decision for them. I'm the wet blanket of the family. I serve no purpose but to make those around me uncomfortable. I stare too hard, sometimes. Think too deeply. It makes people nervous.

What Sutton saw in me, I'll never know.

Or maybe he was always seeing what he wanted to see. He could have been projecting. Convinced he could bring out a lighter side of me by marrying me and making me a family woman, giving me the picture-perfect life I never had.

Ha.

All of that said, I don't suppose it would pain me to spend a little one-on-one time with my father while I'm here, to make him smile the way Sutton once did for me when he sensed my mood needing a lift.

If I'm here to offer my ex closure, I might as well kill two birds.

Especially since, after this, I may never set foot in Monarch Falls again.

CHAPTER 8

Impatience gnaws at me with sharp, kitten-like teeth. I can't get comfortable. I scratch the hives forming on my arms before fixating on a hangnail, and on my way to find a pair of nail scissors in the bathroom, I get distracted by what appears to be a gray hair at my temple.

Or maybe I'm imagining it.

All this waiting has me going insane, coming out of my skin.

I text Campbell Friday morning to see if she and Gigi are up for a walk around the neighborhood.

Fresh air? I send in a second text, adding a smiling emoji. I add a tree and sun but delete them before pressing "Send." Overkill. I don't need to illustrate the mental, physical, and emotional benefits of a leisurely walk-and-talk.

I figure less than seventy-two hours is enough breathing room after Tuesday's weirdness. The last thing I want to do is smother the poor girl or bombard her with this insta-friendship, but I'm genuinely concerned.

The message shows as **READ** within seconds, and I keep an eye on the screen, awaiting some kind of response.

But I get nothing . . . not even three dots indicating a response is on the way.

Chewing my lip, I leave my phone on the nightstand and get changed. If she doesn't text me back in ten minutes, I'm hopping in my car and driving past. At this point, I don't care if it's a psychotic move. I don't care if normal people don't do this sort of thing. I've never been "normal," and I'm not about to start now.

Plus, I need to know she's okay.

Fifteen minutes later—I gave her an extra five just in case—I'm turning the corner to Lakemont, easing up on the gas as I get closer to their brick-blood craftsman. Going too slow would be obvious, but speeding past would get me noticed just as much.

I check my speed and approach the Whitlock residence, palms sweaty on the wheel.

From behind sunglasses, I watch from my periphery.

My heart plunges when I spot Sutton's Toyota in the driveway.

He's back from Baltimore—is that why she's been ignoring me?

Is she not allowed to leave the house if he's there? I wouldn't think so, but after the private phone calls and the fact that he "freaks" if there's a speck of dirt on the floor because he's so particular . . . it's not completely out of the realm of possibility.

I continue on my way, fingers crossed she didn't happen to be gazing out the window at the exact moment I cruised by. The history of our newly minted friendship—if one can call it that—plays like a movie in my head from our very first interaction until our last.

She invited *me* inside.

She accepted *my* coffee invite.

She initiated all this.

Everything was going well until the coffee shop when she just . . . bolted. A hundred times I've replayed our conversation, scrutinizing and overanalyzing each and every question until I'm certain I didn't overstep any boundaries. She claimed Gigi felt feverish—and I might have believed her if it wasn't for the fact that she's been ignoring my texts and blowing me off ever since.

Unless . . .

Unless the two of them talked, and he figured out that her new "friend" is me. And in that case, I can't say that I'd blame him for requesting that she keep her distance. He's probably embarrassed.

By the time I get back to my father's home, I decide enough is enough.

I convince myself it's time to do what I came here to do.

And come Monday, I will.

CHAPTER 9

I swore I wouldn't bother him at work—but that was before.

Now that I'm aware of his controlling tendencies, and now that Campbell knows my face, it's imperative that I run into him solo . . . which is why I'm parked next to his Toyota on Monday, waiting for him to take his lunch.

I called his office earlier, trying to gauge from his receptionist what time he took his lunch, and she cheerfully told me noon to one. Everyone in his circle is too trusting.

I was so prepared to pussyfoot around the question that I wasn't expecting her to drop that information into my lap. I sputtered out a surprised "thank you," ended the call, and booked it here.

The clock on the dash reads 12:01, but I check my phone and verify that it's a few minutes fast.

My skin flushes with anxious heat, and I crank the AC before checking my reflection in the visor mirror. I'm not trying to impress the man, obviously, but when you haven't seen an ex in eight years, there's no shame in wanting to look halfway presentable. Plus, no one takes you seriously when you look like a crazy-haired, wild-eyed maniac who hasn't slept in weeks.

I scan my face in the tiny, dimly lit rectangle, wishing I'd have swiped on another coat of mascara while resisting the urge to fish out a tube of cherry lip balm from my purse. And then I smooth my hair into a low, twisted bun. Neat and clean. As good as it's going to get.

I imagine I don't look all that different than I did eight years ago. My face is a little thinner, having lost some of that early-twenties baby fat. The beginnings of cavernous half moons have formed beneath my eyes. I don't think I had those before. Other than that, my irises are the same shit brown they always were, and my hair is the same shoulder-length, sand-colored bob it's always been. I'm due for a trim, but . . . priorities.

The clock on the dash reads 12:07 now. Sutton was never a stickler on punctuality, but now that he's a white-collar working man, I'd imagine every minute of his lunch break counts.

Any minute now . . .

I tinker with the radio for a minute, trying to find a song to distract me, only they're all obnoxious, so I kill the volume and sink back into my seat, laser focused on the front door.

I want to imagine Sutton running home to enjoy a quick lunch his wife has prepared for him. I want to picture him rolling around on the living room floor with his daughter for a bit, reading her a board book, blowing raspberries on her tummy as she giggles. I want to think that when he's done, he straightens his tie, kisses his wife, and heads back to the office for the rest of the afternoon.

But now all I can imagine is Sutton texting Campbell twenty times a day to check on her, and not because he misses her or wonders what she's up to—but because he needs to know where she is at all times.

I then imagine him rushing home at lunch, slamming the door when he realizes his soup and sandwich aren't ready yet because Campbell's been too busy dealing with a cranky toddler.

I imagine him riffling through a stack of mail before shoving it on the desk in their kitchen with a sigh, a subtle reminder to his wife that he works hard to support them.

Of course that's not the Sutton that I knew and loved.

But Campbell's conduct is textbook. The bruises. The atypical behavior. The way she described him, albeit politely, as a control freak. The math is simple: she's clearly being abused . . . and he's the only person in her life.

Even if he's figured out that I'm in town and that she and I have been talking, even if he's forbidden her from befriending me, it's not right to control someone else like that.

That's his wife, for crying out loud. The mother of his child. Not his domestic servant.

I wait until 12:18.

Then 12:31.

12:47.

At 1:12, I call his office and ask to speak to him—but only as a test. His receptionist patches me through immediately. I hang up before he answers, heart pounding in my teeth.

Exiting the parking lot, I head home, realizing that if Sutton's at work, then Campbell is home with the baby.

Alone.

This could be my only opportunity to help her.

CHAPTER 10

I change into jogging clothes the instant I'm back and hightail it to Lakemont. I'd have driven, given the urgency and potential time sensitivity of what I'm about to do, but driving to someone's house after they've ignored two texts feels . . . aggressive.

I'm rounding the corner, their house in the distance, when apprehension floods my veins. Knocking on the door is forward and presumptive, but if she's in trouble, I'd rather err on the side of making a fool of myself than assuming she's fine and shying away like this is none of my business.

As far as I'm concerned, this *is* my business.

I've turned an angel of a man into a monster—and this is the result.

With quavering thighs, I slow from a jog to a brisk walk before approaching their front steps. I press the doorbell, which I realize now has a camera attached.

This is new.

If Sutton gets real-time notifications on his phone anytime someone presses it, he'll see my face.

I angle myself away from the tiny, eye-shaped lens.

Light footsteps trail from the other side of the door, growing closer before stopping altogether. She's probably peering out the sidelight or peephole or checking her app—seeing who's out here.

A lump lodges in my throat.

I'm no stranger to rejection of the friend variety. Lord knows I'm not everyone's cup of tea and vice versa. But something's not right here, and I refuse to walk away and let *this* be the rest of her life: a prisoner-like existence, married to a man who treats her like a possession, a man who punishes her because she can never be the woman he truly wants.

I reach for the doorbell once more, and then I think better of it, letting my hand fall to my side.

I can almost feel her on the other side of the wall, her energy apprehensive and palpable.

From the inside, Gigi babbles.

A second later, the deadbolt slides and the door swings open.

"Grace. Hi." Campbell is planted on the other side of their screen door. Her gaze falls to the handle. Is she ensuring it's locked?

"Hey." I smile. And then I wave, which is a weird thing to do since we're separated by a couple of feet, but I'm trying to be friendly. And nonthreatening. The poor woman has enough to be afraid of right now. "I was just jogging by. Hadn't heard from you since the other day, so just wanted to say hi."

God, I sound psychotic.

"I'm not sure how much longer I'll be in town," I add before she responds. She's quiet anyway. "So I guess I just wanted to say it was nice meeting you."

Maybe I can instill a hint of urgency into this. If she catches any inclination that I can be her ticket out of this, she'll read between the lines.

Campbell hoists Gigi on her hip and reaches for the handle, stepping outside to join me on the porch. I inspect her face for signs of anything nefarious—bruises, handprints, scrapes, black eyes, caked-on makeup.

But she looks exactly the same as she did last week.

"That's so sweet of you to stop by to say goodbye." Her voice is lighter now, and she shields her eyes from the sun despite the fact that we're standing under her covered front porch. "I'm sorry I couldn't get back to you last week. Gigi's been fussy. Think she might be teething. And then Sutton came back from Baltimore . . ."

Had I not witnessed the private phone calls, had she not confessed to me that he was "particular," had she not ignored me last week, I'd think nothing of this.

I'm convinced there's trouble in paradise.

"When are you heading back?" she asks, lashes batting.

"I don't have a date yet. Soon, though. Maybe in the next week or so? I was going to see if you wanted to maybe grab coffee one more time?"

Her brows meet and her lips start to move, but before she makes a sound, my phone vibrates in my hand. A cursory glance at the screen shows a flashing number with a Los Angeles area code. It takes all of two seconds for me to realize it's the last Sarah Thomas calling me back.

The timing couldn't be worse.

"I'm so sorry—I have to take this," I tell Campbell before backing away. "I'll get ahold of you later, and we can figure out coffee?"

"Sure." She studies me. Gigi waves.

I'm halfway down the front steps, finger hovering over the green "Answer" button on my phone, when I turn back to her and ask, "You going to be okay?"

Without hesitation her expression hardens. "Of course. Why wouldn't I be?"

My phone vibrates in my hand. One more ring and it'll go to voice mail. I tap the green button and lift it to my ear before I lose the caller to a game of phone tag.

"Hello?" I trek toward the sidewalk, glancing back for a moment to find Campbell lingering in her doorway, screen door ajar as she watches me walk away.

"Is this Grace McMullen?" a woman's voice asks.

"This is she."

"I'm Sarah Thomas. You left me a message the other day . . ."

"Yes." I round the corner, and I'm breathless. "This might be a long shot, but are you the woman who nannied for my family twenty years ago?"

Hesitation and quietude settle between us.

Then a long breath.

"Yes," she says. "I am."

My ears burn hot. I grip the phone until my hand aches, as if holding on to it tight will keep her on the line regardless of what I'm about to ask her. Worst-case scenario, I offend her and she hangs up. Best case? She answers all my questions and then some.

"I will say, though, I don't remember much about that time in my life . . . ," she says. Her words are slow, careful, medicated almost. "And honestly, we probably shouldn't even be talking."

I don't ask her why she called me if she feels that way. People have all kinds of weird reasons for doing what they do.

"I completely understand. And I respect that," I tell her, trying to slow my walking pace and steady my breath. "I actually had a few questions about my biological mother, Autumn. I was told the two of you were friends . . . roommates . . . when she was younger."

Sarah says nothing. Perhaps she thinks I'm about to question her about Autumn's disappearance and the murder case the police tried to pin on her.

"First of all, I don't believe you killed her," I say, though it's a lie. I don't know what I believe, but she's not going to give me a single ounce of information if she thinks I'm trying to build a case against her. "Just to get that out of the way. I'm not calling because of that."

Sarah exhales, and I can picture her with vivid clarity—her sandy hair, her average build, the way she'd look at me and tell me I was the most beautiful thing she'd ever seen. She was kinder to me than Daphne was. And she favored me over Rose and Sebastian—a first.

Of course it all made sense years later, when I discovered why she was in our lives.

"I just . . . I want to know what she was like," I say. "My biological mother."

"It's been so long," she says, the undercurrent of an apology in her flat tone. "But I can tell you she was . . ."

Sarah's voice fades into nothing.

"You don't have to sugarcoat anything," I say. "If that's what you're worried about. I can handle the truth."

I'm two blocks from the house, but I veer toward a street in the opposite direction, opting to take the long way home. I wish this conversation could last for hours, but I know all I'll have are a few rushed minutes if I'm lucky. Already she's a woman of few words.

"She was troubled," Sarah finally says.

I release a breath I'd been holding since the last block.

"After she gave you to the McMullens, she was never the same," she adds.

"Can you elaborate?"

"Sad eyes. That's what I remember the most. She was always crying."

There's a tightness in my chest for a woman I've never known. It's strange the way I've always pictured her as a woman, when she was nothing more than a fifteen-year-old child. I try to imagine her as a knobby-kneed teenager. Scared. Frightened. Running out of options.

"She loved your biological father," Sarah says. "So much. She was really heartbroken over that whole thing."

"What do you mean . . . *that whole thing*?"

I'll admit I haven't thought about him much. I suppose I chalked him up to being some blue-blooded, pimple-faced twerp who used my mother to get his rocks off and sailed away from responsibility on his father's yacht.

"He was . . . older. Wish I could give you a name or something. I can't recall if he was a teacher or someone from her parents' church or a neighbor. I'm sorry. It was so long ago. I just remember it was pretty scandalous back then. I guess that sort of thing would be scandalous now, too, but her parents . . . your grandparents, I guess . . . they didn't handle it well. Sent her away like it was the fifties."

"Sent her away?" I had no idea about this. My adoptive parents always made it clear that I was adopted. They told me I was born to a fifteen-year-old girl who wouldn't have been able to take care of me even if she wanted to. The adoption was closed. Not even my parents knew my teenage mother's name was Autumn Carpenter—until Sarah waltzed into our life claiming she was her. Of course, at the time, that detail was shielded from me. Or maybe they were too busy worrying about my mother's upcoming murder trial and what my father was going to do with the three of us.

Everything I know, I learned from that damned book.

"She was always so sad, you know? Like I said. I guess they thought she was going to hurt herself or the baby. They sent her to a private psychiatric hospital. That's how we met. We were fifteen." Sarah's voice grows distant with every revelation, and I wonder how often she thinks about this chapter in her life. "I helped her choose your parents. The agency gave her this booklet with photos and letters from people in the area all wanting to adopt."

"What made you guys choose the McMullens?"

She exhales into the phone, a laugh sort of a thing. "Honestly? Your father was a looker."

I roll my eyes. So my entire fate hinged upon two teenage girls crushing on some twenty-something man in a photo?

"The letter they wrote was nice, too," Sarah adds. "They talked about how they wanted a big family, and how important family was to them. They were both only children. You could tell they were . . . It seemed genuine. And the handwriting . . . the wife's handwriting . . . it was so perfect. I don't know why I remember that, but I do. Pretty and neat, like she put a lot of time and effort into it."

I turn the corner and slow my gait, as if it could possibly stall this conversation further. Uncovering bits and pieces of my own personal history is a foreign, if not exhilarating, sensation.

I don't want this to end.

For every answered question, five more appear out of thin air.

"I didn't kill her. I want you to know that." Sarah's voice has a sharper edge to it that cuts through the receiver. "They . . . they tried to say I did . . . because I was the last person who saw her before she disappeared . . . but honestly, Grace, I don't remember what happened that night at the shore. I just know we went there together—but I came back alone. I wish I could give you some answers. I do. My memories of certain events, certain periods in my life . . . they're not that reliable. And especially now . . . thirty years later? And I've never hurt anyone in my life. I couldn't . . . I couldn't do something like that . . ."

More than anything in the world, I want to believe her. If she truly believed she was guilty, I can't imagine she'd be talking to me right now. She would have ignored my call. Changed her number. Continued to lay low.

"Do you think she's still out there?" I ask.

"Anything is possible," Sarah says without pause.

My entire life, the only thing I've ever wanted was to meet *one* person who shares my blood.

I never once imagined the possibility that it could be my own mother. Sure, I'd hoped. I'd let the occasional daydream slip between the cracks of my reality. But I never believed it could happen.

I want to know if it would feel different.

If *I* would feel different.

"I'm so sorry, but I'm running late for work," Sarah says. "Good luck with your search."

"Wait." I walk faster, irrationally trying to catch up to someone on the other side of the country. "Is there anything else you can tell me about her?"

"I wish," she says. "You ever think about doing one of those DNA test things?"

Many times.

But I would never.

I don't trust them.

Call me paranoid, but working on the dark web and seeing the underbelly of corporate and government intelligence agency corruption, you couldn't pay me enough to spit into a tube and mail it off to a laboratory for eternal safekeeping.

"I really do need to go, though," she says. The background noise crescendos on her end, as if she's strolling into a bustling LA restaurant or one of those trendy open-air markets. I'd love to know what her life has become since that year with us. A conversation for another time. "If you think of any other questions, give me a call. I can't promise I'll have answers for you, but I'll do what I can."

"Thank you. I appreciate that." I end the call and head home, fantasizing about a DNA test I'll never take and all the connections it could lead to. Second, third, and fourth cousins. Aunts. Uncles. Grandparents. Half siblings.

There could be an entire bloodline out there of people just like me—a fact as enthralling as it is terrifying.

CHAPTER 11

"What are you doing over here?" I find Rose lounging in the family room when I return from my walk, a paper-thin tablet in her lap.

My conversation with Sarah has been playing on repeat in my head the past ten minutes, surreal and vivid. I want to rewind it a hundred more times and listen all over again, if only because it gives me hope. A little spark of something I didn't have before. I may never find my biological mom, but the fact that she could be out there is a thought that electrifies my reveries. New food for thought.

She glances up from the screen. "Working."

"Where's Dad?" I ask. "And Bliss?"

Rose shrugs. "Probably at the country club?"

"So you just come here to . . . work?" I ask.

She chuffs. "Evan's working from home today. I'm going over next month's edits. Needed some peace and quiet."

I can't imagine Evan being noisy, but what do I know? Apparently nothing.

"You want to see?" She hands me the tablet before I have a chance to respond. "These are July's edits."

The logo for her lifestyle brand—The Blushing Rose—splays across the top of the page. I swipe through a handful of color-coordinated vignettes featuring tablescapes, outfits, floral arrangements, and menu suggestions for the perfect Fourth of July backyard bash.

I visited her website once before, out of curiosity. And at the time, I found it to be superficial and materialistic with a healthy side of vanity. Everything was so flawless and unspoiled. So curated. So . . . *Daphne*. Not to mention overpriced. The fact that there were people in this world who would shell out almost a hundred bucks for a Bulgarian rose–scented coffee-table candle with my sister's logo on the side blew my freaking mind.

But maybe I judged her too harshly.

Maybe all she wanted was admiration and validation.

It takes a tremendous amount of time and energy and clout to build a brand out of thin air.

"Looks amazing." I hand it back. "Well done."

Her pale eyes shine, aglow for all of two seconds before she digs into the purse beside her and retrieves a small black-and-white photo.

"Got my sonogram yesterday," she says. "Officially eight weeks and five days."

I examine the blurry image and pretend I know what I'm looking at. Aside from her name in the upper left corner, it's all Greek to me.

"Have you told Evan yet?" I ask, giving it back. "Congrats, by the way."

"I did. And thank you," she says. I try to picture her lithe, ballerina-esque figure with a basketball-sized bump.

"How'd he take it?"

Rose exhales. "He was shocked at first. But he's doing okay."

"And how'd Dad take it?"

Her gaze snaps to mine. "I haven't told him yet."

"What? Why not?"

"Just waiting for the right time, I guess. Kind of want to make it a big, fun thing." It's such a Daphne thing to do—make something "a big, fun thing." No denying she's her mother's daughter. "Was thinking tomorrow, maybe? Over brunch? You want to help me? It could be fun . . ."

"If you want me to . . ."

She pretends to swat at me and playfully rolls her eyes. "Don't be like that."

I think of Campbell and I change the subject. "You going to do the stay-at-home-mom thing?"

She wrinkles her nose. "That's random."

It's not random. She's pregnant. It's a valid question.

"Just curious if that's your thing. If you're going to follow in Mom's footsteps, or if you're going to keep"—I struggle to remember her exact title, but then it comes to me—"influencing."

"We haven't thought that far out yet. Why? You want to nanny for us?" There's a hint of jest in her voice and a twinkle in her baby blues. Maybe she doesn't know me that well, but she knows me enough. "I'm kidding."

"Good, because I'd be a terrible nanny."

"You might surprise yourself."

"Speaking of nannies . . . remember Autumn-slash-Sarah?"

"Yeah? What about her?"

I bite the inside of my lip. "I talked to her on the phone a little while ago . . ."

Rose careens her body my way. The screen on her tablet finally goes to sleep. "What? Why? What'd she say? Did you call her, or did she call you? How'd you find her? What's she up to?"

All these years, I assumed Rose had forgotten all about her. Most people don't remember the summer of their seventh year, or if they do, they remember it in inconsequential fragments. Lazy pool days. Bicycle rides. Barbie dream mansions. A favorite Disney movie on repeat.

I take a seat and leave a cushion to separate us. "I used my connections to find her. Just had some questions—mostly about my biological mom."

Rose's gaze softens. Sympathy, perhaps?

"Have you been looking for her? Your bio mom?"

"Not officially. But I've always wondered about her. She was never declared dead or anything . . . just missing. Was trying to find out a little more about her from Sarah, but she didn't have much. Just told me she was troubled and sad and that she doesn't remember what happened the last night she saw her."

Rose is silent, her gaze fixed on the coffee table for a moment, and then she reaches across the cushion that separates us and places her hand on my knee.

"Obviously I don't know what it's like being adopted," she says. "But I know what it's like having an adopted sister—and I can tell you, Grace, I've never thought of you as being anything other than my sister."

Her eyes well with tears, and her voice chokes.

She's always been a crier, ever since we were kids. Everything made her cry. Kid movies. Baby bunnies. Broken toys. Exhaustion. She could go from frolicking around the yard with a grin plastered on her tiny face to turning on the waterworks at the drop of a hat.

Some things never change.

I'm still as a statue, and I avoid making eye contact. I don't do mushy, gushy, or sentimental. It's a language I've never spoken. I couldn't formulate a response if I tried.

"You've been my sister—my only sister—my whole life," she continues. "Adopted, biological, it's all the same to me. Sebastian feels the same. You should know that."

It's strange to think of the two of them having that conversation, and it only serves to make me feel like that much more of an outsider, even if it's not her intention.

She removes her hand from my leg. Though I still feel it there, an indentation of energy.

I clear my throat.

"Thank you for saying that." I stand and adjust the hem of my shirt. I appreciate what she's trying to do, but now I've got a dust storm of sentiments beneath my skin: hot, dry, gritty. It's not even close to dinnertime, and already it's been a day. "I'm going to grab a shower and finish up some work."

"So tomorrow morning . . . you want to run to the store with me?" she asks before I'm out of earshot. "We can grab some flowers and some stuff to make brunch?"

None of that sounds like my idea of fun, but I know it would mean the world to her, and it wouldn't kill me to try to be the sister she so desperately believes I can be.

"Yeah, okay. Sure," I say.

"Pick you up at eight . . ." Her pink mouth arches into a tight smile, but her eyes are still glossy from before. It almost breaks my heart.

I check my texts on my way upstairs, debating whether or not I should reach out to Campbell to set up our coffee date now . . . or if I should give her some more time.

I don't want to come on too strong.

But every day that passes is another day of the poor woman being stuck beneath Sutton's thumb.

Locking the bathroom door, I strip out of my leggings and T-shirt and prep the shower, adjusting the water until it's extra hot. And then I begin to tap out a text—only to have it interrupted by an incoming call . . .

Speak of the devil.

"Hey, you must have read my mind," I answer, inserting a smile into my voice that lets Campbell know I'm glad to hear from her. "I was just texting you. Sorry about earlier, I—"

"Why did you ask if I was going to be okay?" Her tone is low, her question hurried.

"What?"

"When you were at my house earlier, you asked if I was going to be okay . . . Why wouldn't I be?" Her voice is robotic and terse, rehearsed almost.

No. *Coached.*

I pace the space in front of my shower, racking my brain and silently going over all the signs suggesting Campbell's in a bad situation.

"I just . . . I get the impression that maybe . . ." I bite my lip and choose my words with the care of a hostage negotiator. There's also a chance that Sutton's beside her, listening to every word we exchange. I certainly don't want to say anything that could make this worse for her. "I could be wrong . . . but it seems like your husband is a little on the controlling side, and—"

She interrupts me with a single puff of air through the receiver. "I appreciate your concern, Grace. But we're fine. Everything's fine."

Gigi wails in the background, calling for her.

"I have to go. Just please don't . . . don't insinuate that kind of thing again, okay?" she asks, though it's more of a command than a question. The receiver grows muffled for a moment. Gigi's cries are closer. "You don't know the first thing about my marriage. Or me for that matter."

I squeeze my eyes shut, picturing him beside her, nodding with approval.

"You're right. I don't. And I hope I didn't embarrass you by asking. It's just, I'd rather be safe than sorry."

"Sure."

Sure? That's all she's going to give me? He's got to be there.

"Have a safe trip home, Grace," she adds, curt and quick or perhaps distracted. "It was lovely to finally meet you."

The line goes dead.

But her words echo in my head: "It was lovely to finally meet you."

CHAPTER 12

"Should we do pink and blue flowers, or is that cliché?" Rose grabs a bouquet of pale-pink carnations from a grocery store display and holds it up. "Maybe we should just do white? But what does white even mean?"

She returns the flowers to their holder and whips out her phone, thumbs tapping against the screen at lightning speed.

"Purity or innocence," she reads aloud. "Pretty sure that ship has sailed." Moving past the first display, she stops in front of a refrigerated section of various floral arrangements. "Could always do yellow. That's gender neutral . . ."

I lean against the handle of the shopping cart, half-present, half a world away.

"Never mind. Yellow means sorry," she says, half-pouting.

I wonder if it's occurred to her that maybe she should hold off on making this announcement? That many pregnancies don't make it past the first trimester? If I were expecting, that'd be my first thought.

Then again, things always have a way of working out for my sister.

"I'm overthinking this, aren't I?" Rose selects a frilly mix of peonies, hydrangeas, roses, and baby's breath. "This would be so much easier if Mom were here. She'd pick the perfect flowers."

I say nothing because . . . what is there to say? *Mom's not here. She's rotting in a prison. Why torture yourself with wishes that can never be fulfilled?*

"What are we serving?" I change the subject. "For this brunch?"

"Quiche. Fresh fruit. Muffins. Coffee, juice, tea. Nothing crazy." She pulls up a shopping list on her phone and texts it to me. "Divide and conquer? You do the first half; I'll do the second, and we'll meet at the checkout?"

She's listed enough food to feed an army, despite the fact that it'll be six of us—and that's only if Sebastian shows.

"Sounds like a plan." I grab a basket and follow my nose to the bakery department, where I select an assortment of twelve mini muffins.

Oranges are next, and then I make my way to the other side of the store to grab eggs. Once there, I select the pack with the tiniest crack in one of the shells like I always do—an imperfect dozen.

Passing the dairy aisle, I toss a few yogurts into my basket and a pack of string cheese for myself, and then I head to the front of the store to wait for Rose near a display of patriotic-themed snack cakes.

Up ahead, a young mom with a messy bun and neon-print leggings negotiates with her toddler son, who's begging for not one but two bags of Skittles from the checkout. She skillfully ignores his red-faced tantrum and tearful pleas as she loads her items onto the conveyor. Two minutes later, the little boy wipes his alligator tears on the back of his hand, and the two carry on as if none of it happened.

I do a quick search for Rose before shooting off a text, letting her know I'm up front waiting. It occurs to me that I've no idea if she's the kind of person who goes into a store with a list of ten things and comes out with thirty-two. Our mom was that way. She loathed nothing more than feeling underprepared.

A dark-haired man in a Yankees cap steps in line behind the pair, adjusting his cart and reaching into his pocket to retrieve a pacifier, handing it to his messy-haired toddler daughter riding up front. He runs his fingers through her hair, brushing it off her forehead, before bending to leave a kiss on her cheek.

It's a perfectly normal exchange, one that doesn't cause me to think twice. And I almost glance away in search of Rose again—when it hits me.

Sutton.

Gigi.

Heat creeps up my neck in tight little vines, and I almost choke on my spit.

For the first time in eight years, Sutton Whitlock stands before me.

Ten, maybe twelve feet away, he plays peekaboo with Gigi, eliciting giggles so big she almost drops her pacifier on the dirty grocery store floor. He catches it with one swift move, pops it back into his pocket.

Her eyes, dark like his and round like Campbell's, are only for him. She's entranced. In love. A total daddy's girl.

As soon as there's room on the conveyor, he loads their items— milk, butter, oatmeal, cereal, flowers . . . for Campbell?

Is that his MO?

Does he tear her down and build her up?

Does he show her how amazing of a father he is and shower her with flowers and help with grocery store runs so that when she thinks about the possibility of life without him, she thinks twice?

Sutton looks every bit the part of a doting father, from his baseball cap to his lived-in gray T-shirt to his broken-in jeans and tennis shoes. His hair is damp beneath his hat, and I imagine him going for a quick jog this morning before grabbing a hot shower and loading up Gigi to run to the store. Maybe it was a good morning for them. One of the mornings that reminds Campbell why she married him, reminds her that there's a good side to him.

That's what abusers do.

It's a game to them.

The hot and cold, the good and bad, the constant emotional manipulation.

I think of what she said yesterday on the phone: "It was lovely to finally meet you."

At first I thought she was distracted, that it was an erroneous choice of words, but what if it wasn't?

What if she knew about me long before I knew about her?

Sutton was always a sentimental man. There was a shelf in his dorm closet where he kept a box of high school mementos. I'd found it strange that he'd hung on to a dried-up prom boutonniere, a track ribbon, his varsity basketball team photo, and his college acceptance letter, among other things, but he claimed these were the things that made him who he was, and he didn't want to forget.

He said most people went to college to shed their old skin, to become who they thought they were supposed to be. But he didn't want to lose sight of who he was. He didn't want to forget how he got there. He was proud of who he was, who he'd become, and where he was going.

Only now I have to wonder, does he have a box of . . . me?

We spent close to four years together. There have to be dozens of printed and framed photos. A handful of cards. An assortment of random notes and letters. Old T-shirts. Maybe even perfume bottles.

Everything meant something to him.

What if he kept them all? And what if Campbell found them? How would he explain those things to her? It's not the same thing as hoarding a box of high school track ribbons.

Sutton pays for his groceries, tapping a shiny blue debit card against the reader until the light flashes green.

I imagine Campbell finding his box, tearing through his old memories in a state of frenzied concern, studying my face in the photographs and wondering if our resemblance was intentional . . . or chance.

If all of this is true, then she knew exactly who I was when she invited me in to bandage my wounds after our sidewalk run-in.

No wonder she was so persistent.

She was just as curious about me as I was about her.

And once I started prying into her marriage, asking questions directly relating to Sutton, shit got real, and she got the hell out of there.

Oh, my God.

It makes perfect sense.

This is why she's avoiding me.

"All done." Rose's voice startles me into the present moment, and when I glance up, I spot Sutton and Gigi heading through the automatic doors toward the parking lot. She scans the store as he pushes the cart, and I hold my breath in case she sees me and waves. Within seconds, the automatic doors glide closed, and the two are parking-lot bound. I exhale. "You ready?"

I follow my sister to an open checkout, watching from inside as my stranger of an ex loads his groceries beneath the hatch of his Toyota before buckling his daughter into the back seat.

Five minutes later, he's gone and we're heading home to slice fruit and bake quiche and Rose's prattling on about baby names, talking about the size of her bladder, and carrying on like a woman far more than eight weeks pregnant. I indulge her because I'm trying to be a good sister.

On the way home, we pass 72 Lakemont, and I steal a fleeting glance through the open curtains that provide a direct view of their living room.

I spot nothing of interest and no one inside.

But I think about Campbell's phone call yesterday, the defensiveness in her voice all because I asked if she was okay.

"You don't know the first thing about my marriage," she'd said. I was certain she was being coached. Everything sounded so careful and scripted until the end of our conversation, when the tone of her voice sharpened and her words became more surefooted.

Maybe I had it all wrong.

Maybe she isn't a battered, abused woman covering for a controlling husband . . . but a woman fielding a threat? If she knows who I am, knows Sutton loved me first, knows I broke his heart long before she came around, then perhaps she's terrified that my presence will rock the rickety foundation of their marriage?

Maybe she's afraid that if he knows I'm back in town, something will shift inside of him? That the truth will come out? That he only married her because he couldn't have me?

Perhaps she was feeling me out just as much as I was feeling her out, and all her efforts to build a wall between Sutton and me were protective, precautionary measures?

There's a chance that her sugar-sweet naivete was nothing more than an act, and if that's the case, she got me. She got me good. No small feat.

I imagine her putting together the facts piece by piece—Sutton relocating the family to my hometown, naming their daughter after me, marrying a woman the spitting image of the one that got away . . .

All this time, I took Campbell as green and trusting—but maybe it was me.

Maybe it was me the whole time.

Rose pulls into the driveway and releases an exaggerated yawn. I carry most of the groceries in, even though her baby is the size of a raspberry (according to the app on her phone). We make our way to the kitchen, and she arranges flowers in one of Mom's Cartier crystal vases while Dad asks what the occasion is. Bliss offers to help make tea, Evan cracks eggs, and Sebastian pulls up five minutes before the quiche is done.

The *big announcement* is met with happy tears and a round of hugs, which I manage to stealthily avoid in exchange for smiles.

This is, quite possibly, one of the most normal days this family has known.

I allow myself to enjoy it, even if it's the equivalent of a scratchy sweater on a hot day, suffocating but comfortably warm.

Later that night, drunk on expensive wine and emotionally tapped out from an entire day with these people, I fling myself onto my bed and stare at the ceiling, replaying the scene with Sutton and his daughter at the store.

I never should have doubted him, never for an inkling of a second believed he could be anything less than wonderful.

Rolling to my side, I'm about to let the exhaustion of the day wash over me when my phone vibrates on the nightstand. I'm half-tempted to ignore it when it buzzes a second time.

Exhaling, I tug it off the charger and bring the screen to my face, squinting in the dark until the time comes into focus.

11:42 PM.

Pulling up my Messages app, I expect to find something from Jonah or the woman checking my mail back in Portland where it's several hours earlier in the day.

But it's Campbell.

Campbell: So sorry to text you this late . . .

Campbell: Are you still in town?

I sit up, flick on the lamp beside me, and brush the hair from my face. My vision blurs in and out of focus. Too much wine. And the room tilts and spins.

Yes, I text back immediately. A million scenarios flood my mind as to why she would be texting me out of the blue this late, but none of them make sense given what I concluded earlier. What's up?

Campbell: Can you meet me at the park on Hallworth in five?

I don't respond quite yet.

I've spent far too much time on the dark web to know that this is what happens when someone's about to get set up.

I tap out a reply: **It's kind of late . . . Can I ask what this is about?**

A moment later, a photo comes through—a partial image of what appears to be the side of Campbell's face.

She's been crying, as evidenced by the smear of black mascara below her eye.

And a red welt the size of a hand blankets her cheek.

The mere image of her injury evacuates the air from my lungs.

This isn't a setup or an act.

It's a cry for help.

See you soon, I type.

CHAPTER 13

Campbell's dressed in all black, and I only spot her in a picnic shelter thanks to a reflective stripe on the side of her shoes.

"Where's Gigi?" I ask.

"She's at home—she's safe." Campbell's voice carries a hint of congestion, matching the tear streaks on her face. "He has her, but she's fine. He would never hurt her."

"Does he know you left?"

She shakes her head. "No. He's sleeping."

"What's going to happen if he wakes and you're not there?" It doesn't feel like I'm talking about the same man. The vision of the sweet, doting father at the grocery store and the memories of the attentive, selfless boyfriend from my early twenties fade into nothing. "We have to get you out of there. You and Gigi."

I take the spot beside her.

She doesn't smell like me tonight. I catch a hint of dessert wine, though it's possible it's emanating from my pores and not her.

"He's a good man," she says. "He's just been so stressed lately. He wasn't always like this."

I know. "What happened? Can you tell me what happened?"

Campbell exhales, breath ragged, shoulders slumped. "I told him I wasn't happy here. That I wanted to go back to work. That I was lonely. I told him I felt trapped . . . and then he called me an ungrateful bitch."

"Bitch" was never a word in Sutton's vocabulary. I can't recall a single instance I heard him utter the word.

"He told me he's given me this perfect life, and he didn't understand why it wasn't good enough," she continues. "And he's right. Things are pretty perfect. He takes care of us. He loves us."

"That's not love."

She's quiet.

"And you're capable of taking care of yourself," I add. "Lots of people do."

"I can't take Gigi away from her father."

"If he's abusive, you can. And you should. If he's capable of hurting you, he's capable of hurting her. Don't be so naive." I regret the name-calling the second it leaves my tongue, but goddamn it. How can she be so selfish? "You have to get out of there."

"You don't understand . . . I have nothing." She dabs a tear on the back of her hand. "He controls *everything*. I don't have a dollar to my name. Our bank cards? Joint. My car? It's in his name. If I left, he could have it tracked and the engine disabled. And what if he reports me for kidnapping?"

"Listen, you're not the first person to be in a situation like this. There are resources. There are people who can help you. There are ways." I don't know the first thing about those ways, but I'm willing to learn if it means getting them away from the monster he's become. "*I'll* help you. *Let me help you.*"

Our stares catch in the dark and hold for what feels like forever.

"This is going to sound strange . . . I can't help but feel responsible for this." My voice is low, broken.

She's silent.

But it's time we both came clean.

"You know who I am, don't you?" I ask. "You knew this whole time."

Campbell tucks her hands beneath her thighs, eyes locked on the concrete beneath us, and then she nods. "I know exactly who you are."

CHAPTER 14

Three days.

It's been three days since I met with Campbell at the park down the street under the eerie glow of a half moon.

Three days since I saw the red-blue bruise forming beneath her left eye.

Three days since she confessed to living under Sutton's reign.

Three days since she admitted she knew exactly who I was from the start.

I didn't have a second to process her confession before she flew off the picnic table bench, apologized for roping me into this, and mumbled that she had to head home before he woke up and found her gone. She swore she'd be getting ahold of me, but so far it's been radio silence.

The visual of her trotting off in the dark, her reflective sneakers disappearing around the next block, was the last I saw of her.

All my calls, all my texts . . . ignored.

When I jog or cruise past the house, the curtains are pulled tight—doesn't matter the time of day. I've yet to see her car in the driveway, though his has been coming and going throughout the week.

There's no excuse she can offer me to justify why she would lure me out of my house in the middle of the night, drop a couple of bombshells on me, then disappear like . . .

I slam my laptop lid closed.

What if she's . . . *missing*?

She has no friends in Monarch Falls.

Her family's in Connecticut, hours away.

No one would know if Campbell vanished—at least not right away.

Shoving my computer aside, I gather the necessities. Keys. Purse. Phone.

A few minutes later, I'm parked in her driveway, engine idling. Sutton's Toyota is absent—a hopeful sign. Dashing up the front walk, I pound on her door, intentionally avoiding the doorbell in case he gets a text notification.

"Campbell, are you home?" I call out, knocking twice more. "Please. I just want to make sure you're okay."

I knock again.

And wait.

Surely if she'd packed up the baby and run home to Connecticut, she'd have told me, right? Especially after the exchange at the park the other night. No one in their right mind would worry someone with something as serious as that and just disappear without a second thought.

The other side of the door is pure silence. Not a footstep. Not a toddler babbling or cartoon playing in the background. Not a whoosh of a dishwasher or rumble of a clothes dryer. The curtains are still drawn, but it doesn't stop me from peering in, hands cupped around my eyes, as if I've magically summoned the ability to see through fabric.

I knock one last time—in vain.

And before I have a chance to talk myself out of it, I'm halfway to Sutton's office building, praying to God he hasn't left for the day.

Everything I'd originally planned to say to him, everything I came here to say—the apologies, the well-wishes—it all goes out the window as I speed across town.

I'm not sure what I'll say to him now. I don't want to scare him away, but I don't want him to think for two seconds that he can get away with treating the mother of his child like a prisoner.

Because he won't.

Not with me here.

CHAPTER 15

There are people on the dark web who will do this sort of thing for a price—people who will scare the hell out of a piece-of-shit wifebeater or put the fear of God into a neglectful, drug-addicted mother. But I've never been one to leave my dirty work to strangers. Besides, can you really trust someone to accurately convey a message this important? This personal?

"Sutton Whitlock, please," I say to his receptionist before she has a chance to greet me. My knuckles rap on the tall counter in front of her sunken desk. I recognize her voice from the other week, when she cheerfully provided me with his lunch hour and, later, happily patched me through to his office line.

She's on the phone—I didn't realize—but she asks them to hold and cradles the receiver on her shoulder.

"Is he expecting you?" Her hooded blue-gray gaze drifts toward her watch and then back, almost in slow motion. I realize it's the end of the day. She's anxious to go home, and Sutton's likely finishing up a few things before clocking out, but I'm not leaving until we have words.

"He isn't." I force a friendly smile, though my lips are wavy, and I imagine my eyes are tinted a shade of batshit crazy. "I'm an old friend, and I'm only in town for a little while. Wanted to stop by and say hello before I left."

The woman—the plaque on her desk identifies her as Deborah—doesn't blink.

I point to her phone. "If you could page him . . . ?"

"He isn't expecting anyone this afternoon. I'm so sorry."

"Sorry you can't . . . call him and let him know I'm here?" I resist the urge to snort or scoff, and there's a fine line between being rude and being assertive. And making demands won't get me what I want. "Was actually hoping to surprise him. He hasn't seen me since college."

Her eyes scan the length of me, at least the length she can see from behind her desk. I imagine she's piecing together some internal monologue about an ex-flame showing up unexpected, hoping to woo back a former lover.

"Please, Deborah," I say, using her name to make it more personal. "If you could tell him Grace is here. Grace McMullen. I promise he'll want to see me."

Line one blinks on her phone. Someone is still holding.

"You can finish that call first if you need to." I point to the receiver on her shoulder. If I give a little, maybe she'll give a little, too? "I'll wait."

Deborah finally blinks, clears her throat, and presses the flashing button. Fifteen seconds later, she's sent the caller to someone's voice mail and turned her attention back to me.

"Thank you so much." I thank her for something she's yet to agree to do—another psychological trick of the trade—and I cross my fingers.

With the phone flush against her left cheek, she punches in three numbers, keeping her stare trained on me.

"Sutton," she says. "I have a visitor here to see you . . . yes . . . Grace . . . McMullen . . . yes, I know . . . ah . . . are you sure? Yes. Grace McMullen . . . all right. I'll tell her."

Adrenaline heat courses through me, and I wait for her to direct me to his office, only she exhales.

"You said you were an old friend?" Her brows lift, and the lines in her forehead deepen.

I jerk back, vision narrowed, unsure of where she's going with this. "I *am*."

"My apologies, but he said he's never heard of you."

My first instinct is to laugh. This has to be a joke.

But Sutton was never a prankster.

This isn't his sense of humor.

I begin to say something, only nothing comes out.

"Perhaps you have the wrong person?" she suggests with a tempered smile.

"I assure you, I don't."

"Well, he seems to think you're at the wrong place. He's never heard of you." Deborah eyes the door behind me. "Thank you for stopping in. Take care now."

"Wait—"

"No, really. You should go," she says, cutting me off. "Also, we don't welcome solicitors."

Now she thinks I'm peddling something.

"I'm not soliciting. I told you—we're old friends." I tuck my hair behind my ear and step closer, readying to lower my voice. I'm prepared to tell her we dated in college, that he's pretending not to know me because perhaps he's still jaded. I'm prepared to plead, reason, beg, bribe—whatever it takes.

But I stop myself.

Deborah doesn't know me from Adam.

I have no credence with her.

And identifying myself as an ex only serves to make me seem like the crazy one for stopping by—it won't make him seem like the crazy one for pretending he doesn't remember me.

"If you don't leave, miss, I'm calling building security." She's sweet about it, if a person can be sweet about that kind of thing. Mollifying gaze, silky voice. Though maybe the kindness in her tone is more of a defense mechanism—like if you come across a bear in the wild and you're supposed to play dead.

I scare her.

"All right. Well." I take a deep breath, rap on the counter, and prepare to show myself out. "Thank you for your help."

I leave the office suite, but I don't leave the parking lot.

I find his SUV.

And I wait.

CHAPTER 16

I roast in the hellish early evening sun for two hours before the asshole finally emerges.

Dark jeans. Cognac leather loafers. White button-down sans tie. A casual look to match the casual facade he wears as he pretends his wife isn't missing.

I spot him before he notices me. When our eyes lock from across the parking lot, he knows there's no hiding. There's no middle-aged receptionist to shield him from me. No walls or doors to separate us.

His mouth presses into a flattened frown as he makes his way closer. He doesn't slow down or speed up.

"You shouldn't be here." It's been eight years since the last time we spoke, and those are the first words out of his mouth. "Bad idea."

I lean against his driver door, arms folded. "Really, Sutton? Pretending you didn't know me? Did you think that's what it was going to take?"

"What are you doing here? At my office?" His gaze narrows, and the incredulous tone in his words is an insult, as if I'm the crazy one between the two of us.

"We need to talk."

He keeps a generous distance between us. "What could we possibly need to talk about now, Grace? After all these years?"

After all these years—clearly he's harboring resentment.

I don't have time to mince words. "I need to know where Campbell is."

"I don't see how that's any of your business." He takes a step toward his car and waves for me to move, a dismissive karate chop with a flattened palm.

But I don't move. Not an inch.

"Why won't she return my calls?"

He releases an unbelieving smirk. "Are we going to completely sidestep the fact that you're talking to my wife at all? Do you have any idea how inappropriate that is? Maybe we *do* need to talk—about boundaries."

His hand lifts to the side of his head and makes a circling motion, insinuating that I'm crazy. The old Sutton never would've done such a thing. It stings, but not for long.

I'm two seconds from flinging a snarky response his way when I stop myself. This is getting out of hand, escalating faster than it should.

"Is there some place we can go to talk?" I ask, softening my attitude in an attempt to de-escalate this exchange (if that's possible).

He pauses, eyes gliding over me as if he's considering this. "About what?"

"Everything."

"I don't think that's a good idea."

Why? Because his wife is missing, and he doesn't want to risk being seen with an ex-girlfriend?

"Move, Grace." The way he says my name, like he's grinding it between his molars, sends a tightness to my chest. "And I'm only going to tell you this once—stay the hell away from my family."

He reaches for the door handle, which unlocks at his touch, and I have no other choice but to move out of the way.

"I don't know what you were thinking showing up after all this time," he says before jerking the door open. Climbing in, he adds,

"Hope you know you've made things difficult for me, for my family. You should've stayed gone."

He slams the door, and I rap on his window. This isn't over.

To my surprise, he rolls it down. "I mean it, Grace. Just . . . go back to wherever the hell you've been. Stay away from me. Stay away from my wife and my daughter. Just . . . leave."

He's gone before I can offer a rebuttal, and I realize now that closure doesn't seem to be anything he's interested in.

But I'll be damned if I'm skipping town before I find Campbell.

CHAPTER 17

"Mind if I tag along on your walk this evening?" Bliss corners me by the front door as I tie my sneakers. "It's cooled off a little. I could use some fresh air if you don't mind the company?"

As long as I control the route, I don't see the harm in letting her tag along.

"Not at all."

She calls out to my father, letting him know she's joining me, and then she slips into a pair of cloth sandals with yoga mat bottoms and follows me outside.

Dusk has settled and streetlamps glow, swarmed with summer bugs.

"I can't tell you how many times I've tried to get your dad to take walks with me," she says as we hit the end of the driveway. I veer left, and she follows suit; I'm relieved that she's letting me lead. "He says he gets enough walking in at the golf course, but we all know walking to and from the cart doesn't count."

She laughs and waves her hand at no one.

A neighbor rolls past us in her silent electric car, and the two exchange smiles.

"That's Regina Allred," she says. "She's lived here longer than your dad. At least that's what he tells me. You remember her at all?"

I shake my head.

"Probably better off. She's one of those people who'll bake you a casserole when your aunt dies and then turn you in to the association the next day for not putting your trash can out on time." She strides at a leisurely pace. "Not that I speak from experience. You just hear stories about people and they stick, you know?"

"Can't imagine you'd forget something like that."

"I don't know if you know this, but I used to live in this neighborhood before." She checks me from her periphery. "Years and years ago. Back when your parents were still married. I lived over on Lakemont. But it was before they had the fancy new houses. I had an old Victorian. The poor thing was falling apart at the seams. My boyfriend—at the time—he had big plans to restore it to its former glory. Never mind the fact that he couldn't tell a hacksaw from a jigsaw. You give the man a hammer, and suddenly everything becomes a nail. I think some people are like that . . . they just like to destroy things."

I wonder for a moment if she knows more about me than she lets on, but then I deem it impossible and shake the thought from my mind.

"Anyway, I walk down that old street sometimes," she waxes on. "Looking at all the houses. A lot of young families now. New construction tends to attract the younger crowd—the ones whose marriages are still perfect and think they need to have that perfect house to go along with it."

She huffs to herself.

"I'm not bitter," Bliss says. "For the record. I'm just making an observation. From my experiences. You know I was a therapist, right? Back in the day?"

"Back in the day? You act like you're old or something."

Bliss swats my arm. "You're sweet."

She thinks I'm being cute, but I meant it.

We're one corner from turning onto Lakemont, and Bliss is still yammering on, this time about my mother's peony bushes and how hardy they are. She's never seen anything like it. For years she tried to grow peonies like that . . .

I nod and offer the occasional, "Mm-hmm."

She carries on.

By the time we hit Lakemont, she's moved on, asking if I've had a chance to download her meditation app since I've been home.

I consider lying to spare her feelings, and then I think better of it. There are enough liars in this world without adding one more.

"Not yet. I'm sorry," I say.

"Oh, honey. Don't apologize. You're a busy woman. Always working. Always running around. Not trying to give you more to do."

We walk in lockstep. I place a half-second delay into my next step, breaking our perfectly synced strides.

"I always say meditation's not for everyone," she says. "But it should be."

Up ahead, Sutton's home glows from within, lamplight behind curtains. With every pace forward, I watch for something, anything.

A shade, a shadow.

A sign of life.

His silver SUV rests in the drive, just as lifeless as the home itself.

"My house used to sit right . . . *there*." She points to the off-white European-style house next to Sutton's. "Took them three full days to tear it down and haul it away. Couldn't bring myself to drive down this street for months after."

"I can imagine that was hard for you." I offer vague sentiments and half of my attention, the other half consumed by the situation at hand.

"These new houses are pretty and all," she continues, "but they don't have any history. They don't have a story. A past. I guess maybe that doesn't matter to everyone."

I don't ask her what she thinks of the history associated with my father's house.

We pass the Whitlock residence, and I can't help but careen my neck, soaking in every last ounce of the view.

"You like that house, do you?" she asks.

"It's an interesting color," I say. Never mind that it's too dark to fully appreciate its brick-blood hue. "I've seen it in the daytime."

"The little family that lives there is something else," she says.

I turn away from the house. "What do you mean?"

"Husband's supersweet. Friendliest guy you'll ever meet. But his wife . . . I don't like to speak ill of people, but she's not the most sociable." Bliss hesitates. "Introduced myself when they first moved in. The husband talked my ear off for a half hour. The wife just stood there, checking her watch. Huffing and puffing. Eventually she got him to go inside. Kind of got the impression she ran the show."

"The people in that house . . . right there?" I nod to it, opting not to point.

"Mm-hmm."

"Maybe she was having an off day?" People are allowed those . . .

"Maybe?" Bliss shrugs. "I just thought it was strange, you know. Someone welcomes you to the neighborhood, you ought to at least smile, make eye contact. Be cordial. Maybe it's a generational thing."

"Moving is stressful," I say. "Maybe she had a lot on her mind?"

Or she was exhausted. Sore. Overwhelmed. Could be anything. It's impossible to know.

"No, you're right. I should've given her the benefit of the doubt. And normally I do," she says. "But do you ever have an interaction with someone that just feels . . . unsettling? And it sticks with you years later, no matter what? Even if you know it's insignificant or you should brush it off or whatever?"

I nod. "I think we all do."

There are certain experiences no amounts of meditation or spiritual growth can cleanse from the depths of your mind.

"Can't drive down this street now without remembering that icy look she gave me."

Aside from Campbell's phone call a few nights ago and the defensive tone of her voice, "icy" isn't a word I'd use to describe her.

Meek. Mild. Frightened. Lonely. Unsure of herself. Backed into a corner. Perfectly average in all walks of life—that's how I'd describe her.

"They had a baby last year," she adds. "A little girl. I see them around town sometimes—the wife and the daughter. Grocery store. Bank. Dry cleaner. Used to try to wave, but it's like they're in their own world. Stare right through you. Never wave back."

I don't share my suspicions with Bliss. I don't tell her that I suspect Campbell's being abused and controlled. There's a chance her standoffishness is a direct result of her husband's strict, isolative rules.

"Do you see them often?"

She squints into the darkness ahead. "About once a week or so?"

"When was the last time you saw them?"

Bliss's attention snaps to me. "I don't know, last week sometime . . . why?"

I think fast. "Maybe introduce yourself again? I'd be curious if she's always . . . icy . . . or if you just caught her on a bad day."

She swats a hand. "Eh. Not worth the hassle. Easier to live and let live."

We continue on our walk, passing the park where Campbell met me late one night to show me the mark on her face after Sutton had struck her.

I almost ask if she'll keep an eye out for them, but it's a strange request that'll require an explanation I'm not prepared to give.

I respect Bliss, but respect and trust are two separate beasts.

I'm keeping this hand close to my chest for now. Besides, it's my problem to solve, my mess to clean up. No sense in involving anyone else.

Thirty minutes later, we're home. Bliss climbs the stairs, disappearing into the master suite to "run a lavender bath and cleanse her crystals in the moon." I grab my laptop and a joint and settle by the pool.

Sutton's Instaface profile is unchanged—his profile picture still a family portrait of the three grinning Whitlocks standing before their Lakemont arts and crafts bungalow.

I light up, inhale, and call Jonah.

"I need a favor," I say when he answers in the middle of the second ring.

"Again?" There's a light chuckle in his voice, one that suggests I annoy him but he'd do anything in the world for me.

"I made a new friend the other day." No need for specifics, not yet. "And then she ghosted me."

"O . . . okay. And what do you want me to do about that?"

"I need permission to post on the dark web from behind our VPN."

"Holy shit, Grace. You're not going to—"

"God, no. No, no, no. I just need someone—who's not me—to make sure she's okay."

Jonah exhales. "You have reason to think she isn't?"

"I have reason to think her husband is a controlling asshole who hits her."

He's silent. In all the years we've worked together, he's never known me to give this much of a damn about anyone else.

"You know you're behind on the Maylands project. It was due two days ago."

"I'm aware. And I'm almost finished." Working lately has been next to impossible. I can't focus for long periods of time. Everything becomes a distraction. Doors opening and closing downstairs. The faint hum of the TV trailing from the family room. Bliss diffusing different oil blends throughout the house. One minute I'm too hot, the next I'm too cold. My shoulders tense and ache. The sun shines too brightly through my bedroom window at certain hours. On top of it all, my thoughts are hijacked with worry.

"It's not like you to run late." I imagine his lips pressed into a hard line as he takes off his "buddy" hat and slips into boss mode.

"I know. I'll have it to you tonight. I promise. I just need your permission to post on The Black Board using our VPN."

"It'd be a lot less of a hassle for you if you simply called the police and had them do a welfare check."

"I need someone to give me details about what they see. Police can't do that. Not with welfare checks."

He groans, but he's going to give me what I want. I can feel it. He just needs one more gentle push in the right direction.

"I promise I'm not doing anything illegal . . . I just need someone to make a house call, maybe pose as someone selling security cameras or making a delivery or something. I don't know. I haven't thought that far ahead yet. If she won't answer the door for me, maybe she'll answer it for someone else."

"And if she does? What then?"

"Then I'll know she's okay."

"And if she's not okay?" he asks.

"Then I'll involve the authorities." It's an extreme idea, foreign on my lips. Was hoping to be able to handle this on my own as, more often than not, involving police in abusive situations has a tendency to make things worse for the victims. Not always, but sometimes.

He's quiet, but his dog scratches at the door in the background, so I know he's still there.

"Jonah." I attempt to recapture his attention, his favor. "Please. I never ask for anything."

"You swear on your soul it's nothing illegal?" His question is legit. If I'm not breaking any laws, why would I need to use the company's

VPN? I guess when you're accustomed to that extra layer of anonymity, it's difficult to give that up.

Plus, for every kneecap buster on the dark web willing to do your bidding for fifty bucks, there are ten more willing to sell you out for a hundred.

I need the anonymity.

"Yes. I swear," I say.

"Fine. But get me the Maylands project first."

CHAPTER 18

"Have you heard of this show before?" Rose mutes the TV Saturday morning. We're hanging out again, if you can call it that. "*Family Finders.*"

I glance up from my phone, refreshing my email for the tenth time this hour. I posted on a dark site called The Black Board last night, looking for someone to pose as a delivery man. I'll provide him with a khaki uniform, a name tag, and a package containing a prepaid cell phone programmed with my number. If Campbell doesn't answer the door, if he's not able to make contact with her, I'll resort to having the authorities perform a welfare check.

"Nope, never heard of it," I say.

"So there are these people who will take your DNA and find your family for you," she says. "All you have to do is let them document your journey and film the reunion."

"Eh. That's okay." Exploiting other people's trauma and tragedy for entertainment is a sick concept. I'll have no part in it.

Rose leans forward, examining me. She's wearing glasses today—thick rimmed and opaque pink—and her hair is styled in wide, brushed-out curls. I bet she had a photo shoot this morning for her website. "The other day you gave me the impression you were wanting to find your birth mom. These people could help you find her. Maybe. Or at the very least a cousin."

I don't have the energy to explain to her the kinds of things people can do with your DNA or the contract I'd be required to sign, giving away any and all rights to said DNA.

"I appreciate that, but it's fine, Rose, really." I go easy on her. She means well.

Turning her attention back to the TV screen, she leaves it on mute. I check my email—again.

"I'm going to visit Mom next week." Her voice is low, soft, careful. "Was going to tell her about the pregnancy. You want to tag along?"

Tag along . . . so casual.

"Rose."

"I know. I *know*." She places a splayed hand over her heart, and I don't have to look at her to know her eyes are pleading. "For me?"

She's never asked me for anything—except to help her with brunch last week.

But right now, she's asking for the world.

I let my phone fall into my lap and angle myself toward her. "Did you ever read that book . . . *Domestic Illusions*?"

Her pale brows meet, and she shoves her glasses up like a headband. "Parts of it. A long time ago. Why?"

"Mom sold me out, Rose. I can't forgive her for that."

She sinks back into the sofa. "What are you talking about?"

"All that stuff about the nanny, about my biological mom being presumed dead, about Mom's bond—or lack thereof—with me." My hands tremble as I speak, a million tiny earthquakes rumbling to the surface. I always knew I was adopted—that was never a secret. But dis-covering the behind-the-scenes details surrounding that fateful summer in a true crime paperback book was heartless. "She should have told *me* those things, not some random author trying to cash in on our family tragedy. I shouldn't have had to read about them. And what did they have to do with her anyway? Sarah Thomas being in our life for one summer had nothing to do with her hiring some druggie to kill her husband's mistress. Was she trying to make herself look like a saint? A woman with the weight of the world on her shoulders? Was it worth it? Throwing me under the bus like that?"

"Grace . . ." She sucks in a long breath, and her baby blues widen. "You have it all wrong . . . Mom had nothing to do with that book."

Of course Rose's quick to defend her.

"And how would you know this?" I ask.

"Because I remember meeting the lady who wrote it—Dianna something," she says. "She was over here all the time when she was researching. She practically lived here for months, always hanging all over Dad, asking him questions. They'd stay up late and drink by the pool and talk for hours. I was just a kid back then, but I remember. She had jet-black hair down to the middle of her back, and her nails were always some shade of blue. Turquoise, navy, cerulean, sky . . ."

My stomach swells with nausea as my world tilts on its axis.

The last time I saw Daphne, I barreled into the prison on a mission, the dog-eared paperback under my arm. And the second she appeared on the other side of the dividing wall and reached for the phone to speak to me, I slammed the book against the glass—in her face.

And then I yanked the receiver off its hook so hard I smacked myself in the mouth, resulting in a mild fat lip that lasted three satisfying days. A battle wound.

I don't remember everything I said, but I do remember the sharpness of the words I spoke to her, the way they sliced my mouth when I spoke, the way they gutted me straight down the middle. I remember how desperately I wanted her to feel what I felt.

Used.

Betrayed.

Discarded.

Her lips had trembled, and her eyes filled with tears—a confirmation of guilt.

I turned my back on her—sweet irony—and rode out of there without letting her explain. There was nothing she could say to fix it. Nothing she could do from behind bars to make it right. The damage was done. She'd made her choice, and I'd made mine.

"Rose, are you sure?" I tuck my chin. "Are you absolutely sure it was Dad?"

"I mean, we're talking fifteen, twenty years ago, but yeah. I'm positive."

I begin to ask why, but I stop myself. I doubt Rose would have an answer.

I'll ask him in person—when I'm ready.

I let my sister's words sink into my marrow, rewriting a narrative I've lived with almost my entire life. One that's defined my human ego in more ways than I care to admit. One I believed with every rooted inch of my warped little soul.

Now I know—I couldn't have been more wrong.

CHAPTER 19

"I tried twice." He goes by John, but for the purpose of our arrangement real names aren't necessary.

We maintain the smallest amount of eye contact.

"Did you make sure there was no Toyota in the driveway?" I don't mean to insult his intelligence, but the answer matters.

I scan the parking lot to ensure we're still alone. An abandoned plastics factory looms over us as a trailer-less semi whirs past.

I try not to think about what someone like John does on the dark web.

"Yes, ma'am. Driveway was empty both times. Tuesday morning. Wednesday afternoon. I can try again tomorrow, but it'll be an extra fifty. And I'll have my kid with me because it's my weekend. Not ideal for either of us."

It took two days for someone local to respond to my post on The Black Board. A dozen others reached out, but the majority of them were from Brooklyn, Queens, or eastern Pennsylvania and wanted to be handsomely compensated for travel and mileage.

"Did it sound like anyone was home? When you stopped by?"

"House was dead quiet." He shifts his posture. "Sure you don't want me to try one more time?"

"No. You have the package still?"

He hands me the manila envelope containing the burner phone, the one I'd given to him earlier this week when we met at a bar downtown. The fake label is still intact, wrinkled but legible, and I slide out my phone to transfer him fifty bucks' worth of cryptocurrency. I show him the TRANSACTION COMPLETED verification, and he gives me a nod, climbing back into the cab of his black Chevy half-ton. I return to my car and get the hell out of there, a death grip on the wheel as I navigate toward the main road.

At a red light two blocks down, I perform a quick search on my phone, queuing the Monarch Falls nonemergency dispatch number.

It takes me half the ride home to make the call.

"I'd like to request a welfare check on a woman and child at 72 Lakemont Street," I tell the man on the other end.

I pray I don't make things ten times worse for her.

CHAPTER 20

I give myself the rest of the day off and bide my time at a giant bookstore with three floors and meticulous displays, searching for the perfect peace offering.

Three hardbacks rest in the crook of my arm, their virginal spines uncracked, and I stop at a table stacked with dozens of women's literature options. I don't know what my mom reads in prison these days. I don't know what she read before prison, either, or even *if* she read. She was always flitting about, running errands, coming and going. Some people are addicted to busyness. It's an escape. A distraction. I imagine there aren't too many of those kinds of outlets in prison.

I choose a staff recommendation, a historical tome, a book on meditation, and something with an Oprah's Book Club sticker on the cover before making my way to the checkout. Rose gets her used books, which I find interesting because Rose's never been the frugal type, and our mom was used to having nice things back when she had an actual life outside those concrete walls.

Regardless, she's getting new ones from me.

With their smudge-free pages and shiny covers, they're as close to a fresh start as we're going to get.

I part with nearly a hundred bucks and stroll toward my rental, purchases in arm. This morning I overheard Dad talking to Bliss about taking the afternoon off. I've been paying more attention to his sched-ule lately, mostly to prevent our paths from crossing. Ever since Rose enlightened me about our father's part in that *Domestic Illusions* book, I've had to bite my tongue and keep my distance.

The man's giving me a place to stay. I'm not in a position to be confrontational. And even if I were to grab my things and shack up in a hotel for the time being, the nearest accommodations are three miles on the other side of town—a far cry from the three blocks that separate his house from Sutton's.

Like it or not, I need to stay put.

I place the bag of books in the passenger seat and check my phone before pulling out of the parking lot, though it's not like I'm expecting a phone call. The police officer I spoke to earlier said she wouldn't be able to tell me if Campbell was okay, but that if anything wasn't okay, they would proceed with any necessary actions.

When I get home, I camp in the driveway, car idling as I check the websites for three local news stations. I hold my breath and scan the headlines for anything containing the phrase "missing local woman."

Nothing.

I shove my phone into my bag, kill the engine, and stare at the front of the house before forcing myself to go inside. Bliss's car is here. So is Dad's. We're going to have to talk sooner or later.

Once inside, the foyer is silent. No echoes of conversations. No TV in the background. I poke my head into the kitchen, peer through the sliding glass doors, and spot the two of them by the pool in the backyard, none the wiser.

With inaudible steps, I trek upstairs—only to have my phone buzz the instant I reach the landing.

I don't recognize the number, but I answer, a startled pang in my chest. "Hello?"

The family portrait facing me at the top of the stairs has been straightened since the last time.

"Really, Grace? Sending the police to my house for a welfare check?" It's Sutton.

I exhale.

"What exactly are you trying to do here?" The anger in his tone is foreign, much as it was the other day in the parking lot of his office, but everything else about it almost feels like home. A sick, sweet combination. "What's your angle? What do you want? You know what, I don't even care what you want—I just want you gone. Leave, Grace. Stay away from my family before you make all of this worse."

My skin hums and my tongue is electric. "Worse for whom?"

Sutton is quiet for a beat, and then he scoffs. "Do I really need to answer that?"

"Yes." I stand tall and indignant in the safety and privacy of my father's home, simultaneously wishing we were face-to-face once more. "If you love her, you'll let her go, Sutton. You'll do the right thing."

I wait for a response that never comes.

"Sutton?" I check my screen only to find he ended the call seconds ago.

He's never been the kind to insist on having the last word, but now we're two for two.

I call him back now that I have his number.

Three rings and it goes to voice mail.

I clear my throat and wait for the tone. "I'm not leaving."

CHAPTER 21

I reread my newest Black Board ad and press "Enter."

It goes live in under a second—and it goes against everything I stand for.

I could lose my job for this—and if Jonah finds out, I will. No questions asked. No opportunities for apologies or forgiveness. No number of excuses will be able to justify a Watchers and Guardians employee soliciting the illegal services of a dark web hacker.

I offer $500 for anyone who can get me into the Whitlocks' security system so I can view their cameras—$1,000 if they can get me access in under twenty-four hours.

All I want is to make sure Campbell and Gigi are okay.

Nothing more, nothing less.

Within minutes, my messages populate with interested parties, most from Russia and Canada and a handful from the States. I sift through their responses, deleting the ones clearly generated by an AI autoresponder attempting to phish for passwords.

I've narrowed it down to three users when a new message pops up from someone named *Imaginary_Comrade18*.

"I can get you in," he writes. Adding, "One hundred percent."

"Proof?" I type back.

A second later, he sends me an image of a Stone Wall Security Systems employee badge, the face and name blacked out.

He could've gotten that anywhere, or it could be Photoshopped.

"Going to need more than that," I write.

"I can't give you more than that . . ." A moment later, he adds, "Give me twenty-four hours and I'll get you in. Promise."

I know better than to place my hope in internet promises, but I've got a good feeling about him. Or maybe it's desperate hope. My mind is too frenzied to tell the difference.

He sends me an invoice for $1,000, along with his crypto handle.

"I'm not paying you until the job is done," I tell him.

He sends another message. "Obvi. Just sending it through so you have it when I'm done. I require immediate payment upon completion of the work."

I settle against my headboard and nibble at a jagged cuticle.

"Fine," I write back, and then I delete my post on The Black Board.

I need this done ASAP and I don't have time to interview candidates, so I'm willing to give him a chance.

"Just need a name and address," he writes.

Before I talk myself out of it, I've already hit "Send" on the info. When I'm finished, I shove my laptop to the edge of my bed and sprint to the bathroom to throw up.

CHAPTER 22

Imaginary_Comrade18 sends me a link exactly twenty-two hours and forty-three minutes later. I must have checked my messages hundreds of times, holding my breath between each and every refresh.

I click on the site and expect to find a prepopulated log-on—instead I'm met with a live, full-color, high-definition image of the Whitlocks' living room.

I clamp my hand over my mouth and lean in, examining every pixel, zooming in and out on anything I can't immediately identify.

A remote control.

A pacifier.

A teething ring shaped like a giraffe.

The space is empty save for their gray sofa and matching loveseat, their jet-black coffee table with the child safety bumpers on the edges, and a lifeless TV hanging above a white fireplace. Gigi's playpen is folded in the corner, next to a basket overflowing with books and toys.

"How long is this link good for?" I message my guy.

"Security certificate should last a week," he writes back. "If you need longer, it'll cost you."

A week should be plenty. It's not my intention to spy. I'm not trying to be a creep.

I find the payment link he sent yesterday and send the $1,000 before clicking back to the camera footage. Headers at the top of the page connect to six other cameras—front door, back door, garage, kitchen, hallway, and nursery.

I check the nursery first, though it's impossible to know if the diaper pail is full, and other than a folded baby blanket hanging over the side of the crib, there's no way of determining the last time Gigi slept there.

The hallway gives me nothing. Just a dark, narrow space with picture-frame-covered walls and closed doors. At the front door, a UPS package waits, and at the back door, a pink ride-on toy sits sideways in the grass by the patio. I click to the garage camera next, only to find two empty stalls and an oil stain where one car should be.

Save for a pizza box on the stove, the kitchen is pristine.

Sutton, with all his many talents, was never a master chef. Is the pizza sitting out because Campbell's not there to cook for him?

A red flash fills the top of the screen, accompanied by the words SECURITY ALERT. My heart leaps into my throat—I'm certain Sutton is being notified of this breach this very instant—but then I realize it's nothing more than the system letting me know the garage door has been opened.

I swallow my concerns and click on the garage camera, watching the door to the north stall rise slow and steady. Seconds later a white sedan pulls in—and Campbell climbs out of the driver's side.

I don't breathe. I don't move.

Campbell unfastens Gigi from the back seat before retrieving a leather duffel and a polka-dot diaper bag.

She left him.

She obviously left him.

And it explains the ghosting.

It also explains why Sutton was so upset . . . he must have blamed me.

Exhaling, I switch from camera to camera, silently observing as she drops the bags at the door and makes her way down the hall and to the living room. Grabbing a couple of toys from the basket, she carries her daughter to the kitchen, placing her in her high chair and ensuring she's occupied before she begins to fix a snack . . . like it's any other day.

I don't understand.

My phone buzzes with a text from Rose, pulling me out of this virtual reality nightmare, and I glance at the time.

We're supposed to arrive at the prison in an hour.

I power off my computer, grab the books I bought for our mom, and head downstairs.

I'll check on Campbell later . . . one more time . . . just to make sure she's okay.

CHAPTER 23

My adoptive mother has hardly aged since the last time I saw her. I suppose it makes sense, the lack of sunlight and all. Her hair is still the straw-like gray blonde, like before, but aside from the sinking hollows below her eyes, she's virtually unchanged. Same pencil-thin brows. Same humbled, close-mouthed smile.

"Grace." Her voice is tender, and her body swims in her garish orange uniform, a color that does nothing for her. A hint of life colors her irises before fading away as if it was a figment of my imagination.

I think about what it must have been like possessing beauty that couldn't be ignored and a bank account that could afford any of life's luxuries—big and small. And then I think about what it might be like for her now—bartering for hair dye and stomaching third-rate cafeteria food.

"I can't tell you how happy I am that you're here," she says.

We're in a space filled with tables and chairs and guards. There's no glass partition separating us like last time. Her hands and feet are cuffed, but she keeps them tucked out of sight, holding my gaze on hers as if it could keep me from looking.

Rose waits in the next room. I asked for a moment alone with Mom first, and she obliged without question, even offering to take the stack of hardbacks I brought to the security desk for approval.

"Rose told me you didn't have anything to do with that true crime book," I say.

Her eyes, slightly crinkled at the corners, squint, and then she nods.

"Why didn't you deny it? When I came in here that day, you let me say all those terrible things, and you just sat there and took it," I say.

She glances into her lap, then back to me. "You were so angry. And you were hurting. You needed to say those things to me, you needed to get it all out so we could have a civilized conversation." Mom winces. "But you tore out of here before that could happen." She raises her palms in protest, and the silver cuffs glint in the fluorescent light. "I'm not upset with you for any of it. It's in the past. You're here now, and that's all that matters."

"I don't understand why you'd let me believe that lie," I say, "for so long."

I know I need to apologize. And I will. Someday. Right now the words swim around my head before getting lost on the way to my lips.

"I sent you letters. They all came back." She glances at the clock on the wall, the one ironically protected behind metal bars. I can't imagine what it's like mentally calculating the remaining minutes you have to visit someone, watching the second hand sweep all that time away.

"You could've said something to Rose."

"She was so young at the time. It didn't seem right to involve her."

"So you were just going to wait . . . as long as it took . . . hoping I'd figure out the truth one of these days?" I ask.

Her lips press flat and she nods, and I realize the only thing this woman has is time. Time and maybe a handful of items from the commissary.

The weight of this moment is overshadowed by thoughts of Campbell.

"Tell me, Grace," Mom says, adjusting in her chair until her posture is straight and her shoulders are lifted. Leave it to Daphne McMullen to remain poised and proud in the most humbling of situations. "Tell me about the young woman you've become."

I answer her with generic, summed-up responses.

I live in Portland.

I work for Watchers and Guardians.

And I tell her the kinds of things I think she'd want to hear.

I'm happy, healthy, and well.

I don't have the energy to go deeper. The only thing I can think about is Campbell, attempting to wrap my head around the fact that she came back. Trying to surmise what Sutton will say when he comes home and finds her.

Will he reward her for returning?

Or will he punish her for leaving?

"Rose has been waiting . . . I should go grab her," I say to change the subject, and then I leave to get my sister.

The instant she walks into the visiting room, she waves the sonogram like a tiny flag, and Mom begins to cry.

It feels invasive to watch this moment. It has nothing to do with me, and I've never understood the concept of happy tears.

"You're going to be an aunt," Mom says to me later. "How's that feel?"

To be honest, I hadn't thought of that. Not once. Not yet. Our parents were only children. Growing up, aunts, uncles, and cousins were a foreign concept. The kinds of people friends, teachers, and neighbors referred to in conversation and nothing more.

I don't know the first thing about being an aunt.

"She'll definitely be a cool aunt," Rose says. The two of them impart identical smiles in my direction.

I roll my eyes, playful, and point a thumb at my sister. "I don't know why this one thinks I'm so cool."

Mom says something about big sisters being automatically cool. I don't ask how she would know that, given the fact that she never had one, but Rose nods and shares a story about the time she came to Boca Raton for Christmas and I taught her how to kick the vending machine in Grandma's laundry room at just the right moment to get two Snickers bars instead of one.

"*So* Gracie," Rose says. Mom laughs, and I wonder if sharing these memories with her makes her happy or sad. Maybe a mix of both.

I keep an eye on the clock and the guard with the clipboard, and when she walks our way to tell us our visiting hour is over, Rose fights tears and Mom divides her attention equally between us as we say our goodbyes.

On our walk to the car, I'm numb. I liken this visit to meeting a familiar stranger for the first time. Someone from a past life or a lifetime ago.

"She looks good, doesn't she?" Rose asks as we start the drive home.

Rose doesn't remember twenty years ago when our mother was young and her beauty was fleeting but undeniable.

"She does," I lie.

We merge onto the freeway, and Rose quiets the volume on the radio from the steering wheel. Her hands grip at a perfect ten-and-two.

"You doing okay?" She checks me from her periphery. "Awfully quiet over there."

"Aren't I always quiet?" I wink, but she can't see me. She's too focused on the beginnings of New Jersey rush-hour traffic.

"This is true," she says. There's a lightness in her voice that wasn't there earlier. "Think you'll visit Mom again sometime?"

"Sometime."

"It meant the world to her today. I could tell."

I don't know how my sister could know that, given the fact that the two of them were never alone together. Maybe it's an unspoken mother-daughter bond, something they've been cultivating over the past twenty years.

One of these days, maybe I'll get in on that.

"You know, if you think about it, ever since you came back, it's like everything has changed for the better." Rose readjusts her grip and clears her throat. "You should know that."

"I'm glad you feel that way."

I think about Campbell. Her situation isn't better. At least not yet.

Locating my phone in the bottom of my bag, I slide it out and shoot a text to "John," asking if he can try to make one more drop next week. Now that I know she's home, maybe he'll have better luck getting her that burner phone.

Tuesday, he texts back almost immediately.

I darken my screen, shove the phone back, and sink back into the passenger seat of Rose's car.

I can't force Campbell to do the right thing, but I can throw her a lifeline.

If she chooses to drown after this, my hands—and my conscience—will be clean.

CHAPTER 24

It's been forty-eight hours since John made the drop.

If I don't hear from Campbell by tomorrow, I'm booking a flight home and leaving Monarch Falls this weekend. If Sutton wants his knock-off life, if Campbell wants to spend the rest of her life as an abused consolation prize, that's on them.

I did what I could.

I top off the fuel tank in my rental car for the first time since I've been here, and then I head toward a chain pharmacy on the corner. Jonah's birthday is in a few days. He's the only person in the world I'll mail a card to—and it's more of an ironic statement than anything else. Back in the day, he used to tease me mercilessly about my unfeeling demeanor, saying it was nothing more than battle armor to protect the softness inside me. Since then, I've made it a tradition each year to hunt for the mushiest, gaudiest, most sentimental birthday card on the rack just for him.

Twenty minutes later, I find a "Happy Birthday to My Best Friend" card. Pastel blue. Oil-painted flowers. Cursive font. The inside bears a long inscription, a syrupy word salad sure to put a smile on his face. I select an envelope the color of sunshine and head to the checkout, passing a handful of empty aisles on the way.

The shop is quiet, save for elevator music playing over speakers in the ceiling.

"Okay, I think that's everything." A woman says in the next aisle, her cadence unassuming and familiar. "Should we check out?"

There's no way.

I peek my head around, scanning past rows of color-coordinated diapers and boxes of baby wipes, only to find Campbell and Gigi.

"Campbell," I call to her before realizing I'm already halfway there.

Her attention flicks toward me, her eyes growing wide the instant she spots me.

Shock?

Or fear?

"Are you alone?" I keep my voice at a whisper.

She turns her attention to her daughter, hand cinched around her little fist.

"Campbell." I say her name louder this time, still keeping my tone hushed. "Did you get the phone? We have to talk."

She peers around—checking for an audience—before meeting my gaze and taking three steps closer. "Yes."

"Where have you been?" I whisper.

"I was at my mother's. In Connecticut."

"Do you have any idea how worried I've been?" My voice is too loud. I swallow, as if it could possibly erase the volume of the words I've just spoken.

"You should get out of here," she says, turning to check behind her.

"Is he here?"

Before she has a chance to answer, Sutton appears from a neighboring aisle. In less than an instant, he notices me. His lips flatten, and he positions himself between his wife and me.

He takes the pack of diapers from Campbell. "Why don't the two of you go wait in the car."

Campbell hesitates before scooping Gigi into her arms, turning, and disappearing out of sight.

"Are you stalking us, Grace?" he asks when she's gone.

"No." I fold my arms across my chest. Jonah's card bends in the process. "Absolutely not."

Sutton chuffs, offering an incredulous smirk. "I don't know how much clearer I can make this. Leave my family alone. Do not stop at my office. Don't call the police on us. Don't follow us. Don't concern yourself with any of . . . this."

For a moment, I almost blurt out, "What kind of man hits a woman?" because I want him to know that I know . . .

But I zip my mouth. If he finds out Campbell's been telling me about the abuse, he'll take it out on her. That's what happens in these situations. It's textbook.

"If I see you again, Grace, I'm reporting you for harassment and stalking, and we'll file for a restraining order." He speaks through clenched teeth, his voice low. If I didn't know what I know, I'd imagine he's simply being protective of his family. Given the facts, I can only surmise he's trying nothing more than to protect his secret.

The words are on the tip of my tongue like a thinly veiled threat . . . *Don't hurt her again.*

He has no idea what I'm capable of, the kinds of "services" I can purchase on the dark web that would make him think twice about ever putting his hands on her again.

But he's gone.

Once again, Sutton got the last word.

I wait for him to check out, and I watch from the nail polish aisle as the three of them back out of a parking spot in Sutton's silver Toyota and make it through the intersection across the road.

I buy Jonah's bent card along with a single stamp, and then I drive home, the bitter taste of defeat on my tongue.

It's time for me to go.

There's only so much I can do, and at this point, I've done what I can.

Something tells me if I stay, I'll only make things worse.

CHAPTER 25

Bliss teaches Rose a handful of prenatal yoga poses by the pool Friday morning as I search for a direct flight back to Portland.

They aren't cheap, given the short notice, but at this point, I'm tempted to empty my life savings if it'll get me out of Monarch Falls as soon as humanly possible.

Sunlight dances on top of the still waters, and chlorine floats on a breeze mixed with the neighbor's freshly cut grass.

"There you go. You've got it." Bliss supports the small of Rose's back as she struggles to maintain the newest position. For someone as twiggy as my sister, she doesn't have a flexible bone in her body. "Hold it, hold it . . . you're doing great. Five more seconds."

All the girlfriends my father has entertained over the years have brought something unique to the equation. Paris was a marathoner who almost had my father training for an Iron Man. Jada was a vintner's daughter and taught my father the perks of being a wine snob. Tallulah was a preschool teacher fresh out of college. The only thing she brought was a tight ass.

But Bliss brings peace and a willingness to include herself in something that has nothing to do with her—an art form. She's unapologetically, wholly herself. For that, I won't be so quick to write her off.

In fact, I hope he keeps her around a little longer than the others.

I hover over the "Purchase" button for a flight that leaves Sunday afternoon, pausing to consider the things I might miss once I'm gone again.

Rose's pregnancy milestones.

Bliss's random stories and unexpected company.

"Hey, hey." My father steps out to the patio, coffee in hand. Only one this time. Nothing for Bliss. "Yoga by the pool? Where was my invite?"

I've been avoiding him since last week, when I learned the truth about the book. But I can't avoid him forever.

"Morning, Gracie." He uses my nickname again. It's almost like he knows. But he couldn't know. He's too dense. And Rose wouldn't say anything. She wouldn't betray the trust we're building.

"Morning." I don't glance away from my screen.

He takes the spot beside me, and as if on instinct, I one-click the "Purchase" button. I have forty-eight hours to pack my things, forty-eight hours to talk to my father about that book, and forty-eight hours to make internal peace with the Sutton and Campbell situation.

"What's the plan for today?" he asks. "Was going to see if you wanted to grab lunch at the club with us later?"

For weeks I've been home, and he waits until now to invite me out to lunch? Memories of sitting through hours-long meals while my father chitchatted with all his buddies at neighboring tables fill my mind. Today, of all days, I don't have time.

"I've got a few things to finish up," I say. "And then I need to start packing. Going home on Sunday."

He frowns. Bliss and Rose stop their yoga session, slowly rising from their lilac-colored foam mats.

"When were you going to tell us?" Rose asks.

I wait for the confirmation email to come through before closing my laptop, and then I gather my things.

"Now," I say. "Just booked the flight."

"What's the rush, sweetheart?" Bliss asks.

Now I'm getting it from all angles.

I think of Sutton yesterday at the pharmacy. The hardness in his glare, the grit in his jaw. "Don't want to overstay my welcome."

I head inside before they can guilt me into canceling my non-refundable ticket, and as soon as I make it to my room, I realize I've missed two calls from the burner phone, both within the last minute.

Before I have a chance to call back, my screen lights with a third call.

"Hello?" I answer, careful not to use her name in case it's him.

"Grace." It's Campbell. "I have twenty minutes this afternoon."

CHAPTER 26

Campbell's waiting for me at a bistro the next town over, sitting cross-legged at a table for two by the sidewalk. Her sandy hair is twisted into a high bun, and mirrored aviators hide her eyes. The rest of her is dressed for the gym.

"Where's Gigi?" I ask when I take the empty chair.

"I'm supposed to be at barre." She scans the cars that drive by. If she's so concerned about being spotted, why nab a spot outside? "I dropped her off at the fitness center day care and came here. I don't have a lot of time."

Sutton lets her take fitness classes now? I guess I assumed he didn't . . .

Or maybe he doesn't know?

"First of all, why are you still with him?" I ask. "When I didn't hear from you after that night in the park . . ." Preserved images of their home through a security camera lens flash into my mind. "I thought you'd taken Gigi and gotten the hell out of there. I was surprised to see you last week."

"I appreciate your concern, Grace. I do. But I never should have gotten you involved in any of this. Honestly, I wish I hadn't. It's only made things worse between Sutton and me."

"Worse how?"

She slides the sunglasses down her nose and rests them on the table, next to a glass of melting ice water. I scan her face for marks, bruises, swelling, anything, but she's flawless. Not a hint of makeup or concealer anywhere.

Dragging in a jagged breath, she holds her gaze on mine. "I need to be up-front with you about something."

"By all means."

"That night at the park, when I told you I knew exactly who you were," she says before hesitating. Her lips spread into a lightning-fast smile that fades in an instant. "I don't know how to tell you this without sounding completely insane. Also, I feel silly having not brought it up earlier, but the last few weeks have been . . ."

"What? What is it?" My head is light, and my heart trips over its own beats. I haven't the slightest clue what she's about to confess, and every second is torture.

"You and I are half sisters." She studies me, wincing.

I lean back, soaking in her statement, examining her features and mentally overlapping them with mine.

We look similar, yes.

But lots of people do.

"How do you know this?" I ask.

"We share a father." She checks her watch. "When I met Sutton . . . I was actually searching for you. His name kept coming up alongside yours because the two of you shared apartments in college. But by the time I was able to make contact with him, he said you'd ended the relationship and he didn't know where you were." Campbell glances at a passing car, silver like Sutton's, but a Mazda. "We decided to look for you together. He was still in love with you, and I was hell-bent on finding a sister I'd only recently found out existed." She lifts a shoulder, our eyes intersecting. "But we looked and we looked. And it was like you'd erased every piece of your existence from the internet. Your brother, Sebastian, gave us a number, but it was disconnected."

The second I left Sutton, I sanitized every electronic trail that could ever possibly lead him back to me because I knew he'd try. I knew he'd want to talk me out of it. Everything I did was for him, so he could have the life he deserved.

"One thing led to another, I guess," she continues, "and eventually we started dating. We told ourselves everything happened for a reason. That we were supposed to be together. That this was how it was always meant to be."

Fair enough.

"Did you . . . name your daughter after me?" I ask, though saying it out loud paints me rather presumptive.

She hums through a sheepish smile. "We did. We wouldn't have met if it hadn't been for you, so we wanted to honor that."

Words fail to reach my lips as I let the strangeness of that honor wash over me. It's strange. It's flattering. It validates my assumption. But more than all of that, it makes me uncomfortable—the idea of someone walking around as my namesake all because I broke her daddy's heart once upon a time.

"Everything was amazing those first few years," she continues, speaking to me but peering over my shoulder. "Shortly after we got married, though, he changed."

Campbell checks the time again.

"Controlling. Obsessed. Angry," she says. "So angry." Clearing her throat, she adds, "He wasn't like this before we moved here. Before Monarch Falls, he was . . . perfect."

I'm inclined to believe her claims about him because that's the way I left him, perfect.

But her claim about us being sisters? I'm hesitant to take her word for that. This world is full of liars and people who believe their own lies. I'm going to have to do the deepest digging before I buy this.

"I thought it was odd that out of all the cities in the world, he snagged a job in your hometown, but he told me it was here or Erie,

Pennsylvania, and I didn't want to be farther away from my family in Connecticut." She slides her sunglasses over her nose. "I'm so sorry. I'm sure you have a million questions, but I have to get back to the center to pick up my daughter."

She rises. I rise.

"You can't just leave," I say, though I know damn well she can. "Why won't he let you talk to me? If he knows we're sisters? He can't keep you from your family."

"You don't know him." She slips her bag over her hunched shoulder, voice defeated. "Not anymore."

"So you're just going to stay? With that monster?"

"I know it's hard for you to understand," she says. "But yes."

"What about your daughter?" I think of myself at Gigi's age, blissfully unaware that I was nothing more than a pawn.

"You don't think I've thought about that a million times?" Her brows intersect, and her arms fold across her chest. Her stare is pointed, as if my question is out of line.

"You want her growing up thinking *that's* normal?" I point at her. "You want her thinking it's okay to be reduced to nothing more than a spineless domestic servant?"

The words glide from my mouth before I have a chance to stop them, but I manage to bite my tongue before I say something worse.

Apparently self-centered parenting is a trigger for me.

"Is that what you think of me?" Her tone softens and her face tilts. She reminds me of a helpless puppy with the saddest eyes, and I can't help but wonder if she does this little trick to Sutton when he's going off on her.

"Why'd you want to talk to me today, Campbell?" I change the subject. I will not be manipulated. I refuse to pity someone who willingly chooses to raise her daughter with someone like Sutton.

I don't understand.

And I don't know what it'll take to get through to her, to make her see the danger of this situation. Does she want her daughter to grow up like me? To never know a loving marriage? To be nothing but a pawn between two dysfunctional human beings?

Without thinking, I shove the contents of our tabletop to the ground.

A cacophony of broken glass is followed by frigid water soaking through the top of my tennis shoe. Two ladies at the table behind us gasp. Campbell takes a step back.

I'm not okay.

Not that anyone is asking.

"My entire life, I've wanted to meet one person who shares my blood. *One*." I speak the words I've never spoken out loud before. Not to anyone. "You're not my sister. You couldn't be. You're too weak."

I wrestle cash from my wallet and place it on the table to cover the damage, and then I leave.

On the way home, I think about believing her.

I *want* to believe her. My God—a sister. A *blood* sister.

And her story is quite compelling. Convincing too.

But I've been lied to before.

CHAPTER 27

I flick through Campbell's Instaface photos until I find one of her sandwiched between a couple in their late fifties to early sixties. It's dated last year, but the caption says "RIP DAD!"

I zoom in on his face, then out. In and out. Everything about him screams boring, retired white guy. Thinning silver hair that fades to nothing on top. Generous double chin. Nondescript, generic features that don't so much as hint at whether he was an attractive man in his younger days. Not even a logo or detail in the background from which to infer a profession or whether he was working-class or upper-class or comfortably in-between.

It's the only photo she has with him in it.

I sift through eighty-nine comments until I find one that mentions his name.

Anthony Beckwith.

A quick Google search brings me his obituary, a short and sweet paragraph that mentions he managed a cold shipping warehouse for thirty-four years, was married to his high school sweetheart, Gabby, for forty-two, and had one daughter—Campbell.

Had I not gone off on her so quickly, I probably could have siphoned a few more answers out of her, but at the time, all I saw was red and all I felt was a distracting amount of everything.

Even if I wanted to believe we were half sisters, I don't know that history would allow me to. The only definitive proof would be a DNA test, and I'm firm in my stance on those.

I chew the inside of my lip. Sometimes the only thing more terrifying than the unknown is the truth. The truth changes things. It rearranges the way a person interacts with the world. Am I ready for that? Say Campbell *is* my half sister—what would change? Would I become a lighter soul? Would I walk on clouds and spot rainbows everywhere? Would I laugh more? Hide away less? Would I stay in one place for longer than six months at a time?

I close out of her profile, pull up my email, and double-check my flight departure time for Sunday afternoon.

Dad and Bliss are outside by the pool, their voices carrying up the side of the house and into my open window. Staying planted in my room, face buried in a computer screen, is doing nothing but delaying the inevitable. And it's not that I'm afraid of his response, I'm simply dreading that face-to-face I'm about to have with reality, and all those years I've spent loathing Daphne for something she didn't do.

I promise myself I'm going to pull him aside tonight.

No matter what.

Worst-case scenario, if it becomes a big thing and I explode and he asks me to leave, I can spend the next two nights in a hotel.

Best-case scenario, he apologizes for being a selfish asshole and we can figure out a way to move forward.

I perch cross-legged on the edge of my bed, fingers rapping against the side of my face as I stare at my laptop screen. There's a chance I'm subconsciously looking for one last excuse to keep me from having to trot downstairs and pull my father aside.

Logging on to the Watchers and Guardians VPN, I check a few work messages and clean out my inbox until all that remains is a handful of old emails from Jonah—and the link *Imaginary_Comrade18* sent to the Whitlocks' security cameras.

It's been over a week. The security certificate should have expired by now. But with a cocktail of curiosity, boredom, and procrastination coursing through me, I click anyway.

The screen refreshes twice as I wait for an access denied message—that never comes.

An image of the Whitlock kitchen fills the page. A messy kitchen table. A pot of something simmering on the stove. A refrigerator door cocked open, leaking a vertical sliver of light.

Sutton circles behind Campbell as she rinses something in the sink, his arms flying in the air. I can't see his face, can't hear a damn thing, but she keeps her back to him, hunched. Gigi plays in her high chair, oblivious.

I zoom in when Sutton turns, and I study his face as he paces from the sink to the peninsula, his hand flying to his temple and back. My eyes burn and I squeeze them tight, giving them a few seconds of rest. When I focus on the moving image again, I find his hands are on her shoulders. He spins her to face him, his fingers digging into her shoulders—at least from what I can tell. And she's crying. Shoulders heaving. Red-faced. Cheeks saturated in tears.

My heart sprints, my muscles jerking with sparks of adrenaline urging me to move. To get up. To go there.

To do something.

But what?

Both Sutton and Campbell have made it abundantly clear they want me out of their lives, that my mere presence has only made things worse. I could dash to my car and speed over there to intervene, but how could I explain what I've witnessed? Hacking into a security system is illegal, I'm sure. And Sutton's already threatened to have me reported for harassment and stalking.

I close my laptop and wear a path into the pristine carpet of my childhood bedroom. Bed to dresser. Dresser to nightstand. Nightstand to bathroom.

The pit of my stomach hollows with nausea.

I've done everything I can do. I've crossed boundaries, blown through a chunk of my personal savings, and broken laws. I've done things I'm not proud of, and it's all been for nothing.

These people don't want help.

And they especially don't want my help.

I splash cold water on my face before making my way downstairs, tilting the family portrait ever so slightly on my way. The house is quieter than it was a half hour ago. Dark with dusk.

"Hello?" I call out when I hear someone's voice—female. "Bliss?"

No answer.

"Rose?" I ask, louder.

A million seconds later, someone calls my name. "Grace? Is that you?"

I release a held breath. It's only my sister.

"In the family room," she adds.

"Where's everyone else?" I ask when I find her flipping through a home and garden magazine, illuminated by lamplight. "And what are you doing here? Where's Evan?"

"Dad is having drinks with some of his friends downtown. I don't know where Bliss is. Evan's prepping some online summer class he's teaching. Now that we're having the baby, he thinks he needs to take on some extra courses." She rolls her eyes and flips to a new page. "You still leaving this weekend?"

"Yeah." I take a seat.

"That's too bad." She offers a smile, half-sad, half-apologetic. "It's been nice having you around."

"You can come visit me in Portland anytime." I don't mention that my lease expires in three months. That I don't have a guest room or pull-out couch. Or that the idea of being in extreme close quarters with anyone else is so suffocating it almost makes me hyperventilate in anticipation.

But I'd suffer through it for her.

"You don't look so hot," she says. "You okay?"

Rose has asked me that question more in the past couple of weeks than anyone's asked me in the past eight years. The only other person who used to ask me that on a regular basis was Sutton, and I never had to answer him because he always knew the answer. He could take one look at me and know, and while it always freaked me out, it comforted me at the same time.

No one's been able to do that since.

Except maybe Rose.

She folds her magazine and returns it to the coffee table. "Talk. Tell me what's on your mind."

I think of the used books with the cracked spines. I think of the worn pages smudged with fingerprints. And I think of how many people have shared those stories, the experiences between the pages, the depths and the highs and the lows and the joys and the pains . . . and I decide maybe I've been missing the point all along.

"How much time do you have?" I ask.

Rose's pink lips curl in the corners, and she pulls her knees against her still-flat stomach. "For you? All the time in the world."

I retrieve a bottle of water for Rose and pour myself a glass of wine and settle back in, telling my sister everything, from the moment I left Sutton eight years ago to my conversation with Campbell at the café when she confessed to being my half sister.

"Do you believe her?" Rose asks.

"I don't really believe anyone about anything," I say with a sniff and a smirk. "But what would it benefit her to lie? What's in it for her?"

Rose shrugs, wide-eyed as if she's seeing me in a whole new light. And she is. I've never opened up like this to anyone, least of all her.

"Do you look like your dad?" she asks. "Your biological dad, I mean?"

I shake my head. "I can't tell. There was just the one picture."

I don't like her referring to him as my "biological dad." It doesn't fit. Not in my mind. And until there's scientific proof . . .

Sure, the Beckwiths are from Connecticut and my biological mom grew up in Connecticut, but other than that, it's going to take some thesis-level research to unearth a definitive connection, and even then . . .

It's not like I can call up my biological grandparents—whom I've never spoken to in my life and who are still likely grieving their missing daughter—and get them to confess that their sweet Autumn was impregnated by some older man. The fact that they sent her away to have the baby means they wanted to hide the truth. Thirty years later, I doubt that's changed.

Sliding my phone from my pocket, I pull up Campbell's Instaface account and scroll through her profile pictures until I find the "RIP DAD!" photo.

"His name is Anthony Beckwith." It's strange to say his name out loud, though I'm not sure why. He's nothing more than a dead stranger and a possibility.

Rose leans close, taking my cell and zooming in on the image. Her pale eyes dart from the image to me and back. "That's tough. I don't know. Genetics are weird, though. Sebastian looks like Dad's twin. Can't even tell Mom was a part of that equation. Maybe you look more like your mom than your dad?"

"If he's even my dad . . ."

"You'll have to do a DNA test, compare it to her," Rose says. "That's the only way you'll know for sure."

"I don't see that happening." I don't feel like explaining all the potential ways DNA testing can ruin a person's life. In certain circles, it's akin to discussing UFO conspiracy theories. Only this isn't a conspiracy theory. I've witnessed firsthand how nefarious government intelligence agencies can be and exactly whose hands that information can land in for the right price.

Her brows knit. "Don't you want to know?"

"Of course," I say. "But we didn't exactly leave things in an amicable place. I'm not about to ask her to spit in a tube."

Nor am I about to spit in a tube.

"Maybe she's got some other kind of proof? Obviously she homed in on you for a reason. She has to know something. And you do look similar."

I top off my wine. Sip. Reflect. Scrutinize.

"You should reach out to her again, ask her more questions," Rose says.

"She asked me not to bother her anymore."

Rose places her water on a marble coaster with a smack. "She doesn't get to do that to you. She doesn't get to play victim for weeks, drop this bombshell in your lap, then expect you to fade into the background."

I've never seen sweet Rose this fired up.

I must admit I enjoy this side of her.

She almost reminds me of . . . me.

"Call her," she says. "Call her and demand your answers. Ask about your dad. Ask anything you want to know."

The crystal clock on the fireplace mantel settles at nine PM, and I'm certain this day is refusing to end to spite me.

"I hate to pack up, but I told Ev I'd be home by nine and it's already past," Rose says. She rises from the sofa, fluffs the pillows behind her back into place, and adjusts her top. "But I'm serious. Call her. You have a right to know what she knows."

I let Rose hug me, and I inhale the remnants of her floral perfume and the faded fabric softener that clings to her blouse.

"We'll talk tomorrow, and you can tell me all about it," she says with a wink as she slips a camel-colored crossbody bag over her shoulders. I recognize the rose emblem on the side. It's from her personal line of merchandise, and I kind of love that she wears her own label. Speaks volumes about her character.

The fullness of pride silently—and unexpectedly—wells in my chest as I watch her leave.

And as soon as the front door latches closed, I head upstairs and make that phone call.

CHAPTER 28

I call Campbell on the burner, and I don't expect her to answer. But in the middle of the first ring, she does.

"Grace," she whispers. "Oh, my God. I'm so glad you called."

Muffled noises fill the background. Shuffled feet. Heavy things being thrown about. The quick slick of a zipper.

"What are you doing?" she asks.

"Packing."

I'm confused, but I don't pry. "I just had a few questions about your dad . . . our dad . . . that whole thing."

"I'm sure you do." She's breathless. There's a second zipper followed by a muted thud. "And I want to apologize for all of that. For the way you had to find out. I wanted to tell you, but there was never a good time. And then when Sutton found out you were back . . . he didn't like us talking."

Of course not.

He knew me, and he knows I'd never put up with him treating someone like that—especially if there's a chance they are my own flesh and blood.

He was right to fear my presence.

I didn't go quietly. But I am going.

He won. And I'm not proud.

"Listen," she says. There's another zipper, then silence. "I'm leaving him."

"Again?"

"I didn't leave before—I went to my mother's in Connecticut," she says. "I needed him to cool down. We needed space. And it was her birthday, so the timing worked."

"So why couldn't you talk to me then? Why couldn't you tell me that? You couldn't have called when you got there? Do you know how worried I was when you weren't returning my phone calls?" I don't mean to go off on her, but the questions hurl themselves with minimal effort.

"He monitors all my phone calls and texts," she says. "I couldn't risk him knowing we were still in contact."

Even if that's true, couldn't she have called me from her mother's phone? Borrowed a landline at a local diner?

I take a seat on the floor and pull my knees to my chest. "So you're actually leaving him now? You and Gigi? For good?"

"Yes. But I need a favor."

"Okay?" My heart races. I imagine hers does, too. I'm good at leaving people—it's kind of what I do . . . but I've never helped anyone else leave. This could get tricky. Dangerous, even. Dampness blankets my palm. I move the phone to my other hand and wipe my hand on my thighs.

"I have a friend with a cabin in Sussex County, about eighty miles north," she says. "I'd order a taxi, but they don't take cash. And they don't go beyond a sixty-mile radius of here. Also, it wouldn't be hard for him to trace any of those transactions and figure out where I went."

"So you need me to take you to this cabin? When?"

"Tomorrow night," she says. "I'm going to crush up a couple of Ambien and put it in his wine at dinner. He'll be out cold in an hour, two at the most. By the time he wakes up, we'll be gone. I'll leave my phone. He'll have no way to trace us . . . Gigi and me."

"When I said you should leave him . . . I meant divorce him. Move out. Kidnapping your own kid, Campbell . . . I don't know if I can help you do that." My temples throb. I pinch the bridge of my nose, hard, to transfer the pain.

"You said he was a monster," she counters, voice trembling. "'Monster' doesn't scratch the surface of what that man has become."

I bury my face against the tops of my knees. Inhale. Exhale. Still as a statue. Basking in dread. Knowing I can't *not* do something—I'd never forgive myself if something happened to either of them.

"I'm flying out Sunday," I say. An hour or two in the car will give me ample time to ask about our supposed sisterhood and my alleged father. "But I can drive you to the cabin tomorrow night."

"Thank you, Grace. Keep your phone on you tomorrow night . . . I'll text when we're ready." Her voice is broken, grateful. "Again, I'm so sorry for everything."

CHAPTER 29

"I hate that you're leaving so soon," Bliss says over dinner Saturday evening. She pouts as she reaches for her wine. "Feels like you just got here."

My father dabs his mouth on a cloth napkin before laying it in his lap. "Sure you don't want to stay a little longer?"

My watch reads 7:08 PM. Campbell said she was going to slip Sutton some sleeping pills at dinner and call me once he was knocked out, but I have no clue when they eat and I've yet to hear from her today.

"I wish I could," I say to appease them both.

I cross my legs to keep my knee from bouncing and try to chew a bite of Bliss's dry chicken marsala, but I can't focus long enough to eat and my stomach is rock hard, too full of nerves to have room for sustenance.

When we're finished, I clear the table and wash the dishes, checking the time after I dry the silverware and return it to the tray in the drawer. By eight fifteen, Campbell still hasn't reached out.

"Thank you, Grace," Bliss says when she shuffles into the kitchen to refill her drink. "For cleaning. I appreciate it."

I nod. "Thanks for dinner."

With an elbow propped against the marble island, she studies me. "I've really enjoyed getting to know you these last several weeks."

She hasn't gotten to know me, not in the slightest.

I wish Rose were here to cushion some of tonight's awkwardness, but she and Evan had a double date with an old friend of hers in town from college. Tomorrow morning we're meeting for brunch—just us sisters—at a little café called Meadowlark in the trendy Westridge section of Monarch Falls.

Dare I say, I'm looking forward to it?

"Maybe your father and I can take a trip out to Portland sometime? See your side of the world?" Bliss's eyes light. "Of course it's up to you. We don't want to intrude."

I dry a plate, my back toward her. "We can figure something out."

She lingers, just a moment longer, before padding outside, securing the sliding glass door behind her and settling into a pool lounger. Party lights hang from the pergola, giving off a glow like a silent invitation to join her, to relax.

My father's heavy footsteps coming from the next room remind me there's still one thing I need to do before I go. I'd been waiting for a moment alone with him today, but every time I found one, he'd be on the phone or on his way somewhere, key fob dangling in his hand. Or Bliss was beside him, talking his ear off about this new mantra she's testing.

"Hey, Gracie," he says.

I place the last dish away and face him, anchoring him with my gaze. "Dad."

He grabs a drink from the fridge. Green glass bottle. Fancy label with cursive writing. Upshore Pale Ale. Sounds exactly like something he'd drink. I don't doubt the name alone was enough to sell him on it.

"I need to talk to you about something," I say.

He slides a barstool out from beneath the island and takes a seat, his thumb running along the wet label of his beer. "What's on your mind?"

I check my watch, then the screen of my phone. Procrastination, I suppose. And then I gather a breath.

"Remember that book that came out a while back? *Domestic Illusions*?" I ask.

His brows meet, and then his forehead creases. "Yeah. I do. Why?"

"I read it," I say.

His lips flatten, and his hand rests statue-still on the bottle. "Ah."

Ah?

"That's all you have to say?"

His dark eyes rest on mine. "So let's talk about it."

"Rose told me you were the one behind it. She said you helped that Dianna Hilliard, fed her all that information, all our personal family business."

"A lot of it was public record. I had to clarify a few things. Clear up some rumors and such."

And such . . .

"Would've been nice if you could've left me out of it." I slide my hands into my back pockets and glance away. I can't look at him. And if he's not going to own up to the magnitude of what he did, this conversation is going to be a waste of both of our time. "Reading about Mom's difficulty bonding with me, how I was *hard to love* . . . do you have any idea what that did to me?"

Deep lines crease along his forehead, as if he's genuinely confused.

"It was never about you. I was trying to portray your mother in a certain light." His voice lowers. "To be honest, I didn't think you'd read it."

"You didn't think I would? Or you hoped I wouldn't?"

"Both." He takes a sip, and we finally make eye contact again. "At the time, I was thinking of it as an apology, of sorts, to your mother. For what I put her through. She sacrificed a lot for this family, and she deserved better than me."

No wonder the story portrayed her as a saint and him as a charming womanizer.

"You couldn't have written her a letter? Visited her in person and told her how sorry you were?"

"She wanted nothing to do with me after everything. Wouldn't take my letters or let me visit," he says. "After all we'd been through, I wanted her to know I still loved her. That I forgave her for what she did."

"For having Marnie Gotlieb murdered, you mean?" My words slice the thick air that separates us. The coward can't bring himself to say her name, so I'll do it for him. "Or for her part in tearing up our family?"

"All of it." His eyes apologize, but the rest of him is stiff as a board. "And I guess I was hoping for her forgiveness, too."

"And the only way to do that was to sell us out?" I ask. "Excuse me—sell *me* out."

His shoulders rise. Exhaling, he hesitates. "I'm sorry, Grace. I'm so sorry. If I could take it back, believe me, I would. But I can't. All I can do is apologize. And ask for your understanding."

I can't look at him. Biting my tongue, I glance away.

"I never meant for you to get hurt in all of this," he says. His pained gaze glides to my hand. If I were Rose, he'd likely reach for it in an attempt to comfort me. But he knows better.

My eyes well. I squeeze them until it stops. All these years, I could've had a relationship with my mom. I won't get that time back. And whatever relationship we have moving forward will be forever changed because of it.

"Dianna donated a portion of the proceeds to you kids," he says. "I told her it wasn't necessary, but I think somehow it made her feel justified in writing this book and making money from it. Anyway, I placed your third in an account, where it's grown quite a bit over the last decade. Doubled almost. I was waiting for the right time to tell you about it, but I guess—"

"I don't want it."

"Grace." He scoffs, as if he can't fathom the idea of someone turning down free money. Only this money isn't free. It came at a price.

"I mean it. I want nothing to do with that book. With what you did." I shoot him a look, only to realize there are tears in his eyes. Real tears. But as far as I'm concerned, our conversation is over. I said what I needed to say. He apologized. No need to drag this out or turn it into some Hallmark moment. I won't hug him. I won't offer him clemency.

There's nothing the man can say to undo what's been done, and he'll never understand the full effects of his actions or how they've trickled through me and spilled over to the Whitlocks. I've said it before, and I'll say it again: the man is bulletproof.

Everything ricochets off him.

Everything.

I leave my father alone with his tears, and I head upstairs to wait for Campbell's call.

CHAPTER 30

It's three minutes to midnight when she calls.

I sit up on my bed, in a pitch-black room, in a silent house. I must have passed out.

"Hey," I answer.

"We're ready," she whispers. "He's finally out."

"I'll leave now." I push myself off the bed and locate my purse on top of the dresser.

"Pick me up around the corner." Each syllable is whisper soft, at times inaudible. "I don't want him to see your car—on the driveway camera."

Five minutes later, I'm idling around the corner from 72 Lakemont, under a black patch of darkness between two streetlamps, when Campbell appears out of nowhere, run-walking toward my headlights with a sleepy Gigi on her hip, an overflowing backpack on her back, and a car seat in her arm.

I climb out and help her load up. She hands Gigi a sippy cup and buckles her seat into the middle of the back seat.

The moon is full, and the street is asleep.

Not a single car coasts by.

"I'm sorry it's so late," she says when we're fastened in the front seat a minute later. "We had a late dinner, and it took him longer than

I thought to fall asleep. I wanted to make sure he was really out before I made any noise."

He was always a light sleeper.

Pulling out her phone, she types an address into the GPS. A voice comes from its tinny speaker, telling me to proceed to the highlighted route, but I can't see her screen.

"Go left at the stop sign." She glances back at Gigi, keeping her voice soft.

"Where's the burner?" I ask.

"In my bag," she says. "This is a satellite phone I picked up a few days ago. My friend said cell service is terrible at the cabin."

She crosses her legs in the passenger seat, making herself small, compact. I imagine she's scared.

"How are you feeling? About all of this?" I ask once we turn left. The GPS tells us to stay straight for the next five miles. "You doing okay?"

Campbell nibbles at her thumb, nodding.

Is she scared of starting over?

Or scared of what Sutton will do when he wakes up to find his wife drugged him and ran off with their daughter?

My eyes squint and water, hypnotized by the stretch of gray road ahead, and I avoid checking the time. I'm aware that it's late. It would've been nice to have left a few hours ago, but nothing I can do about that now.

"Do you mind if we stop for a coffee before we hit the interstate?" I yawn at the sight of a twenty-four-hour gas station ahead.

"Of course not," she says. "I could use one myself."

I pull into the parking lot of the Quik Stop-n-Go on Highland. The only other car here is parked behind the building, its driver's door a different color than the rest of it. Campbell stays with Gigi, and I run inside to grab us a couple of watered-down cappuccinos, a granola bar, and a bag of crackers. I couldn't possibly eat right now, but I should have something on hand just in case.

Ten minutes later, a weak boost of caffeine hits my system. I haven't yawned for miles. I check Campbell in my side view and determine she's as wide awake as I am.

"You mind if we talk?" I ask. "I'd turn the radio on, but I don't want to wake Gigi."

"Not at all," she says.

Good.

Because I have questions.

I grip the wheel at a nine-and-three position, not a perfect ten-and-two. And softly clear my throat.

"There's no easy way to ask you this," I say, "and I don't want to sound paranoid, but what makes you . . . how did you . . . why do you think we're sisters?"

Campbell melts back in her seat, adjusting her posture, taking her time. "My dad—our dad—told me after he was diagnosed with esophageal cancer, about ten years ago or so. He thought he was going to die, I guess. Didn't want to die with this secret."

I think of his smiling, generic face in the "RIP DAD!" picture.

"He ended up living another seven, eight years after that," she says. "It got him the second time around."

Road noise fills the silence between us.

"My mom still doesn't know," she adds. "He never wanted to hurt her. She thought I was his first daughter, his only daughter. It would've devastated her to know he lied to her. It took them a long time to have me. They were almost forty when I came along. Total surprise. Anyway, Dad kept tabs on you your whole life. He told me your name, where you grew up, told me we looked like twins."

I try to do the math, but my brain is on cheaply caffeinated fumes. "My mom was fifteen when she had me. And you're, what . . . a couple of years younger than me?"

She's quiet, and then she nods. "He said he'd had an affair with a younger woman. I never realized how young she was until I read that book about your family."

I imagine Campbell poring over that tell-all book, devouring facts about me and my childhood, and a shiver runs through me, as if I'm naked, exposed. I hate that anyone can waltz into a bookstore and grab a story so personal, so unauthorized.

"So your dad was more than twice my birth mother's age," I say.

Campbell sighs. "He had demons. And he was far from a saint."

Maybe my darkness and contempt for societal norms are inherited, like a gnarled, broken gene. This would make sense.

"I don't want you thinking you missed out on some amazing fatherly experience," Campbell says as she angles toward me, the whites of her eyes reflecting in the headlights of an oncoming car. "He loved whiskey more than anything in the world. But when he wasn't drinking, he'd embarrass me in front of my friends with corny jokes or take me fishing at the lake. Typical dad stuff. But those days were few and far between. There were more whiskey days than anything else."

I try to imagine a different childhood, one with fewer floral arrangements and ballet lessons and more corny jokes, fishing trips, and drunken fatherly advice.

"I wish we could've met sooner," she says. "Before all of . . . this."

"Do you have any pictures of him?" The image from her Instaface account flashes in my head. I don't share a single feature with that man, and I wouldn't say Campbell shares much with him either—which would suggest she takes after her mother. But age and time have a way of warping those things. And genetics can be complicated.

"I'll dig some up for you sometime, sure," she says.

Sometime . . .

There's no urgency or guarantee in her voice. Then again, her priorities in this moment have more to do with safety than convincing me of something she already believes to be gospel.

I conjure a memory of Sarah Thomas and how she lied to me before, and the thought brings a tightness to the back of my throat. Sarah was disturbed and unwell, though, and Campbell is unassuming and benign. What reason would she have to make this up? I don't have anything to offer anyone. No fame or fortune. No mansion by the sea. No political influence. No connections. Nothing about my life is remotely enviable. There's not a single thing Campbell could gain by claiming to be my half sister.

There's a chance her father lied. Or maybe he had his information wrong. Maybe my mother slept with another man, and her father simply assumed the baby was his? Stranger things have happened. And people spend their entire lives believing things are one way only to find out (or never find out) that they were wrong.

"I hated being an only child," she confesses with a breathy smile. "I was so lonely all the time. Dad was always working, and when he wasn't working, he was drinking. Mom was this social butterfly—always fluttering from book club to bake sale. Not only that, but we lived in the country, so . . . no neighborhood kids to run around with or ride bikes with. Would've been nice to have a big sister to bother."

People have a tendency to idealize the past, what it could have been. I gave up on that time-wasting practice a lifetime ago.

"What was your childhood like?" she asks. "After . . . everything?"

"Unremarkable." I know I'm lying the second the words leave my lips. But I'm not lying to her. I'm lying to myself. It's what I've done my entire life. It's why I loathe coming home. It's why I've avoided getting to know my younger siblings in their adult years. All of it represents a past that is anything but unremarkable. "After my mom went to prison, I went to live with my grandma in Florida. Graduated from high school. Went to college. Got a job. Here I am."

Campbell sniffs. "Something tells me you're skipping over all the good parts."

Good . . . or unpleasant?

"My grandma lived in this retirement village," I say. "Fifty-five and older. She took a lot of heat for taking me in, but I laid low, stayed quiet and out of the way, and eventually her neighbors got used to me. I got pretty good at being invisible. Mostly hung out by the pool, rode my bike around the parking lot. Sometimes I'd walk dogs for a few of the neighbors or weed flower beds to make some cash, but other than that, I was a loner," I say. "Trust me when I tell you, you didn't miss out on some profound experience of having me as a big sister."

Campbell laughs. "I'm sure I'm glamorizing it. I probably would've been the worst kid sister anyway. I was terribly shy—to the point of having an invisible friend until I was eight or nine. When my cousins would come for a week in the summer, I was so starved for attention I'd follow them around until they'd get sick of me. Clinging to them, copying them, never letting them out of my sight."

I snort. We were both a couple of weirdos. True misfits. Whether we are or we aren't sisters, we've got that in common.

Her GPS tells me to take the next exit, and I glance down at her coffee for a split second. She hasn't taken but maybe one or two sips for the past half hour. I imagine she's had a long day, nerves spiking and adrenaline dropping and sinking her into exhaustion.

"So what's your—" I begin to ask her where she's going from here, what her next move is . . . when I discover her eyes are closed and her head is pressed against the passenger window. Slow, quiet breaths escape her half-open mouth.

My questions can wait.

I take comfort knowing she feels safe with me.

I slide the satellite phone from her lap and check the ETA.

We'll be there soon enough.

CHAPTER 31

We pass a sign for 145th Avenue, and the GPS tells me to turn right in two hundred yards. I press the brake, coasting slower and watching for a turnoff. Aside from the glow of the moon, it's darker than midnight out here—and almost two AM.

Gravel pings the underbelly of my rental, and Campbell stirs awake, sitting straighter, rubbing her eyes.

"You have arrived at your destination," her phone announces when I stop outside a log cabin so quaint and dark, a person could easily mistake it for part of the surrounding forest.

"Wait here." Campbell climbs out and shuts the door with a quiet click, phone in hand, and she makes her way to the front of the structure, punching a code into a lockbox. A second later, the front door swings open, and she disappears into the darkness.

A small light by the porch blinks on.

Campbell returns, moving to grab Gigi from the back seat. I climb out and get her bag, following them in.

A thick flood of musty air invades my lungs the instant I step inside. I say nothing as I close the door behind me. Sweat collects along the nape of my neck. It's at least eighty degrees in here, if not more. I reach for a hair tie from my wrist before remembering I didn't bring one.

Gigi stirs, eyes half-open, and Campbell cradles the back of her head, shushing her as she rocks her in place.

"I'm going to lay her down," she whispers. "I'll be right back."

I anchor myself in the middle of a cozy living room, one barely big enough for a sofa and overstuffed armchair. A bookshelf rests against the wall where a TV could go, filled with aging board games. Monopoly. Aggravation. Life.

Campbell makes a beeline for the kitchen when she returns, flicking on a dim light over the stove and peeking inside the refrigerator.

"I'm starving," she says. "You hungry?"

I shake my head and don't mention the bag of cheese crackers I ate while she slept. The coffee was wearing off, and I needed something to do to keep from falling asleep behind the wheel.

I check the time on my phone. By the time I get home, it'll be close to four AM. I'll be lucky to get a few hours of sleep before I have to meet Rose for brunch.

"What's your plan?" I ask. "From here?"

She swipes a bottle of water from the fridge. A bag of groceries rests on a Formica table shoved up against the windowed wall in the kitchen. There must be someone else involved in this.

"My friend who owns this place," Campbell says between drinks of water. A rivulet drips down her chin, and she swipes it away with the back of her hand. "She and her husband are coming to pick us up sometime tomorrow."

"Where are you going to go?"

"I've spoken to my aunt in Denver," she says. "We're going to stay with her for a while. Until we can get on our feet."

"What about Sutton?" I ask. "What are you going to do when he finds you?"

She steps toward the window, peeking out from behind a gingham curtain. "If—and when—he finds me, I'm hopeful he'll be in a reasonable place so we can have a discussion on where to go from here."

"So you're *not* leaving him?" I ask. "What, did he threaten you? Did he say he'd take Gigi? Help me understand . . ."

Campbell lifts a shoulder, gaze pointed at the linoleum floor. "I'm doing what I have to do. There are things in our marriage that aren't working for me. This is the only way I can get his attention."

I squint. "You don't think all of this will make him worse?"

I can't imagine a scenario where a woman kidnapping a man's child would help him "cool off."

"He'll be livid when he wakes up and realizes what I've done. No question." Her voice is an uncertain whisper, almost as if she's speaking to no one but herself. "But once he calms down, we can talk. This is for the best. For him. For me. For our daughter. When it's all over, he'll realize that."

Yawning, I peek at the time again, only to be met with a black-and-white message across my screen: **LIMITED CELL SERVICE**.

"If you're all settled, I should probably take off," I say. "I've got a flight tomorrow . . ."

Campbell paces toward me, placing her hand on my arm. "It's so late. You sure you want to head back now? There's a spare bedroom you can have if you'd rather drive home in the morning?"

With no cell service and no GPS in the rental, I wouldn't begin to know how to get to Monarch Falls from here. It'd be easier to leave in the morning. I'd be more awake, too. Less likely to fall asleep behind the wheel and make all of this ten times worse.

"Here." She takes my hand and leads me down a short hall until we end up in a bedroom the size of a large closet. A double bed with a sunken middle and a vintage quilt anchors the space, accessorized with a blue painted nightstand with a frilly white lamp, the kinds of things you'd find at a secondhand store or in a grandmother's attic.

Releasing my hand, she heads for the window, propping it open to let the tepid summer breeze mix with the stuffy, humid air to make the room breathable.

Nothing about the bed screams comfort, but the alternative is an eighty-mile drive with blaring music and rolled-down windows and gas station coffee—and that's if I can find my way out of here in the dark.

Campbell moves for the bedside lamp. One soft click later, an inviting glow floods the space like a visual lullaby, beckoning me to settle in for the night.

"I'd feel so much better about all of this if you stayed." Campbell pleads with her eyes. "For your safety." She steps closer. "Please, Grace. Stay."

The weight of the day blankets me in exhaustion. She's right—it's safest to stay here tonight and leave in the morning.

"All right," I say, already imagining peeling out of my jeans and climbing beneath the covers.

"Sorry for falling asleep earlier, by the way." She winces. "That cappuccino was . . . questionable . . . and I was worried it would upset my stomach even more than it already was."

"It's fine."

"It's crazy . . . I was so tired earlier, but now I'm wide awake." Campbell examines me. "You up for talking? Just a little bit? Before you nod off?"

"Oh . . ." I don't want to talk. I want to sleep. I need to sleep.

But I also have more questions.

"I saw a bottle of sauv blanc in the fridge," she says. "I doubt they'd care if we tapped into it. And I wouldn't mind a little toast to this new chapter . . ."

Can she call it a chapter when it's nothing more than coercing her husband into being a better man?

The light in her eyes is infectious, and her smile stretches wide. She's unbraced for disappointment or rejection.

"One drink," I say. I could use a nightcap to give me that final shove into a hard sleep.

I ask her to point me to the bathroom to get washed up. When I come out, she's perched on the side of the guest bed, a glass of white wine in her hand.

"Yours is on the nightstand." She points, gathering her legs onto the bed and settling in. "It's delicious, by the way. Don't judge, but I'm already on my second glass."

I didn't think I was in the bathroom that long. She had to have chugged it.

Anxiety hits us all differently.

I take a sip, letting the sweet notes linger on my tongue before swallowing, and then I slide in beside her. Outside the window, crickets chirp and the moon peers in.

"You know, I've thought about you every single day for years," she confesses, a slow, sheepish smile drawing across her mouth. Whatever her father told her, she believes him with all her heart. It's painted sweetly in her eyes when she looks at me. "Probably to the point of being obsessed." She laughs under her breath. "So when you showed up in my neighborhood . . . I thought I was dreaming. You'd become such a fictional character in my head, and then you were there. In the flesh."

I take a drink, then another.

Sleep calls to me.

And I'm ready to go home—to Portland. The sooner this is over, the sooner I can make that happen.

"It's easy to build people up in your mind when you don't know them," I say.

"I don't know, Grace. I think I probably took it a step past that." She chuffs at herself, taking a long sip.

"You don't strike me as the obsessed type."

Her demeanor fades, and lamplight shadows paint her expression. "You don't seem like the kind of person who cares about other people. Guess we're both full of surprises."

I bury my face in my wine, taking another swallow. Maybe she's had too much to drink? Maybe she's taking this "sister" thing a step too far and trying to test our bond? Not that we're bonded. I've been down this road before, and I'm going to need more proof than her dead father's word of mouth.

"I care more than most people realize," I say.

It's why I place distance between myself and anyone who remotely tries to care about me. It's the ones who care about us who can hurt us the most—and it goes both ways. It's why I stay away.

"You didn't just break Sutton's heart, you know." She peers out the open window. "You annihilated it."

"I know."

"I had a lot of pieces to pick up," she says with a huff. "Took a lot of work to get him to a good place."

"And I feel terrible for that." I swallow the lump in my throat, tasting the linger of sweet wine along with the cheap, metallic aftertaste of a screw-top lid. "That's why I came back . . . to apologize."

Campbell slides off the bed, her glass empty, and she disappears to the kitchen, returning with a fresh top-off.

"Sutton was a shell of a man when I met him," she says when she sits down again, diving back into her oration—one that feels strangely practiced.

"We're still talking about him?" I half laugh. She's growing more inebriated by the minute, and I've had friends like this before—the ones who go on never-ending man-hating tangents after one too many tequila shots.

"I showed him he was worthy," she continues. I brace myself for a rant, something to do with all the years she sacrificed for him, their beautiful life together that he ruined, the betrayal of being physically and emotionally damaged by the person who promised to love you forever. "I taught him how to love, how to be loved again. When you stopped loving him, he—"

"He was always loved." I finish the last of my drink and place the glass on the nightstand. "I made that clear to him when I left. I would always love him, but I could never be the wife he wanted. I couldn't give him the family he always dreamed of."

"And yet deep down, he never gave up hope that you were going to change your mind and come back." Her words snip through the dark, flavored with more resentment than sweet wine.

"How could you know that, though?"

"I found a box."

"Sutton had a lot of boxes of a lot of things," I say. "He's sentimental. Was always keeping things."

"This box went beyond," she says. "Imagine four years' worth of relationship *junk*, all piled into a clear plastic waterproof container, hidden inside another clear plastic waterproof container, then shoved into a cardboard box labeled summer clothes, and hidden on the top shelf of the guest room closet?"

I have no words for Sutton's extreme measures, for the lengths he took to keep Campbell from finding that box.

"We'd been together two years when I found that," she says. "Two years. We'd just moved in together. We were talking about getting engaged, making plans for the future. And he was holding on to that . . . *stuff* "—Campbell wrinkles her nose—"behind my back that whole time."

"Maybe he didn't want to hurt you?" I shouldn't defend him after everything he's done to Campbell, but she's working herself up.

"He promised he'd get rid of it after that," she continues. "But guess what? A year later, I found it again."

I wince.

"I'd never felt so stupid," she says, gaze skimming the ceiling. "For years, I stayed beside him, loyal as a dog, only to find out he was still waiting for you to come back. That he was hanging on to that ridiculous shrine—which I made him burn, by the way."

The idea of Sutton dumping his box of me into the fire makes me feel for the both of them. How demeaning it must have been as a couple to share a moment like that.

"He cried, Grace." She lifts a hand in the air, grabbing a fist of nothing. "The man wept. Like a baby. On his knees."

My chest squeezes so tight it hurts.

I don't want to know these things . . .

I don't *need* to know these things . . .

I place a gentle palm on her shoulder. "Maybe we should get you to bed now? It's been a long day. And I'm sure Gigi will be up—"

She pushes my gesture away. "Don't."

"Campbell."

My eyelids are heavy. I don't have the energy to sit here and listen to her drunk ramblings that grow more pointed with every breath.

Folding my arms, I say, "I can't control the fact that *I* came into his life first or that *you* fell for *my* ex. I also can't control that he kept a box of things that reminded him of me. I know you've had a rough several weeks, and it's been a long day. You've had some wine. You've vented. Now it's time for you to get some rest. Your daughter's going to need you in a few hours."

Her gaze is unfocused, landing over my shoulder. "Do you have any idea what it's like to be used like a pawn by the one person who was supposed to love you?"

I remember the book, the chapter about Daphne adopting me as a marital Band-Aid, and I think of my father selling our secrets for his own personal agenda.

"I know exactly what that's like."

"I gave up hoping you and I would ever meet. I made peace with that. I moved on. *He* moved on. We were finally happy." Her dark eyes turn glassy, and she swipes a tear before it rolls down her cheek. "All you had to do was stay away."

There's fault in her logic.

My presence didn't cause the problems in her marriage. Her perception of my presence did. And Sutton may have struck her, but I didn't lift his hand.

I slip my hand into the bend of her arm and lead her to the bedroom where her daughter sleeps peacefully in a small playpen in the corner. I draw the covers of the queen bed and help her in, searching my soul for every last ounce of compassion. Closing the door when I'm done, I return to my room at the end of the hall, body weak with exhaustion as I crumble into a heavy heap on the vintage quilt.

In the seconds before I pass out, I set my alarm for seven AM. A few hours of sleep and some sunlight are all I need to get out of here.

CHAPTER 32

Hot tension sears through my forehead, shocking me awake the next morning. When I open my eyes, I'm alone. The air is thick and stale in my lungs. The sole window in the room—the one Campbell opened last night—is closed tight. But the curtains remain undrawn.

Sunlight stings my vision, and I recall setting my alarm. I think of my flight. Brunch with Rose. Bits of last night trickle into my memory like a dream, much of it slipping away the harder I try to remember.

A heady scent fills the air—coffee? And outside, birds chirp.

I sit up—or I try to, only to be met with the burn of thick rope against the flesh of my wrists and ankles.

I'm tied to the bed.

"Campbell!" I scream.

This isn't real.

I lift my head, and the compact space around me spins. Every gasp of air is like trying to breathe underwater. There's no ventilation, no circulation.

She drugged me.

The crazy bitch drugged me.

She must have slipped something in my wine—the same way she did to Sutton.

"Campbell!" I yell for her again.

The sound of running water—the bathroom maybe—gives me hope that I'm not alone, that she didn't leave me here. A minute later, the door swings open.

"What are you doing? What is this? Untie me!" I tug at the ropes. It only stings worse. "Campbell."

The coward won't look me in the eye.

"I don't understand," I say. "All I did was help you . . ."

Her expression twists until it matches the one she wore in the middle of the night as she vented about Sutton, about me. All that misdirected anger. All that . . . hatred.

"Pretty sure I made myself perfectly clear last night." She makes her way around the bed, inspecting the knots that keep me from moving more than a handful of inches.

"You were drunk," I say. "You said a lot of things, none of which made sense, to be honest."

Campbell shoots me a sharp look, a silent *Watch yourself.*

Gigi calls for her from another room, and without a word, Campbell leaves, closing the door behind her. For a moment, I contemplate screaming at the top of my lungs—until I remember the drive here, the miles upon miles of nothing and no one. The void and the darkness.

No one would be able to hear me.

My left hand tingles with the beginnings of numbness. I pull as hard as I can, desperate to slip my wrist from the knot, only pain shoots to my fingertips, and traces of blood push through broken skin.

Heat pricks my eyes, a threat of tears, but I refuse to cry.

I'm not going to die.

Not here. Not today.

I think of Rose sitting at the café, waiting for me. How long will she wait before she assumes I've stood her up? Will she think it's simply me being me? Flaking out on my goodbyes like I've done so many times in the past? Will she swallow her disappointment, pay for her coffee, and go back to her day-to-day life?

If anyone checks my bedroom, will they glance over the pristinely made bed and the vacuum tracks in the carpet and ignore the fact that my suitcase is still shoved in the closet?

My father will make the same assumption—I left without saying goodbye. And he won't think twice if he doesn't hear from me for the next six months.

And Jonah—I told him I'm coming back to Portland this week, but it's not unusual to go a week at a time without checking in. By the time he realizes I'm missing, it'll be too late.

The scents of cinnamon and maple syrup waft from the other side of the door. Campbell must be feeding Gigi breakfast . . . like it's any other day, like she doesn't have her husband's ex locked away in another room like a crazy person.

I swallow the burn of bile in the back of my throat, stare at the ceiling, and wait.

Though for what, I can't be certain.

CHAPTER 33

It's impossible to know how much time has passed since Campbell was last in here, but the way the sunlight peers into the room, glaring yet indirect, I can only surmise it's close to noon. It's been hours, easily. My bladder is growing uncomfortably full, though I can't imagine she'll do more than give me a bedpan if I'm lucky.

I've called her a handful of times, only to be ignored.

She's waiting for something.

Or maybe for someone.

Last night she mentioned her "friends" were going to pick them up today and drive them to Denver. But it doesn't make sense. If she's leaving her husband, what does she gain by doing something to me? Is it revenge? Is she wanting to ensure I don't swoop in and steal him while she's gone? And if he's so horrible to her, why would she want to keep him?

People do worse things for lesser reasons.

"Campbell!" I yell for her again.

Light, quick footsteps come to an abrupt stop outside the door, which flings open a second later. The handle smacks the wall, leaving a noticeable indentation. The unexpected thwack elicits a startled gasp from each of us.

"Quiet," she says, hushed but not quite whispering, narrowed gaze pointing as if it were my fault. "I just laid Gigi down for a nap so you and I can have a civilized discussion."

"There'll be nothing civilized about this discussion as long as I'm tied up like an animal."

"I'm sorry you feel that way."

"I imagine I've already missed my flight, but if you let me go, I'll leave here, book the next one home, and you'll never see me again."

She sniffs, glancing at the closed window. For a moment, I assume she's as hungry for fresh air as I am, but she remains planted.

"You don't get it," she says. "It's not enough that you're gone. As long as you're still out there, living, breathing, existing . . . that man has hope. Even if he looks me in the eyes and tells me he hates you—which he's done—the fact that you're out there somewhere . . . it's going to haunt our marriage the rest of our lives."

"If he's so awful to you, why does it matter? I thought you were going to leave him?"

She cocks her head my way, a condescending smile slipping over her lips. "Don't be so dense. Do you really think I'd go to all this trouble if I had no intentions of saving my marriage? He's the only person that matters to me, and this marriage, my family . . . they're the only things I have."

"If your marriage is broken, that's between the two of you. You can't put that on me."

"It's absolutely on you, Grace," she says. "You've been a cloud over our relationship since the day it began. I've tried and I've tried, and I can't get out from under you."

"Maybe you should try counseling?"

"What makes you think we haven't?" She snorts. "All that did was open up an entirely different can of worms. You put Sutton in a safe space, and he makes all kinds of confessions. Did you know he imagined *I* was *you* on our wedding day?"

She paces at the foot of the bed.

"He also confessed that he hated you. That he wished he'd never met you. That if he could erase you from his memory, he'd do it in a heartbeat," she says.

I've always known I hurt him, but the idea of him hating me has never crossed my mind.

Sutton was never a hateful person. He was a walking, talking, turn-the-other-cheek, forgive-and-forget cliché of a man, and I loved that about him. He was so much better than me in those ways.

But people change.

They evolve.

They do what they have to do to survive, to chase that ever-elusive concept of happiness.

"We were in a good place after that. He was finally accepting that you two were over. That his life was with me. That you weren't coming back—*and then you came back.*" Red blotches cover her neck, and she stops pacing to take a few breaths. "As soon as I told him you were in town, that you'd been coming around our house, that we'd been talking—he lost it. I'd never seen him so angry, Grace. And I knew then that he meant what he said when he told me he hated you."

His face that day in the parking lot of his work—so tight, so indignant. I thought he was protecting his secret. I thought he hated that I'd uncovered it. Turns out I'd barely scratched the surface of what that man was going through when his steeled gaze bored into mine.

"He told you to stay away," she says. "Several times. But you refused. You wouldn't listen. I have to believe, Grace, that we wouldn't be here right now had you just stayed the hell away like he told you to."

"I was trying to protect you." I try to sit up, forgetting that I can't. "You said he was hurting you. You said he was controlling. I was worried about you!"

Campbell clucks her tongue. "Do you honestly, truly, in your heart of hearts believe that man is capable of hurting someone? Especially the mother of his child?"

No.

I don't.

I never did.

Until the phone calls in private, the confessions over coffee, the welt on her face . . .

"So you hit yourself that night?" I ask. "When you had me meet you in the park?"

"I did what I had to do."

She's insane. Deranged. Unhinged. "Who *does* that?"

"A woman hell-bent on preserving her family," Campbell says without pause. "I'm sure your mother can relate to that. She had her husband's mistress killed because she saw her as a threat to the beautiful life she created."

"And look where that got her."

"Her first mistake was trusting someone else to get the job done." Campbell circles back to the side of the bed and takes a seat.

"You think killing me is going to make all your problems go away?"

She shrugs and nods, as if the answer is so obvious she doesn't need to say it aloud.

"Sutton would never forgive you," I tell her.

She stands. "Did you not hear me a minute ago? He hates you. He wishes he could forget you. I'm doing him a favor."

The fire in her eyes makes her unrecognizable. Arguing with her is getting me nowhere, and reasoning with a crazy person will be akin to banging my head against a brick wall. I need to approach this from a different angle.

"You're hurting." I infuse as much manufactured compassion into my tone as I can manage, and I speak to her as if I'm not tied to a bed, awaiting a death sentence. "I'm so sorry for everything you've been through. I wish things could be different. But this isn't the answer. If you do this . . . things will only get worse for you."

Gigi calls for her from the other room, up from her nap already. Or maybe she hasn't fallen asleep yet due to all the noise coming from our end of the hall.

Without a word, Campbell leaves, closing the door behind her. I rest my head on the pillow, my neck strained. The water-stained ceiling above me reminds me of my apartment back in Portland with its leaky plumbing and dated kitchen and decades-old carpet. It was the only unit in the building that hadn't been updated, and that was precisely why I chose it. It was perfectly imperfect, all its flaws in plain view. It wasn't trying to be anything other than what it was.

The ropes burn against my flesh once more. I do my best to stay still.

From the moment she claimed to be my half sister, I knew better than to believe her. And I asked myself what she'd have to gain by lying.

Now? I have my answer.

She had a plan all along.

And because the smallest part of me secretly hoped for a blood connection to someone, anyone, I gave her the benefit of the doubt every step of the way, every moonlit mile to this cabin in the middle of a rural county.

Closing my eyes, I transport myself beyond these four walls. Eventually Campbell will be back to do what she's going to do. I could have hours. I could have minutes. My mind floods with all the things I'll never get to do, all the things I'll never get to say. If I die here, today, never to be found, Rose will spend the rest of her life thinking I stood her up. I'll never get to apologize to my mom for hating her all these years. I won't get to find my biological mother, the real Autumn Carpenter. I won't learn to forgive my father for the book. I won't get to see what becomes of Sebastian once he finishes law school. There'll be no thanking Jonah for everything he's done for my career, for being not only a boss I can respect and look up to, but a friend as well.

Funny how quickly death puts everything into perspective, big and small. It shows you who you really are underneath life's armor.

It's ironic—I came back to Monarch Falls to tell Sutton how sorry I am for hurting him.

I wanted to make everything better.

In the end, I made everything worse.

CHAPTER 34

I'm not sure how much time has passed when Campbell returns, but I've managed to make some form of peace with the inevitable. With eyes closed tight, I've played half a dozen mental scenarios in my mind— apologies, exchanges, conversations that will never take place—grasping a sliver of comfort.

"Can we get this over with?" I ask when she closes the door.

Reaching into the back of her jeans, she pulls out a small handgun. I wince. I've spent enough time on the dark web to know that the type of gun she wields is nothing more than a threat stopper. It'll take multiple bullets to kill me, and unless she aims at exactly the right place, my death could be slow and agonizing instead of quick and painless.

A shotgun would be better—at least for me.

It'd be messy, but it would be fast.

And then it would be over. For both of us.

Years ago, I was tasked with filtering a website that linked graphic images of murders along with their respective definitions. Patricide. Senicide. Filicide. Honor killing. Suicide by cop. There are a hundred ways to be killed, and I've witnessed photos of them all.

I know what this is going to look like when it's over. The blood spatter. The soaked mattress. The wide-eyed expression on my face. I think about the person who'll eventually find me—whether she leaves me here or somehow manages to drag my body into the woods. Two years back, I cleaned images off a dark site where a young EMT would post photos of dead bodies, mostly from car accidents and crime scenes. The goriest circumstances. He'd wait until no one was looking, snap a gruesome shot with his cell phone, and post it online for other sick fucks to enjoy.

"You know, once I'm reported missing," I say with the phony confidence of someone who fully believes she'll be reported missing, "they're going to connect the two of us. The police will figure out you were the last person with me. Plus, my rental car? It's got a satellite locator. It'll lead them here."

I leave out the fact that Rose knows I've been talking to Campbell. I'm leaving her out of this—for her safety.

"One step ahead of you." Campbell isn't fazed. She doesn't hesitate. Doesn't blink. "Of course your car is here. You're obsessed with me. And my husband. You're his delusional ex who flew three thousand miles across the country to try to get him back. You showed up at his work. You called and texted his wife. And when none of that worked, you kidnapped us at gunpoint and forced us here. Don't worry. I've got ample evidence to show what a crazy bitch you are and how you refused to leave us alone."

"So when the police arrive and find my rental car . . . and not me . . . what are you going to say then?"

"Oh, they'll find you," she says. "Right here. In this room. I had to defend myself. You were going to kill me. And my daughter."

"Good luck proving self-defense when they find the rope burn on my wrists and ankles . . ."

Campbell squints out the window, quiet and contemplative. In all her scheming, did she not take that simple detail into consideration? The only alternative would be to march me out into the woods where no one would hear a thing, and then bury me in a shallow grave covered by branches and foliage, praying the elements and wildlife get to me before I'm discovered by some hiker or hunter.

But she wouldn't leave her baby in the house alone.

Would she?

She's about to say something when the crunch of tires on gravel commandeers her attention. Rushing to the window, she pushes the curtain aside and peers out. And then, shoving the gun into the back of her jeans, she says, "Don't say a word."

This visitor must be unanticipated, a possible wrench in her plan. But I stay quiet and listen. I know better than to get my hopes up. I've been burned before.

Closing the door with a soft click, Campbell leaves me alone once more.

On the other side of that door lies freedom . . . or death.

All I can do is wait.

CHAPTER 35

Two voices: one male, one female. The hushed, muffled arguing takes me back to my childhood, when my parents would throw on smiling, nonchalant faces and save their battles for the end of the night when doors were closed and children were supposed to be sleeping.

It's impossible to decipher the words, but I'm familiar with the conversational rhythm of discord.

For a moment, I envision a scenario where Rose knew I wouldn't stand her up, went to our father's home, found my suitcase in the closet, and immediately called the police—but this is real life, and things don't fall into place like perfectly placed rows of dominoes. From the time the police are contacted, it could take hours, if not days, to piece everything together. There would be questions and interviews—warrants to be signed off on before they could begin to locate my rental car or trace my cell phone activity to the nearest tower.

If it were a police officer at the door, Campbell wouldn't be arguing with him.

She mentioned a friend who owns the cabin . . .

Shuffled footsteps outside the door tell me I won't have to wonder much longer, and when it swings open a second later, I have my answer.

Campbell stands in front. Behind her, Sutton. Animosity colors her wild eyes, but his expression is unreadable. Indifferent. He isn't here to save the day—at least not *my* day.

Sweat prickles along my hairline, and I force a thick swallow.

Campbell's words play in my ear, silently reminding me of Sutton's hatred.

The man has two choices in this moment—save the woman he hates, or cover for the woman he married so he can keep his family intact. If he chooses family—and he will—he'll have no choice but to go along with his wife's diabolical plan.

Sutton steps out from behind her, looming over the edge of the bed, his hands on the metal footboard. His prismatic gaze runs from my wrists to my ankles as he assesses the situation, and he releases a heavy breath.

"You're not a killer," I tell him. I keep my voice low, as if it's just the two of us here, a subtle reminder of intimacy past, of a connection born a lifetime ago. "You don't have to do this."

"Yes, he does," Campbell says from the doorway. She takes the spot next to her husband, her hand on his arm as she leans in. "It's too late to back out. We have to do this."

I know what she's thinking—if they let me go, how can they be sure I won't run to the police and tell them what happened? They can't let me live. It's a liability. It defeats the purpose of everything that led Campbell to this moment.

Sutton pinches the bridge of his nose. Rubs his eyes. I wish I knew what he thought this morning when he woke up to an empty bed, discovered an empty crib, and came upon his wife's cell phone. I imagine him rushing to the garage to find her car resting in its stall—missing Gigi's car seat in the back.

But how did he know she was here—of all places?

Campbell is a master manipulator. A skilled, cunning liar. If she lied about her abusive marriage, why wouldn't she also lie about drugging him so she could leave?

Perhaps this was part of the plan all along.

"Give me the gun, Campbell." He keeps his voice low. "And take Gigi in the bedroom. Don't come out until I call for you."

She peers at him through squinted eyes, almost as if to challenge his instructions. Maybe she wanted to see him shoot me. Maybe she wants a front-row seat to my demise, the satisfying end to her marital discontent.

"You're going to do this," she says to him, and she isn't asking.

His lips flatten. He nods.

The heaviness of this moment sinks me into the mattress.

I try to make eye contact with him, but he refuses.

"Campbell, *go.*" His voice booms through the small room. The number of times I've witnessed this man yell in my life, I can count on one hand.

"Gigi's fine. She's in the playpen. I want to—"

He lifts a hand . . . not to hurt her, but to silence her. "She's my problem. Not yours."

Her brows knit as she attempts to read his face.

"I want a word with her first. Alone," he says. "A few things I need to say before we do this."

She starts to say something, but he quiets her with a tender kiss, his hand cradling her tensing jaw, fingertips slipping into her messy hair. When they're finished, Sutton whispers into her ear, words not meant for me to hear.

They lock gazes.

She hands him the gun.

Disappears into the hallway.

He's made his choice. He chose his family over doing the right thing. Though I suppose in his mind, choosing family *is* doing the right thing.

Sutton closes the door.

This is it.

CHAPTER 36

"Did she drug you last night, too? Or were you in on this all along?" I ask. I don't suppose it matters. I don't suppose anything really matters when you're standing this close to the end.

He paces, his attention occasionally landing on my ankle or wrist, his grip firm and secure on the gun. His free hand tugs a fistful of hair.

I know him . . . he's unraveling.

"You can't live with this on your conscience," I tell him. I'll spend every last breath I have coaxing him to the reasonable side of this. "This isn't you. You're a good person."

He stops patrolling and turns to me, moored at the foot of the bed. "Let me do the talking."

I'm prepared to say whatever it takes to stay alive, even if it's nothing.

"When you ended things the way you did, completely out of nowhere, not a warning, not a sign it was coming . . . it was devastating for me," he says. "I loved you more than life, Grace. I didn't know how I was going to go on." His jaw sets. "I met a side of me I never knew existed. An ugly side. A dark side. For years, I thought about you. I missed you. I told myself you'd come back eventually. Yet at the same time, I forced myself to move on . . . even if I was going through the motions." He turns toward the window, staring into the distance.

"Every milestone, every achievement, every memory these past eight years has been plagued by . . . you. Thoughts of you. Because even if you weren't there, I found myself wishing you were. Wondering what it'd be like if you were. Fantasizing about how different that moment would feel if it were you standing there and not Campbell."

"I'm sorry," I say.

"She's a good woman," he says. "She loved me and stood by me when she didn't have to. She dealt with my demons, my obsessions, with the patience of a saint. And she's an incredible mother to my child. She's better to me than I deserve. And I almost lost her because of . . . this. Because of you."

He tucks the gun into the back of his pants and reaches for my left ankle. I flinch at his touch.

He's untying me.

"Don't move," he says when he works the other restraint.

I stay still. I don't speak. I hardly breathe. Tension in my jaw pulses with every heartbeat when he works on my right wrist, then my left.

When he's finished, the air stings my skin, but I'm free.

For now.

"For so long I wished I never met you," he says, reaching for the handgun. "And honestly, Grace, there were times I wished you'd died, because it would've been easier losing you to a car accident or cancer than to accept the fact that I wasn't good enough for you, that I couldn't make you happy, and you were never coming back."

He has it all wrong.

"You were good enough for me," I speak, even if it's a dangerous decision. "You were too good for me."

Didn't he listen to a word I said when I left him that day?

I explained it all.

At the end of the day, we can say everything we need to say to someone, but we can't control how they receive it.

"Get up." He points the gun from me to the floor.

With tight muscles and a bladder about to burst, I slide my legs off the bed, feel for the warm wood of the floor, and push myself upright. The room spins for a moment. I tilt. He steadies me, his hand on my arm, but only for a moment. The minuscule wince on his face tells me he doesn't enjoy touching me.

"We're going for a little walk." He motions toward the window, though I know he means the woods. "I know you're good at running, Grace, but now's not the time for that. Don't try to be brave. Just do exactly what I say, and it'll all be over soon."

CHAPTER 37

He leads me out of the guest room, the nose of the handgun pressed against the small of my back. The door to the other bedroom is closed. Campbell sings to Gigi, a familiar nursery rhyme I can't place, one I'm certain Daphne sang to me once upon a time.

The air is fresher in the hallway, breezier in the living room. Curtains dance in front of open windows in the kitchen, sunlight pouring in. Dirty dishes rest in a bubble-filled sink, and I catch a whiff of green apple soap.

Never in my life have I craved the ordinary, the everyday, the mundane . . . as much as I do in this moment.

He told me not to get brave.

He told me not to run. I couldn't if I tried—the intense build of pressure in my bladder makes it nearly impossible to so much as walk.

"Can I use the bathroom?" I ask. "Please. I haven't gone since last night, and it's really hard to walk like this . . ."

It's a silly if not pointless request because I know what happens when you die. I know bodily fluids seep, no longer held by muscles and functions. But every minute I delay this is another minute Sutton has to come to his senses.

He pushes a breath through flared nostrils and doesn't agree—at first.

"Please," I whisper.

His hand loops into my elbow, and he leads me back to the hallway, where he examines the bathroom, removing a men's razor from a drawer—as if I could possibly defend myself with that. He closes me in the windowless room, and I shove my pants down with seconds to spare.

I've barely flushed when he knocks and asks if I'm almost done.

I wash my hands with soap that smells of lavender and honey—another silly, pointless endeavor in the grand scheme of things—and give myself one final look in the clouded, vintage mirror that hangs above the sink.

My skin is sallow, and my hair hangs limp around my face. I tuck it behind my ears. I think about splashing water on my face—one final slice of something normal before I die, but he knocks again.

Harder.

"What are you doing in there?" His voice is so clear and cutting he might as well be in here with me.

I take a deep breath and return to the hall.

"Thank you," I say because I need to humanize us in this moment. "I feel much better."

He nods toward the front door and positions the handgun against my back once more. "Get your shoes on. It's time to go. And don't ask me to stop again."

A minute later, I'm halfway between where the cabin ends and the forest begins, marching to my fate.

CHAPTER 38

It's a good day to die—if there were such a thing.

Sunlight trickles through heavy treetops. Birds sing. The sky is a pristine blue, not too dark, not too light, not a cloud to be found. I can't recall a time when I've felt more alive, so aware, so present . . . than I do in this moment.

Life has a twisted sense of humor that way.

Tall weeds scratch my exposed ankles, but I deem that the least of my problems.

We make our own path through the woods, stepping over mossy rocks and ropelike tree roots, ducking under branches. Me first. Always. His presence is weighted, palpable. I don't have to turn around to know he's there, holding the gun steady on my back.

If I'm lucky, he'll fire off a round without warning.

He'll make it quick.

I can't imagine he wants to draw this out longer than necessary. Despite his stoic expression and the void of compassion in his words, I know he wants this to be over as much as I do.

Then again, I spent eight years clueless as to how much our breakup mentally tortured him. I was living my life, flitting from city to city collecting experiences and tethering myself to nothing and no one . . .

while he was trying to make a life for himself in the cold shadows of what might have been.

I swallow the lump in my throat, realizing I may not know him as well as I thought.

There was an article on the dark web once, a man describing the difference between male and female murderers. Not unlike sex, men prefer to watch the face of the other person in the midst of all the action. Women, statistically, are more likely to sneak up from behind or to poison their victim. The less mess, the less noise, the less fanfare, the better.

I think of the snuff films I've seen—the real ones, not the fake ones bored film-school assholes post, hoping their project looks real enough to get a reaction from some stranger on the other side of the world. I think of the dirt. The blood. The gore.

Does Sutton have the stomach for what he's about to do? We went fishing once, a lifetime ago, and the mere act of baiting the hook sent the color from his face.

The scent of earth fills my lungs.

I try to focus on that.

We approach a small incline, and my legs ache. I'm certain we've been walking forever. Above, a hawk soars over the trees. I picture a stream nearby. A brook with clear water. Something peaceful.

I want my last thoughts on this earth to be beautiful, and if that's not possible, then at least neutral. I refuse to die screaming, crying, terrified.

My lower lip quivers, an indication that my mind and body are on two separate pages. Even if I don't want to die in a mess of tears, I may not have a choice. It's human nature, the urge to constantly control. I cut myself slack. It might be the last time I have a chance to do so.

"Can you just . . . do it?" I ask.

Twigs snap and leaves crunch under the weight of his footsteps.

"Keep walking," he answers. "We're not there yet."

"I really am sorry for hurting you." It's funny how such a powerful word can lose its meaning the more you say it.

I'm sorry.

I'm sorry.

I'm sorry . . .

"That's all I came here to tell you," I say, careful to choose my words. "I looked you up online, and I saw what your life had become . . . that you moved to my hometown, married a woman who looked like me, and named your daughter Grace. I was worried about you."

He says nothing.

Leaves still crunch and twigs still snap, and we're still marching on.

"Anyway, that's all I came here to do. I didn't mean to run into your wife or disrupt your life in any way." I'm about to continue when something catches my eye ahead.

A dirt path trail.

No rocks, twigs, or leaves.

People hike here. Maybe we're close to a state park?

I think of all the souls who have hiked these woods. Couples. Families. Adventurous loners. I think of all their wonderfully ordinary lives, all the things they still get to do . . . all the things I still want to do . . .

I don't want to die.

This can't be the end.

I stop in my tracks and turn to face him, my hand splayed over my thrashing heart, skin hot with adrenaline, shallow breaths filling my chest.

"You deserved better than a life with me," I tell him.

Our gazes hold.

He keeps the gun trained on me—pointed toward my sternum—but he's listening.

"I can't sit still. I can't stay in the same place for more than six months at a time or I go crazy," I say. "Your parents live in the same house they bought when they were first married. That's the kind of life you wanted. I can't keep a houseplant alive. You wanted enough kids to fill a soccer team. The idea of being pregnant makes me physically ill. All you ever wanted was to be a father. I loved you, Sutton. And I never stopped. But my decision wasn't—"

He lifts a palm. I silence my narrative.

"Grace. I know these things." Sutton nods for me to turn around, motions for me to keep going. "We're almost there."

CHAPTER 39

The path is long out of sight. I've yet to see another human. We've walked for an hour, maybe, if I had to guess? Which puts us somewhere around two or three miles out from the cabin. Deep in the woods. A world away from civilization or anyone who could hear a gunshot or two.

The never-ending thicket of trees surrounding us is disorienting, but the way my thigh muscles ache tells me we're on an incline. He wouldn't shoot me on a hilltop, would he? The earth is rockier, harder to dig, the trees less dense.

A faint droning in the distance makes me glance up to the sky in search of an airplane, momentarily spiking my hope, until I'm met with that same clear-blue sky from before.

But the humming continues . . . louder, closer with each arduous trudge forward. We're climbing higher, steeper into the hillside. While each step is harder than the one before, my muscles screaming for rest, I focus on the noise.

Noise means people.

He won't shoot me if we're not alone.

Twenty yards ahead, the tree line thins. I take longer strides, desperate to make it to the other side in search of life. He hasn't noticed my increased pace. Not yet. The hard metal of his gun no longer presses into my back, and from my periphery, I notice there's space between us for the first time.

He could swipe at me and miss, especially if I ran.

He told me not to get brave. But when have I ever listened to anyone?

My heart whooshes in my ears, pounding in my teeth, drubbing in my fingertips. The burn of adrenaline flushes through my veins. I promise myself I'm going to run from him or die trying, and I glance back one last time to make sure I'm still out of arm's reach—only to find him standing still.

Eight, maybe ten feet separate us now.

His hand rests at his side, gun pointed at the ground and not me.

"You're free, Grace." He crouches, slowly, and places the handgun carefully on a bed of flattened leaves and broken sticks. "Go."

I sprint.

I tear away from Sutton, nearly tripping over myself as I dash toward the top of the hill. He doesn't chase me, but I run anyway. Faster, harder, ignoring the exhaustion that gnaws through me with each breathless second.

He let me go.

He let me go . . .

Adrenaline courses through me, reducing me to actions. I can't think. I don't have time to question why he's done this.

I can only run for my life.

When I get to the top of the hill, there's a guardrail, metal and chipped with red paint, and to my left, I spot a highway in the distance— the source of the strange noise from before.

And then I hear a voice.

A car door.

And another.

More voices.

Someone yells my name.

Beyond the guardrail, at the bottom of the incline, is a blacktop parking lot, along with a large wooden sign identifying this as **SADIE MILES STATE PARK**.

A county police car blocks the entrance, lights flashing but no sound.

I count three black SUVs, six officers, and an ambulance.

Today might have been a good day to die.

Fortunately, that's not going to happen.

CHAPTER 40

They don't arrest him.

I sit in the back of Officer Conrad's SUV, the door open and my legs hanging out. After a quick check-over and vitals, a paramedic noted my chattering teeth and full-body trembling and handed me a thermal blanket, though I assured her it was nerves.

Two vehicles over, a couple of the cops talk to Sutton. No one rests their hands on their duty belts or looks remotely like they're about to ready their cuffs. They're just . . . chatting.

"Is there someone we can call for you?" Officer Conrad asks from the passenger seat. He's young, easily the youngest of the group with his scrawny build and peach-fuzz goatee, and I'm assuming he's been tasked with staying with me. If only he knew how accustomed I am to being alone, he'd know this isn't necessary.

I shake my head.

My phone is back at the cabin. The only number I have memorized is Jonah's, and there's nothing he can do from the other side of the country.

I keep my gaze trained on Sutton, on the situation between him and the officers. I don't understand why they aren't apprehending him. The man held a gun to my back and marched me through a forest. At the very least he should be charged with an accessory to kidnapping or attempted second-degree murder.

As if he feels the weight of my stare, he glances my way, but only for a moment. And in that flash of a second, he almost looks sorry. Is he sorry for holding a gun to me for the last hour? Sorry for all the things he said? Sorry for marrying a psychopath? Or is he sorry for all of it?

A voice comes over the radio on Officer Conrad's shoulder, someone saying they've got the suspect in custody as well as a small child.

Campbell.

Gigi.

I don't understand . . .

Did he turn himself in? Did he turn *her* in? And when?

"Can I talk to him?" I ask. "To Sutton?"

Conrad angles himself toward me, lips pressed flat. "I don't think that's a good idea."

"So is that a no?"

He offers an apologetic wince. "Yeah. It's a no."

"I'm just trying to understand what just happened . . ."

Officer Conrad nods. "He saved your life, that's what just happened."

CHAPTER 41

My phone battery blinks to a sufficient 98 percent. I pluck it from the charger I borrowed and give it back to the woman in the pink scrubs behind the nurse's station. This hospital is the size of most clinics back in Portland, but it's buzzing with activity for a Sunday afternoon.

"Thank you," I say.

The police confiscated my rental car as evidence and insisted I get a thorough examination at the municipal hospital in the next town over—protocol. Everything checked out, aside from mild dehydration, and they gave me a tiny white pill to help calm my nerves, though the trembling has yet to subside.

The first chance I got, I called Rose. I told her I was stranded and that I needed a ride. I promised to fill her in later. No sense in getting anyone worked up when I'm perfectly fine, and the worst is over.

She said she was on her way, and that was over an hour ago.

I replay the events from earlier, marching through the forest at gunpoint, the police, Sutton letting me go . . .

. . . the cop claiming Sutton saved my life.

I've yet to get an answer.

I've also yet to rectify how someone could go from doing something so vile to being my personal hero.

I grab a magazine from a nearby pile, opting to conserve my phone's battery while I wait. An article in *Psychiatry Now* catches my eye— "The Psychology of Obsession"—but I make it through two paragraphs before deciding it hits too close to home. I fold the magazine, toss it back on the stack, and watch the circle drive for Rose's car.

An ice-blue minivan creeps up to the curb, stopping to allow a frail older woman in a floral smock dress out of the back. Cane assisted, she makes her way to the automatic doors of the urgent care side. She disappears inside and another car pulls up; this one I recognize.

It's Rose.

Standing, I slip my phone into my bag and check my surroundings, making sure I didn't leave anything behind. I'm halfway to the exit when the passenger door swings open—and Bliss emerges. She scans the glass doors, and when she spots me, she presses a hand against her heart. The other holds a crumpled tissue. A second later, she's all but running toward me.

We meet outside the automatic doors.

My father enters next, wearing an expression I haven't seen on him since my mother's guilty verdict—something that straddles terror and relief.

"I know you don't like hugs," Bliss says, eyes welling. "But I'm going to hug you."

It's strange, this moment. But after the day I've had, I allow it. I don't have the energy not to.

I let someone hug me—and for the first time in a long time, it doesn't kill me.

In fact, I've never felt more alive.

CHAPTER 42

I wake from a Valium-fueled sleep on my father's family room sofa later that night. The house is quiet, though voices carry from the patio. Rose, Bliss, and Dad picked me up from the hospital earlier, and when I got home, Evan and Sebastian were waiting.

It turned out Rose *did* find it odd that I stood her up for brunch, and given what I'd told her about Sutton and his wife, she knew something wasn't right. She called the police immediately, and when they sent an officer to the Whitlock residence, Sutton told them his wife and child had disappeared overnight.

They knew we were together—it just took a while to pinpoint an exact location.

And as for Sutton, he was helping the police the whole time. At least that's my understanding. I hope to speak to him soon—if he'll even speak to me. I want to know why. How. I need to make sense of what happened.

As soon as everyone had a chance to hear the full story and give me a once-over to ensure I was fine, I popped a pill to quiet my mind and curled up on the sofa for a thousand-year nap.

The clock above the mantel reads eleven PM.

I slide the blanket off my lap, sit up, and peer into the dim, lamplit space as I get my bearings. My throat is parched, and my neck is kinked from sleeping in a strange position. I rise up to grab a water and make my way upstairs, only I stop when I find I'm not alone.

At the end of the sofa, sleeping softly with her head in her hand . . . is Bliss.

I study her for a moment. At the hospital, she was the first to jump out of Rose's car and wrap her arms around me. And on the ride home, she insisted she sit in the back, next to me. The instant we made it home, she ran around, fetching herbal teas and extra pillows and lighting a candle she said was supposed to cleanse the bad energy of the day.

Her eyes blink, slowly, as if she senses me watching her, and she sits up, finger-combing her long waves into place.

"You're allowed to leave my side, you know," I say.

She smiles. "Sorry. I don't mean to smother you. I was just worried I'd never see you again."

I hesitate. This isn't the first time someone's taken a peculiar interest in me.

"I appreciate it," I say, "but I have to admit I'm confused . . . you've known me a handful of weeks, but you're taking this worse than everyone else. Why do you care so much?"

"It's a conversation for another day." Her tone is light, but her stare is unfocused, lost in thought. "You've had enough excitement for one day, don't you think?"

I cock my head, examining her, recalling the preliminary research I did on her back when she and my dad first started dating. I do background checks on all his girlfriends, despite the fact that there isn't much need. They can dig his gold all they want, but he's smarter than that. His financial situation is locked tight, and it'll be a subzero day in hell when he marries again. Even if he did marry, he'd require an ironclad prenup.

"I looked you up last year," I tell her, "online."

"Find anything good?" There's a glint in her eyes.

"*You* didn't exist until about twenty years ago," I say.

"Sounds about right."

"So who are you?" I fold my arms. I don't mean to be overly defensive to a woman who's shown me nothing but grace and kindness since the instant we met, but there's no room in my life right now for crazy.

She pats the sofa, an invitation to sit, but I prefer to stand.

"I don't often talk about who I was before," she says. "Because I'm not her. I haven't been her for a long time. And there was nothing special about me. I was your typical rebellious teenager who couldn't stay out of trouble for more than two seconds at a time. I hated my parents. I ran away more times than I could count. Everything was always someone else's fault. I loved making people worry about me—convinced it would prove whether or not they truly loved me. When I was seventeen, I ran off with this guy to prove some kind of point to my parents, I guess. But six months later, they died in a car accident. Gone. Just like that. I didn't get to tell them goodbye. Didn't get to apologize for putting them through hell. Spent the next ten years hating myself. Making my life harder than it needed to be. And one day I just . . . woke up . . . and decided I didn't want to be that girl anymore. The name change was more symbolic than anything else. A blank slate. My old name was Karen Delgado—if you're so inclined to know. But I can assure you, that woman is dead. Figuratively. Obviously. I know you probably look things up about people online, so you have my full permission. But you're not going to find anything. That version of me didn't do anything halfway worth documenting. Now, Bliss, on the other hand . . . she's moved mountains."

Bliss places her hand over her heart, lips spreading into a slow smile as she gazes up at the ceiling and gathers in a long breath.

"People change, Grace. They change all the time. You can move out of the darkest part of yourself and into the light," she says. "Reinventing myself was the best thing I ever did. I'd even go so far as to say it saved my life."

I don't know the first thing about reinventing myself—but she makes it sound lovely. Medicinal almost. Like changing your name is akin to taking a pill to fix what ails you.

Bliss exhales, glancing toward the sliding door, where Dad, Rose, Evan, and Sebastian converse under the glow of party lights.

I'm unsure of what to say. I fix my gaze outside, focusing on my grinning father. She makes him happy. Happier than the last few, for sure.

"Does my dad know who you really are?" I ask.

"He does."

"And he's okay with it?"

She laughs a soft laugh. "He is. He understands. He accepts me for who I am, no matter how crazy I may seem sometimes." Her laughter fades. "You know, he's changed quite a bit, too. At least from what he tells me."

I think of his apology. And the real tears.

"You know, I see so much of myself in you," she adds. "My old self."

Rising from the sofa, she makes her way close and cups my face in her hands, tender and compassionate.

"You've been through quite the ordeal, Grace," she says. "You doing okay?"

Her eyes search the depths of mine, as if she's gazing into my soul. And warmth blankets me with a sensation I can only describe as home, despite the fact that she and I are mere strangers in this world, sharing not an ounce of blood or a single memory other than what has transpired over the past several weeks.

And still, there's almost a connection between us.

Almost.

Maybe one of these days, I'll allow myself to feel it.

"Yeah. Just tired," I say.

Tired of running. Tired of pushing. Tired of keeping those closest to me at an arm's length.

"Lie back down, sweetheart." She helps me get situated, fluffing my pillows and straightening my blanket. And she disappears into the kitchen, returning with a glass of ice water with a sprig of mint and wedge of lemon. "Get some more rest. I'll be here when you wake up."

I close my eyes and still my mind. For as long as I can remember, I've had an emptiness deep inside me. One that no amount of love or compassion could fill. An incompleteness that gnawed at my soul. I spent years hating my past. Convinced that I'd become a whole person, that everything would settle into a better place, once I found my birth mother.

But that aching void is gone. At least in this moment. And for the first time, I have something I've never had—acceptance that the past was perfectly imperfect, knowledge that the future will be, too, and hope that I'll be around to experience every raw, beautiful minute of it.

I fall asleep with Bliss's idea of reinvention floating through my head.

Maybe I will, maybe I won't.

The only thing I know for sure is that I'm keeping my name.

I can't imagine being anyone else but Grace McMullen.

CHAPTER 43

I shouldn't be here, standing at Sutton's door, but I was passing by on my run, his car is in the driveway, and I have questions.

Also, I want to thank him—if he'll let me.

Four days ago, Campbell was arrested and arraigned. The fact that he's yet to bail her out gives me hope that he might not slam the door in my face.

I press the doorbell and face the camera, attempting to keep my expression light, which is difficult given the circumstances, but I manage.

He doesn't keep me waiting. Within seconds, the doorframe fills with his presence. A brown bottle rests in his left hand. He hasn't shaved since the last time I saw him.

"I was hoping you had a minute to chat?" I use "chat" instead of "talk," hoping it'll put him more at ease.

He scans me from head to toe—contemplating his decision, maybe—and then, without saying anything, he motions for me to enter.

"I just laid Gigi down for a nap," he says, monotone.

The place isn't a mess, but it's less neat than before. A nonfiction book on a sofa cushion. An empty sippy cup. Toys thrown near the toy basket but not quite inside it.

"I don't plan to stay long," I tell him, sitting on the couch because this isn't the kind of conversation you have standing up. "I just had a few questions . . . about last week . . . I'm trying to make sense of it, I guess. The timeline. What's true and what isn't. The police said you saved me."

He lowers into an armchair and rests his beer on a coaster. "Yep."

The man across from me is a different version of the one I once knew, and a different version of the one I've come to know. The bags under his eyes suggest little—if any—sleep lately, and I assume he's trying to piece together what remains of the life he knew less than a week ago.

"First of all . . . thank you." It's strange thanking a man who, days ago, held a gun to my back and marched me through miles of forest, implying he was going to kill me. But from what Rose has told me, Sutton was instrumental in figuring out where we were. He was able to make a few phone calls to some friends of theirs and narrow it down to the cabin in north Jersey long before the police were able to serve a warrant to the car rental company to perform a satellite locate. He hightailed it out there before the police arrived, knowing that he could handle her better than any hostage negotiator because he knew more than anyone what she needed to hear. The police weren't too thrilled with his decision, initially.

"She was obsessed with you." He reaches for his beer, stopping to graze his thumb over a peeling corner of label. "To the point that it drove her insane."

"Clearly."

His eyes flash to mine. "No. Long before this. When we first started dating, when she saw a photo of you on my phone, she was fascinated by the fact that the two of you looked alike. And it was pure coincidence. That or I guess I have a type. But she fixated on it. And years later, she found this old box I kept of . . . things . . . from college. And it sent her over the edge."

"She told me you hid it from her, and after you promised to get rid of it, you kept it anyway."

"That's true." His mouth flattens. "But it wasn't like that. I've always been . . . sentimental."

"I know you are."

"I've got boxes of stuff from elementary school, junior high . . ." He lifts his beer, gesturing behind him. "I hold on to everything. Everything that makes me *me*."

"I remember." Still, I can't imagine it'd be easy for a wife to come across something like that.

"She didn't believe me when I said I was over you," he says. "And I guess, why would she? That box of old stuff was pretty damning. Caused quite the rift, especially the second time she found it. She actually made me burn it."

"I know. And she said you wept."

His brows meet. "I can be a sappy son of a bitch sometimes, but believe me when I say I didn't shed a tear. Maybe she saw what she wanted to see—or what she needed to see. She never brought you up again after that."

"She had me believing a lot of things." I pause, anchored by the weight of that revelation. "And that's not easy to do."

"I can imagine. She was good at that—she could make anyone believe anything."

"What was with the bruises I saw on her?" I ask.

He sniffs. "She's got this condition that makes her prone to blood clots . . . takes a prescription blood thinner . . . can't bump into anything without it leaving a mark. We used to joke about how it looked. Guess it was funny to us since I'd never laid a hand on her. Not so funny now."

"She told me she was my half sister," I say. "And I almost believed her. I think that was only because I wanted to . . ."

"Are you serious?" He shakes his head.

"She told me she met you when she was looking for me. That the two of you bonded during your search."

Sutton leans forward in his chair, elbows on his knees, peering over the bridge of his nose. "We met on a blind date. She's the cousin of a guy I used to work with. And Grace, I never searched for you. I knew you too well. Once you were gone, you were gone."

"Wow . . ."

"What else did she claim?" he asks. "Just out of curiosity."

"Aside from you being controlling and physically abusive? Let's see . . ." I take a deep breath. How much time until Gigi wakes? "She told me you two moved here for your work. Is that true?"

"We moved here because she claimed she found her dream job managing a pediatric ER downtown." He speaks from the side of his mouth, takes another swig. "I found a job here only because of her. A month after we got settled, she got pregnant. Wanted to quit her supposed dream job right away so she could stay home."

"Why'd you name your daughter Grace?"

"*Campbell* named her Grace," he corrects me. "She told me she made some promise to her grandmother years ago before she died, said she'd name her firstborn daughter after her. I never met her grandma, but she insisted. I thought it was strange, personally. Especially given her fixation with you earlier in our relationship, but I went with it as long as she agreed to let me call her Gigi. It would've been too weird to call her Grace."

I sit with these facts for a moment, burying my head in my hands, breathing through my fingers. "Why do you think she did those things? Was she trying to punish you? Test you?"

Sutton shakes his head. "I imagine something like that. She had demons, I guess. When we first met, I thought it was nothing more than an insecure streak. Once we got married, had Gigi, I realized how deep those demons lived in her. How much they ran her life. For a while, things were getting better. We were settling here, she seemed happy, I thought there was hope for us. That we could salvage this . . . then you showed up, and it set her off."

"I didn't mean to."

"I know." He takes a sip of beer, then another, then places the empty bottle on the coaster. "You couldn't have known. I just wish you'd have stayed away when I told you you were making things worse."

"You have to understand . . . she had me convinced you were hurting her. I thought when you told me to stay away, you were threatening to make things worse for her."

"Yeah. I can see how you'd think that now." He chuffs. "She almost had me convinced for a while that you were obsessed with her, that you were stalking her. I told her to stay away from you because, to be quite honest, I didn't know why you were back. I was just trying to keep the status quo around here, trying to hold on to what we'd spent years building."

"I came home to apologize for leaving you the way I did."

He tilts his head, expression softening. "Grace . . . we were twenty-two. We were kids. Yeah, it hurt, but life goes on."

The man saying these things clearly hasn't met the man at the cabin, telling me he wished I were dead.

"All that stuff you said . . ."

"I had to say those things. She was listening in the next room. I needed her to think I was going to go through with her plan."

Lying in that bed Sunday afternoon, hearing the crunch of tires on gravel, seeing the shock on Campbell's face as if she wasn't expecting someone, and then listening to the murmur of discord in the next room—it makes sense now.

He found us.

He came to stop her.

They argued about what to do next—and he chose me.

He chose to do the right thing, even if it didn't seem that way at the time.

"When have I ever been one to dwell?" he asks. And he's right. He was always daydreaming only of the future, leaving the past where it was.

"True."

He pushes himself up, shuffles to the kitchen, and grabs a fresh beer from the fridge.

"She hadn't slept in weeks," he says when he sits. "An hour or two here, an hour there. I was out of town that first week, but when I got back, I knew something was different about her. By the time she told me you were in town, that she'd been talking to you, I started to keep an eye on her. That's when I told her to stay away from you. And I told you to stay away from her. And neither of you listened."

Sutton shakes his head and uncaps his beer with his bare hand.

"She asked me to meet her at the park one night," I say. "Implied that you'd hit her. She'd been crying. There was a welt on her cheek."

"Ah," he says. "She had a couple of violent episodes the last few weeks. Sometimes she'd hurt herself. Sometimes I had to restrain her."

I think of the kitchen camera that day, Sutton's hands on her shoulders. He must have been restraining her, not shaking her.

"I just want you to know," I say, "that I'm sorry everything turned out this way."

"Grace, don't be sorry. You didn't cause any of this. Not directly anyway."

"If there's ever anything you need . . ." I don't know what I could possibly have to offer him at this point, but he needs to know he matters to me. The man saved my life.

"Appreciate it." He eyes the hallway, where his daughter sleeps behind a closed door.

I rise from the sofa.

He walks me to the door.

"You going to be okay?" I ask when I step out to the porch.

He leans in the doorway, elbow resting on the jamb, and leaves me with a bittersweet smile. "We'll be fine, Grace. Maybe worry about yourself now for a change?"

I amble home, taking my time, dissecting his words as they echo in my head.

All this time I thought he wasn't okay. He took one look at me and knew it was the other way around. And he's not wrong.

For weeks, I thought I'd broken him.

Turns out I'm the broken one. While I ran away from love, Sutton embraced it. While I preferred to numb my feelings and avoid anything that could remotely disturb my emotional bluntness, he sprinted toward his future, eyes wide shut and arms wide open. He welcomed the good, the bad, the easy, and the hard. The certain and the not so certain.

Sutton had it right this whole time.

And me? I had it all wrong.

At thirty years old, I know now that I haven't been living. I've merely been alive. And that's the difference between him and me.

Ten minutes later, I stride through the front door of my father's home, inhaling the lemon dusting cleaner. The hint of lavender. The scent of leather dress shoes. Breathing in the vintage rugs, the essence of time, of years gone by.

And for the first time in my life, this house feels like home.

EPILOGUE

Three Months Later

"So much for Charleston, eh?" Jonah crowds the last moving box into the passenger side of my U-Haul and carefully closes the door.

When I told him I was moving across the country, he insisted on driving down from Seattle to help. I almost turned him down, until he reminded me that my only other option involved paying strangers to touch my things.

He knows me too well.

"Someday," I say. Charleston was going to be my next stop after Portland. I'd always heard it was slower paced than the West Coast, crammed full of history and charm with a side of those relaxed drawls I'd only ever heard in the movies. After that? Miami. Someplace vibrant and tropical.

But for now, I'm moving home—to Monarch Falls.

In a few months, Rose will have her baby, and she's already asked me to be his godmother. She even asked me to choose his middle name. I told her I have horrible taste in names, but she insists. I hope for the kid's sake she changes her mind before he comes. I'm making a list, just in case.

That said, I'm quietly excited to be an aunt. It's not something I broadcast to strangers at the coffee shop or the woman cutting my hair, but I think about it often, this next chapter for Rose, the next generation of our family. And I've caught myself ambling into baby boutiques a handful of times, always walking out with something small to give after he's born. A onesie with a dancing elephant. A sterling silver rattle. A muslin swaddle covered in sailboats.

In silence, I try to imagine Jonah as a dad, but I can't. He's as awkward and uncomfortable around tiny humans as I am. We both get tongue-tied and never say the right thing. Plus, neither of us is warm or fuzzy. Some people aren't meant to become parents, and that's perfectly okay.

I lean against the driver's side door, arms folded, not quite ready to say goodbye yet.

"Let me know if you ever want your job back," Jonah says.

"Appreciate it, but I hope it doesn't come to that." I chuckle. For ten years I've chased the dark side of the human psyche, spending my days in the underbelly of the internet. But it's time to move on. It's time to focus on other things—like getting to know my parents. And spending time with Rose and Sebastian.

For the first time in my life, I'm willing to accept the family I have and stop wasting precious energy wishing anything could have been different.

I'm also making peace with the fact that I'll likely never find my biological mother. If she were still alive and had she wanted to be found, I imagine it would have happened by now.

Maybe I'll never meet a blood relative, but Bliss likes to remind me that it doesn't make me any less complete. I'm whole just the way I am, she tells me in the inspirational texts she sends me several times a day.

Jonah clears his throat, blanketing me with a weighted stare.

"You still going to send me those god-awful cards?" he asks.

"Only if you want me to."

We exchange a wordless smile, our eyes catching.

"You're going to be okay," he says, as if he knew I needed to hear it. Lifting a balled fist, he offers me a bump instead of a handshake.

I push it aside and hug him instead.

He's tense. I'm tense.

It's unnatural and awkward and wonderful and sad. It's all the things, all at once.

I breathe him in—peppermint and aftershave—and I realize that in all these years of knowing him, I never got close enough to know what he smelled like. It's a strange thought, but I make a silent resolution from this day forward: to allow myself to get close to people. It won't happen overnight, of course, but it's something to think about as I drive east and start this new phase in my life.

I'm shunning my darkness and shedding my armor.

"I should get on the road if I'm going to avoid rush hour," I say, letting him go.

"Right. Yeah." He draws in a long breath and looks at me as if it's the last time he'll ever get the chance. "Good luck with everything."

"Thanks, Jonah."

I climb into the truck, plug in my phone, program my GPS, and cue my playlist. In a couple of days, I'll be back in Monarch Falls. I text Rose to let her know I'm leaving, and she texts me back saying she found me the "cutest little apartment."

The other day I was browsing the housing market online, and I happened to notice Sutton's house was for sale. I imagine he wants nothing to do with that place. The house, the town, the life he created. All that it represents.

I think of Gigi sometimes—my little namesake. And I think about her mother rotting in a prison cell, same as mine. While Campbell isn't serving a life sentence, she's going to miss out on the next twenty-five years of her daughter's life. I only hope for Gigi's sake that she's a better person when she gets out.

Sutton's a single father now, but I doubt he'll stay single for long.

He's a good man.

Some would even say he's perfect.

ACKNOWLEDGMENTS

To my agent, Jill Marsal, whose calm, no-nonsense demeanor and top-notch professionalism are always appreciated. To Jessica Tribble-Wells, an ace at taking a manuscript and seeing the whole picture when I'm in too deep. To the entire team at Thomas & Mercer—thank you for your continued support, cheerleading, and all the behind-the-scenes craziness that goes into putting my stories in the hands of readers all over the world. To Charlotte—your discerning eye for detail and invaluable feedback are second to none. To Ashley, thank you for your brutally honest feedback that always manages to stroke my ego at the same time. Ha! To Max and Kat—thank you for always being there when I get stuck on something (or when I'm in a procrastinating mood). To my husband, Jamel, and our three beautiful kids—thank you for eating frozen pizza when you'd much rather be eating something I found on Pinterest. To my readers, bloggers, and bookstagrammers—thank you so, so much for spreading the word about my books and for your kind and supportive messages and emails. I truly couldn't do this without you. Lastly, to the lovely and talented Jennifer Jaynes, who supported, encouraged, and advised me long before anyone had ever heard my name. I'd give anything for a chance to thank you one last time. This book was written in your memory.

ABOUT THE AUTHOR

Photo © 2017 Jill Austin Photography

Minka Kent is the *Washington Post* and *Wall Street Journal* bestselling author of *When I Was You, The Stillwater Girls, The Thinnest Air, The Perfect Roommate,* and *The Memory Watcher.* She is a graduate of Iowa State University and resides in Iowa with her husband and three children. For more information, visit www.minkakent.com.

I DIDN'T EVEN SEE HIM DRAW HIS SWORD.

WH-WHEN DID HE ATTACK...?

I SEE. SO HE ISN'T ORIGINALLY FROM HERE.

HOW LONG HAS THAT PRIEST WORKED HERE?

UM...HE CAME TO THIS TOWN TWO DAYS AGO AS A MISSIONARY FROM KRAIN CASTLE...

D-DAMN YOU! DON'T GET COCKY JUST BECAUSE YOU BEAT ME!

HEY, SEIYA. HOW DID YOU KNOW THE PRIEST WAS AN UNDEAD?

SIMPLE LOGIC.

IN OTHER WORDS, HE WAS GOING TO BE UNDEAD SOONER OR LATER.

THAT PRIEST WAS THE OLDEST, FEEBLEST ONE HERE.

WHAT KIND OF REASONING IS THAT!?

"HE WAS GOING TO BE UNDEAD SOONER OR LATER"!?

WHEN THEY ARRIVE TOMORROW MORNING, THIS TOWN WILL BE REDUCED TO ASH!

FOR HE HAS OVER TEN THOUSAND UNDEAD SOLDIERS!!

"TEN THOU-SAND"!?

GENERAL DEATHMAGLA HAS ALREADY CONQUERED KRAIN CASTLE AND IS ADVANCING ON THIS TOWN WITH HIS UNDEAD ARMY AS WE SPEAK!

HEAR ME AND DESPAIR!

WELL, I'VE GOTTEN ALL THE INTEL I WANTED FROM HIM.

UH-HUH.

ENJOY THE REST OF YOUR SHORT LIVES!

WHAT!? WHY DO WE HAVE TO RUN!?

BATA

BATA (FLAIL)

-BATA

?

EVERYONE, RUUUUUN!!

HA (GASP)

GUESS IT'S TIME TO CLEAN UP.

Y-YEAH, HE'S SICK...

JUST HOW CAUTIOUS AND SUSPICIOUS IS THIS HERO?

YOU COULD HAVE BEEN SWITCHED OUT WITH AN UNDEAD WHEN I WASN'T LOOKING.

WHY DID YOU POUR HOLY WATER ON ME TOO!?

YEAH. WHY ARE YOU STARING AT US LIKE THAT?

WHAT'RE YOU LOOKIN' AT?

JI (STARE)

DO YOU SERIOUSLY THINK THERE WAS ENOUGH TIME FOR THAT!?

GAAA (ROAR)

I SHOULD CHECK TOO!

SEIYA MUST BE USING SCAN ON THEM TO CHECK THEIR STATS.

OH!

HEY!? THESE PEOPLE ARE STARTING TO CREEP ME OUT!

JIIIII (STAAAARE)

THEY'RE A LOT MORE... AVERAGE THAN I EXPECTED.

I FIGURED THEIR STATS WOULD BE A LITTLE BETTER, SINCE THEY'RE OF DRAGONKIN BLOOD...

ELULU
[LV] 7
[HP] 355
[MP] 195
[ATK] 98
[DEF] 160
[SPD] 76
[MAG] 189
[GRW] 36
[RESISTANCE]
Fire, Water, Lightning
[SPECIAL ABILITY]
Fire Magic (LV: 4)
[SKILL]
Fire Arrow
[PERSONALITY]
Optimist

MASH
[LV] 8
[HP] 476
[MP] 0
[ATK] 206
[DEF] 184
[SPD] 101
[MAG] 0
[GRW] 28
[RESISTANCE]
Poison
[SPECIAL ABILITY]
ATK Boost (LV: 3)
[SKILL]
Dragon Thrust
[PERSONALITY]
Brave

THEIR STATS AREN'T EVEN ONE-TENTH OF SEIYA'S... BUT MAYBE THEY'LL GET STRONGER WITH TIME?

CHIRA
(GLANCE)

HYUOOO
(HWOOOO)

GYO
(STARTLE)
!?

WHAT DID YOU JUST SAY?

HUH...?

DON'T NEED THEM.

I'M SURE YOU HAVE!

SO PLEASE DON'T CRY, ELULU!

I'VE BEEN TRAINING SO HARD SINCE THE DAY I WAS BORN, BUT HEEE...!!

WA...

BIEEEEEE (SOOOOOOB)

I CAN'T TAKE THIS ANY-MOO-OOO-ORE!!

PYAAA (GUSH)

WAAAAA-AAAAA-AAAH!! "I DON'T NEED YOU"!? "KEYS" !?

COULD YOU SHUT UP FOR A SECOND !?

WHAT IS THIS, A DAY CARE? RIDICU-LOUS.

I HAVE TO DO SOMETHING! IT'S MY DUTY AS A GODDESS TO FIX THIS!

AHHHHHH! CAN THINGS GET ANY WORSE!?

H-HUH!? WHAT THE...!?

EVERYONE, LOOK!

I NEED TO CHANGE THE SUBJECT...

KYORO (GLANCE)

KYORO

I WONDER WHAT IT COULD BE!

ZA

ZA (STOMP)

SOMETHING'S COMING THIS WAY!

ZA

ZA

WE RECEIVED WORD THERE WAS SOME NOISE COMING FROM THE CHUR...

THE CHURCH HAS BEEN BURNED TO THE GROUND!

WHAT HAPPENED HERE!?

THE NUN'S UNCONSCIOUS!

LOOK OVER THERE!

BA

BA (BAM)

ZA

ZA

THE HERO IS OVERPOWERED BUT
OVERLY CAUTIOUS

YOU SEE...

UM...

WELL...

EXPLAIN YOURSELVES!

NOBLE KNIGHTS.

!

...WHAT HAPPENED HERE.

ALLOW ME TO EXPLAIN...

パチ PACHI

パチ PACHI (CRACKLE)

CHAPTER 7
BREAKDOWN

HERE'S WHAT ACTUALLY MATTERS— WHAT CAN YOU DO ABOUT ALL THIS?

YOU DIDN'T EVEN GET ONE PART RIGHT!

GREAT.

MASH THE HERO FROM NAKASHI VILLAGE!!

ORGANIC MUSHROOM FROM NAMASTE VILLAGE.

MAAAAASH!!

WH-WHAT DO YOU MEAN?

HUH?

I...!

...CAN YOU DO ANYTHING ABOUT THE TEN THOUSAND UNDEAD SOLDIERS HEADING THIS WAY?

LOOK...

GOT IT? THEN GO BACK TO NAMASTE VILLAGE.

BUT I CAN.

THERE IS NOTHING YOU CAN DO TO CHANGE THE SITUATION.

LISTEN.

M-MASH, WHAT SHOULD WE DO?

YOU CAN AT LEAST HANDLE THAT MUCH, RIGHT?

AND IF YOU DON'T WANT TO, STAY HERE AND PROTECT THE TOWN WITH THE KNIGHTS.

FORGET HIM! WE'RE GONNA TAKE MATTERS INTO OUR OWN HANDS!

LIKE HELL I'M GONNA FOLLOW ORDERS FROM YOU!

ZA (STOMP)

BYUN
(WHOOSH)

DON'T YOU DARE UNDERESTIMATE A GODDESS!!

......

HEY, MASH...? WHAT ARE WE GOING TO DO NOW?

GU
(STRAIN)

GRRR! LIKE HELL I'M GONNA LOSE TO SOMEONE WHO DOESN'T EVEN HAVE WINGS!!

WH-WHAT THE...!?

HIGU (SNIFF)

IT LOOKS LIKE I CAN'T BEAT HIM EVEN USING MY DIVINE POWERS...

I EVEN GOT PERMISSION TO USE THE SPIRIT WORLD'S EMERGENCY MEASURE...

HIGU

HYU (HUFF)

HYU

I LOST.

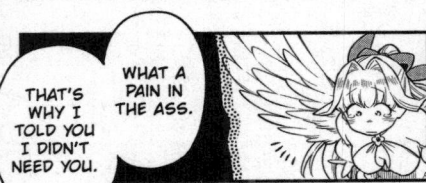

THAT'S WHY I TOLD YOU I DIDN'T NEED YOU.

WHAT A PAIN IN THE ASS.

LET'S GO.

COME ON.

WHILE HE WAS PROBABLY DOING IT ON A WHIM...

...THE KINDNESS HE SHOWED BY WAITING FOR ME AND THE WARMTH OF HIS HAND WRAPPED AROUND MY WRIST...

BUT...

AND I WAS GETTING TIRED OF HOW OB-SESSIVELY CAUTIOUS HE IS.

I WAS PISSED THAT HE LEFT ME BEHIND.

SEIYA...

IT...

SEIYA...

HE'S EVEN HANDSOMER UP CLOSE!

...IT KINDA TURNS ME ON!!

HAAAH!

HAAAH!

AND HE'S HOLDING MY HAND! IT'S ALMOST LIKE WE'RE ON A DATE!

RISTA.

!!

HE USUALLY JUST SAYS "HEY YOU" OR SOMETHING TO GET MY ATTENTION!

WHAAAT!? SEIYA JUST CALLED ME BY MY NAME!?

HYUOOOOOO
(HOWL)

I GET WHAT YOU'RE SAYING, BUT... THERE AREN'T ANY FIGHTER PLANES OR BOMBS IN THIS WORLD.

...SINCE IT WOULD ONLY TAKE ONE BIG EXPLOSION TO WIPE THEM ALL OUT.

I WOULD HAVE DIVIDED THEM UP TO AVOID RISK...

SO THEY'RE MARCHING TOGETHER TO LOOK INTIMIDATING.

IT'S AN IMPRESSIVE SIGHT, BUT FOOLISH.

GROAN...

GOOOOOO
(BOOOOOOM)

ZU
(CRASH)

GUESS I SHOULD DROP ONE MORE FOR GOOD MEASURE.

......!!

IT CAN ONLY BE USED IN VAST OPEN SPACES WITH NO PEOPLE, AND YOU NEED TIME TO CONCENTRATE.

WHILE POWERFUL, IT'S A SPELL WITH MANY RESTRICTIONS.

W-WOW...!

IT'S NOT VERY PRACTICAL.

I FEEL BAD FOR MASH AND ELULU, BUT SEIYA REALLY IS ON A WHOLE OTHER LEVEL...

IT CAME TO ME WHEN I WAS PRACTICING MY MELEE STRIKES BY STRADDLING CERCEUS AND PUMMELING HIM IN THE FACE.

WHERE DID YOU LEARN SUCH A POWERFUL SPELL?

I CAN PROBABLY SAVE GAEABRANDE WITH THIS HERO ALONE...!

ANY-WAY...

UH...HE'S THE DIVINE BLADE— SHOULDN'T YOU HAVE BEEN PRACTICING SWORDS-MANSHIP ...?

OKAY! LET'S GO BACK TO SEIMUL AND REST AT THE INN!

I USED TOO MUCH MP. I NEED TO REST A LITTLE.

ARE YOU OKAY!?

!

FURA (STAGGER)

I DON'T BLAME HIM, THOUGH. I MEAN, HE JUST USED THAT EXTREMELY POWERFUL SPELL TWICE IN A ROW!

SEIYA LOOKS LIKE HE'S IN PAIN...

THIS IS BAD....!!

YEAH, I THINK YOU'LL BE FINE!

I HAD 15,000 MP...BUT NOW I'M DOWN TO ONLY 13,500...

IT'S BEEN THREE DAYS SINCE WE RETURNED TO TOWN.

SEIYA LOCKED HIMSELF IN HIS ROOM AND HASN'T COME OUT SINCE.

SEIMUL'S INN

ELULU?

...?

UH...?

KONKON
(KNOCK)

ガチャ
GACHA
(KERCHK)

UGH! ARE YOU FINALLY READY?

... YOU'RE RIGHT!

ナデ (NADE PAT) ナデ ナデ NADE

SO IT'S PRETTY UNLIKELY HE'S IN ANY TROUBLE!

I'M SURE HE'S FINE! BESIDES, THE UNDEAD ARMY IS LONG GONE!

YEAH, I GUESS YOU COULD SAY THAT...

HE REALLY IS AMAZING, ISN'T HE!?

IT'S ALL ANYONE'S TALKING ABOUT.

I HEARD ABOUT WHAT THE HERO DID.

...WITH SYNTHE-SIZING THINGS.

ESSED ...

EVER SINCE WE GOT BACK, HE HAS BEEN OBSEE

GET THIS...

WHERE IS HE NOW? THE ROOM NEXT DOOR?

R-REALLY!?

NOW PAY UP.

I WON'T BE NEEDING THEM. THE UNDEAD ARMY HAS BEEN DESTROYED.

THE REST OF THE ROSEGUARD IMPERIAL KNIGHTS WILL BE HERE SOON!

SIR HERO!

...AND I HAVEN'T SEEN HIM SINCE.

I SHOULD AT LEAST TELL HIM WE'RE GOING OUT, THOUGH.

I'LL BE TESTING OUT THE ABILITY "SYNTHESIS" FOR THE TIME BEING.

I SHOULD BE ABLE TO BUY A LOT OF EQUIPMENT WITH THIS.

DOSA (CLINK)

LET'S GO LOOK FOR MASH TOGETHER!

I'M COMING WITH YOU!

HUH...? "WE'RE GOING OUT"?

I'M SURE I'D NEVER HEAR THE END OF IT IF I DIDN'T LET HIM KNOW.

GACHA (KERCHK)

SEIYA, YOU'RE IN THERE, RIGHT?

I'M COMING IN.

RISTA, LOOK AT THIS SWORD.

WHOA!?

WHAT THE HELL HAPPENED HERE!?

GOCHAA (CLUTTER)

I NEEDED TO CHANGE MY PERSPECTIVE.

W-WOW! WHAT IN THE WORLD DID YOU COMBINE TO MAKE THIS!?

DON'T TELL ME...IS THIS A PLATINUM SWORD!?

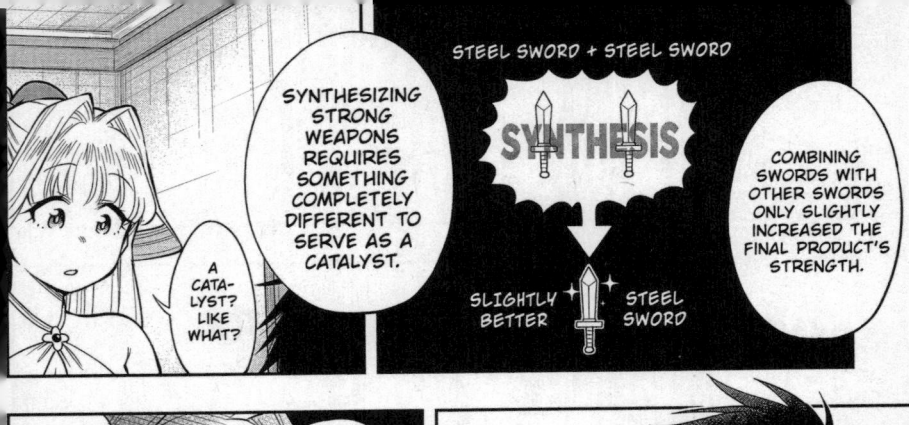

SYNTHESIZING STRONG WEAPONS REQUIRES SOMETHING COMPLETELY DIFFERENT TO SERVE AS A CATALYST.

A CATALYST? LIKE WHAT?

STEEL SWORD + STEEL SWORD

SYNTHESIS

SLIGHTLY BETTER STEEL SWORD

COMBINING SWORDS WITH OTHER SWORDS ONLY SLIGHTLY INCREASED THE FINAL PRODUCT'S STRENGTH.

YOU USED MY HAIR...? YOU WENT INTO MY ROOM...?

I THEN SYNTHESIZED IT WITH A STEEL SWORD TO MAKE THAT PLATINUM SWORD.

THE HAIR OF A GODDESS.

I—I KNOW, RIGHT?

WOW!

EVEN YOUR HAIR IS MAGICAL!? YOU'RE SO COOL!

I FOUND SOME IN YOUR ROOM WHEN YOU WERE OUT.

I'D BE BALD IF YOU TOOK THAT MUCH!

SO I'M GOING TO NEED AROUND A THOUSAND STRANDS OF YOUR HAIR, ROOT AND ALL.

AT ANY RATE, I WOULD LIKE TO MAKE SOME SPARES.

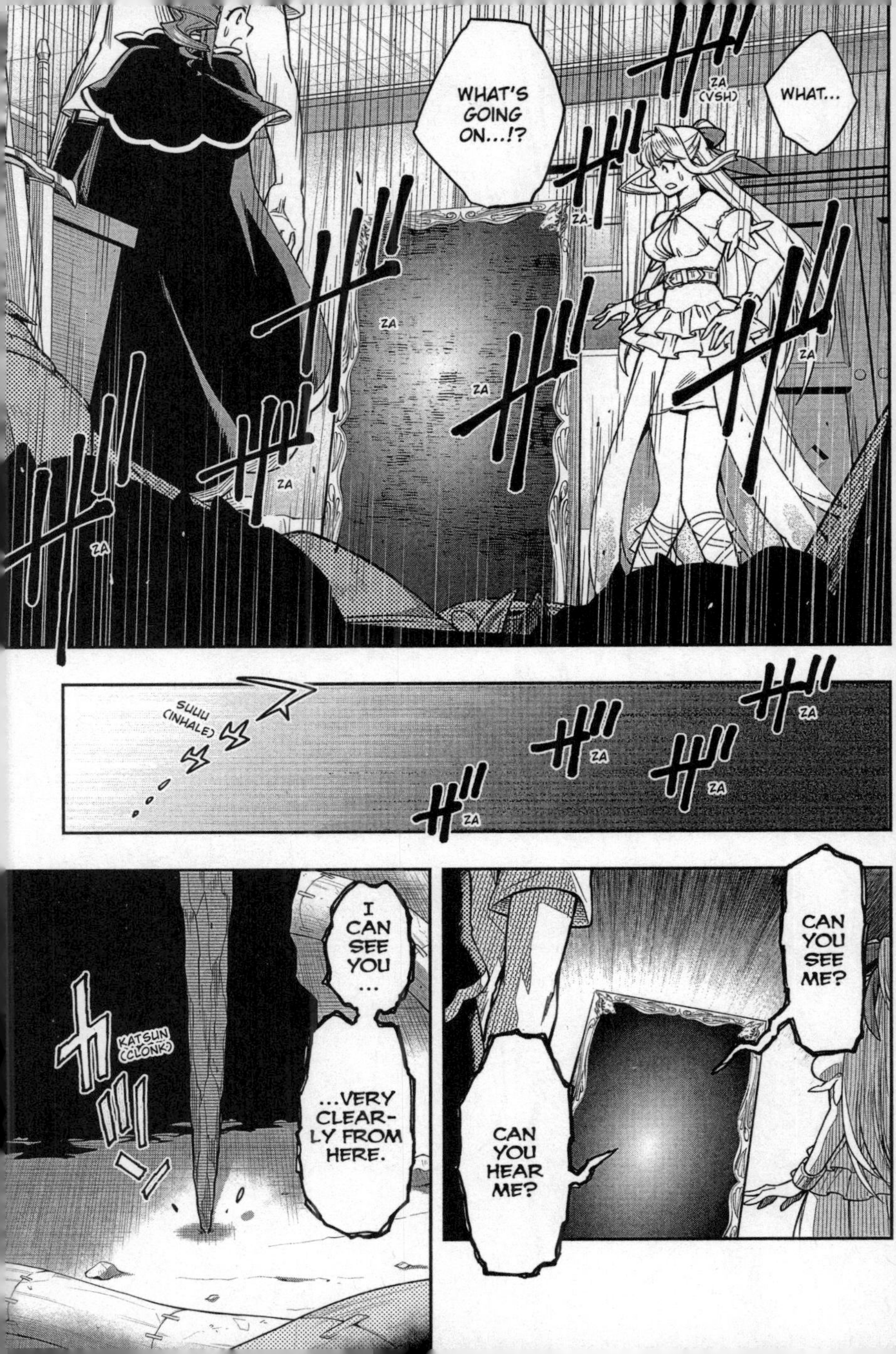

WHAT'S GOING ON...!?

WHAT...

ZA (VSH)

ZA

ZA

ZA

ZA

SUUU (INHALE)

ZA

ZA

ZA

ZA

KATSUN (CLONK)

I CAN SEE YOU...

...VERY CLEAR-LY FROM HERE.

CAN YOU HEAR ME?

CAN YOU SEE ME?

THE HERO IS OVERPOWERED BUT
OVERLY CAUTIOUS

YOU'RE A PIECE OF SHIT, BUT YOU'RE A TRUE HERO!

I CAN'T EVEN COMPARE!

SO PLEASE...

PLEASE...

SAVE THE WORLD IN MY PLACE...!

CHAPTER 9
A BLADE'S REACH

OH YES. REMEMBER THIS, WON'T YOU?

...YOU STILL FAILED TO SAVE A SINGLE HUMAN DEAR TO YOU.

EVEN THOUGH YOU WERE ABLE TO DESTROY AN ARMY OF TEN THOUSAND...

I HEAR YOU ARE QUITE THE CAUTIOUS ONE...

BA (STARTLE)

DON'T TELL ME YOU'VE ALREADY DISCOVERED WHERE I AM AND SENT SOMEONE TO STOP ME!?

OH MY. LOOK AT YOU, HERO.

...

YOU'RE STILL CALM EVEN THOUGH I'M ABOUT TO SLIT HIS THROAT.

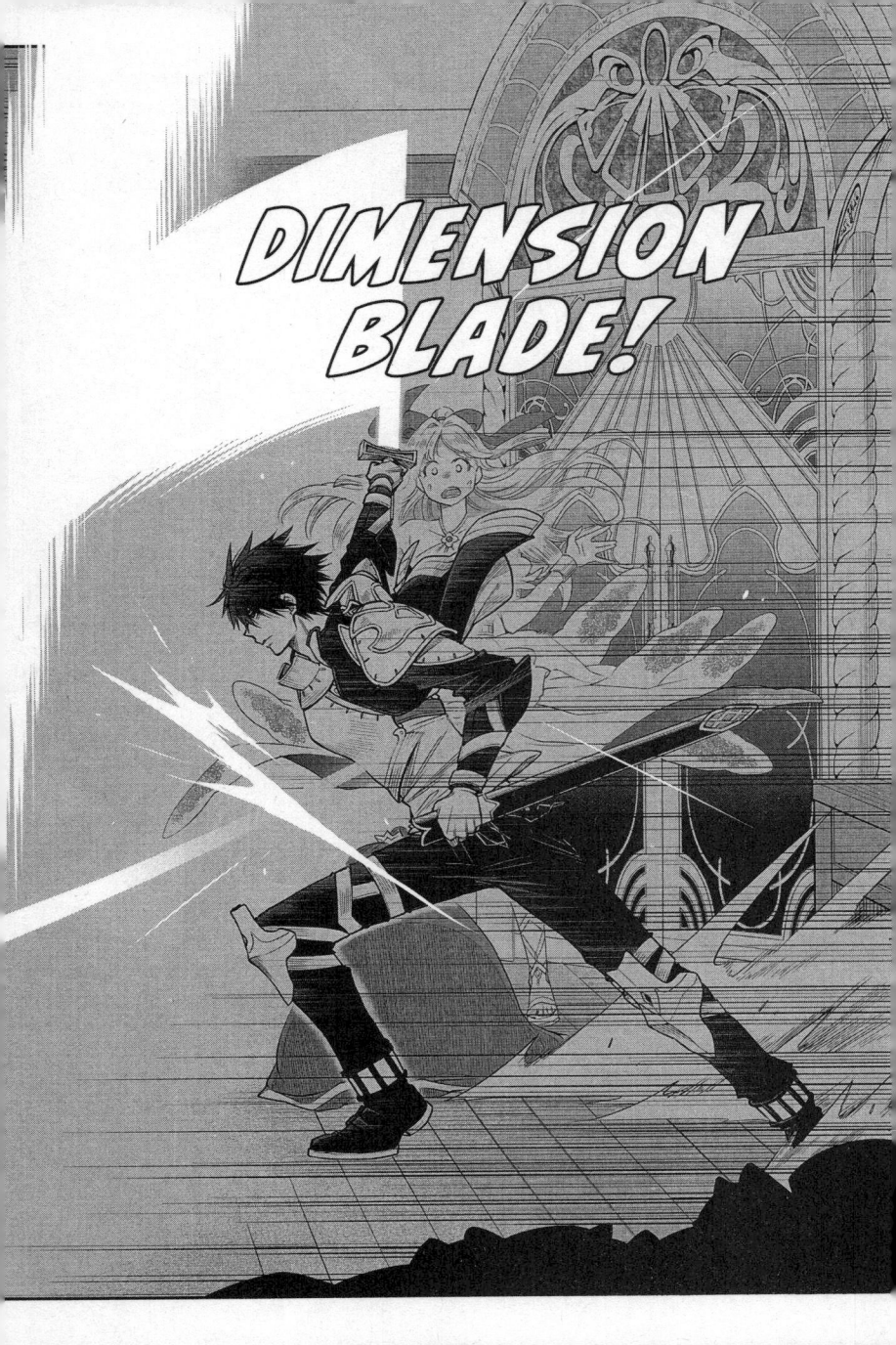

DO
(SLASH)

STOP DAY-DREAM-ING.

WHAT THE HELL!?

GOCHIN (BONK)

THIS HERO'S POWERS ARE ALREADY GODLI—

OOF!?

THE REAL FIGHT STARTS NOW.

THAT'S WHY WE CAME TO THE SPIRIT WORLD, WHERE TIME FLOWS AT ONE-HUNDREDTH THE SPEED OF WHAT IT DOES ON GAEABRANDE.

G-GOOD POINT! WHAT ARE WE GONNA DO!?

ONCE HE CALMS DOWN, HE'S GOING TO TAKE HIS ANGER OUT ON MASH AND KILL HIM.

ALL "DIMENSION BLADE" DID WAS CUT OFF ONE OF DEATHMAGLA'S ARMS.

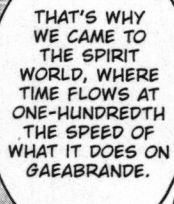

...STARTING NOW, WE HAVE FIFTEEN MINUTES TO FIND A WAY TO GET TO WHERE THEY ARE AND SAVE MASH.

IN OTHER WORDS...

AT THE VERY LEAST, IT'S GOING TO TAKE HIM AROUND TEN SECONDS BEFORE HE SNAPS OUT OF HIS CONFUSION AND TRIES TO KILL MASH.

YOU TALK TOO MUCH.

I'LL MAKE THIS BRIEF.

GUI (SHOVE)

I HAVE COME HERE TODAY TO MAKE A REQUEST TO—

WE NEED TO FIND MUSHROOM IMMEDIATELY.

LISTEN, GRANDMA.

SEIYAAA! DID I NOT JUST TELL YOU TO KEEP QUIET!?

SO OPEN A GATE THAT TAKES US TO HIM.

PLUS, HIS NAME ISN'T MUSHROOM! IT'S MASH!

YOU MAKE IT SOUND LIKE WE'RE MUSHROOM HUNTING!

IN SHORT, YOU WISH FOR ME TO FIND YOUR FRIEND.

CORRECT?

HOH HOH HOH.

AND YOU WERE SAYING HIS NAME RIGHT UP UNTIL A FEW SECONDS AGO, FOR CRYING OUT LOUD!

HMM...

I SUPPOSE NOT, NOW THAT YOU PUT IT THAT WAY.

SURELY THERE'S NOTHING WRONG WITH THAT?

ALL YOU NEED TO DO IS OPEN A GATE TO A SPECIFIC POINT IN GAEABRANDE LIKE THIS WOMAN ALWAYS DOES.

YET THE EXCESSIVE AID OF HUMANS IS PROHIBITED BY SPIRIT WORLD LAW...

I FOUND HIM.

HE IS IN AN UNDER-GROUND VAULT IN THE FOREST NEAR KRAIN CASTLE.

WANT THE GATE TO TAKE US TO AN AREA SLIGHTLY AWAY FROM THE VAULT LIKE LAST TIME?

SO WHAT DO YOU WANT TO DO, SEIYA?

W-WOW, YOU'RE AMAZ-ING!!

IT APPEARS HE IS BEING HELD CAPTIVE.

WE'RE GOING TO MAKE IT WITH TIME TO SPARE, EVEN!

TEN MINUTES HAVEN'T EVEN GONE BY SINCE WE CAME TO THE UNIFIED SPIRIT WORLD.

RIGHT IN FRONT OF HIM, YES?

VERY WELL.

ZUZU (THRUST)

NO. THINGS ARE DIFFERENT THIS TIME.

RIGHT IN FRONT OF THE ROTTING MUSHROOM WILL DO.

YOU'VE GROWN.

......

BUT I BELIEVE THIS IS THE FIRST TIME WE'VE MET...

YOU MAKE IT SOUND LIKE YOU'VE KNOWN ME FOR SOME TIME.

GWAAAAAAH!?

BUO (FWOOSH)

HELLFIRE!

MASH!!

ALL RIGHT! THERE AREN'T ANY ENEMIES IN SIGHT!

AND HE'S MISSING PLENTY OF TEETH...

HIS BODY'S COVERED WITH BURNS... HE'S HAD HIS FINGERNAILS RIPPED OUT...

...!

ARE YOU OKAY!?

MN

Y-YEAH...

THEN ...!

THE ATTACKS ARE GOING RIGHT THROUGH HIM! IS THAT A GHOST-TYPE MONSTER!?

BOBO

SEIYA! TRY RUBBING HOLY WATER ON YOUR SWORD AND ATTACKING!

BO

ZA (THUD)

IT ALREADY HAS HOLY WATER ON IT.

BUT IT'S NOT WORKING.

I CALL IT DARK FIRUS.

HYA-HYA-HYA! THIS ISN'T A GHOST.

ZUZU
(MENACE)

IT IS MY PARTNER, BORN FROM COUNTLESS EXPERIMENTS USING HUNDREDS OF MONSTERS.

AND IT IS THE STRONGEST OF ALL FIRE-TYPE MONSTERS!

DARK FIRUS

[LV] 74
[HP] 80,187
[MP] 9,215
[ATK] 31,559
[DEF] 135,875
[SPD] 10,741
[MAG] 8,377
[RESISTANCE]
Fire, Wind, Water, Lightning, Earth, Holy, Dark, Poison, Paralysis, Sleep, Curse, Instant Death, Status Ailments

[SPECIAL ABILITIES]
Null Physical (LV: Max)
Null Fire Magic (LV: Max)
Null Wind Magic (LV: Max)
Null Water Magic (LV: Max)
Null Lightning Magic (LV: Max)
Null Earth Magic (LV: Max)
Null Holy Magic (LV: Max)
Null Dark Magic (LV: Max)
[SKILL]
Deadly Flames
[PERSONALITY]
Only obeys Deathmagla

THE HERO IS OVERPOWERED BUT
OVERLY CAUTIOUS

CHAPTER 10
EVEN MORE TERRIFYING

DO YOU WANT TO CHECK ITS STATUS? GO AHEAD.

ALL WE HAVE TO DO IS CHANGE TACTICS NOW THAT WE KNOW IT'S NOT AN UNDEAD MONSTER!

I GUESS THAT MEANS YOU PEEKED AT SEIYA'S STATS, DIDN'T YOU?

UNLIKE CERTAIN COWARDS, DARK FIRUS DOESN'T USE FAKE OUT TO HIDE ITS ATTRIBUTES.

WELL, HIS FAKE OUT'S LEVEL IS FAR TOO HIGH FOR ME TO SEE HIS REAL ATTRIBUTES.

BUT THAT WON'T BE A PROBLEM.

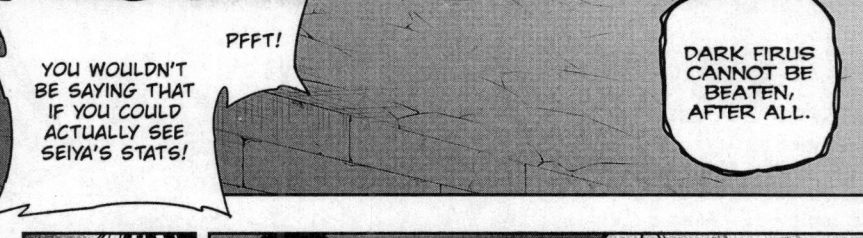

PFFT!

YOU WOULDN'T BE SAYING THAT IF YOU COULD ACTUALLY SEE SEIYA'S STATS!

DARK FIRUS CANNOT BE BEATEN, AFTER ALL.

...

BUT HIS STATS SHOULD BE FAR HIGHER THAN THEY WERE WHEN HE FOUGHT CHAOS MACHINA.

PLUS, I DON'T WANT TO RISK GOING BLIND AGAIN.

I CAN'T AFFORD TO WASTE MY DIVINE POWERS, SO I HAVEN'T SEEN HIS STATS LATELY.

THIS CAN'T BE...

DOKUN (BADUMP)

IT'S NO USE...

KIII! (SCREECH)

GATA

GATA (TREMBLE)

HE CAN'T...

HE JUST CAN'T...

...BEAT THAT THING...!

ITS...

WIND BLADE WON'T WORK FOR OBVIOUS REASONS...

SEIYA'S FOCUS IS FIRE MAGIC.

ZU (FWSH)

DO (BURST)

AND ATOMIC SPLIT SLASH HAS EARTH PROPERTIES...

ZU

ZU

THE ONLY THING THAT CAN DAMAGE THAT MONSTER IS...

YES...

TO MAKE MATTERS WORSE, SWORD-BASED ATTACKS WON'T WORK EITHER.

ICE MAGIC.

BUT I'M A NICE GUY. I'LL TELL YOU HOW TO DO IT.

YOU CAN'T JUST START CASTING ICE SPELLS AND EXPECT THEM TO WORK.

BUT THERE'S AN ORDER TO IT.

...THAT MONSTER STILL HAS AN IMPENETRABLE DEFENSE...

EVEN IF YOU SOMEHOW MIRACULOUSLY HAD BOTH SKILLS...

THE CHANCE OF YOU DEFEATING DARK FIRUS...

...IS ZERO!!

EXACTLY!! I TOLD YOU BECAUSE IT WAS IMPOSSIBLE!

I JUST WANTED TO SEE THE LOOK OF DESPAIR ON YOUR FACE!

...WAS A FIRE-TYPE MONSTER WHICH HAS NO COMMON WEAKNESS WITH THE UNDEAD!

YOU CAME PREPARED TO FIGHT UNDEAD MONSTERS, BUT WHAT AWAITED YOU...

HERO! I WAS STARTLED WHEN YOU TELEPORTED HERE STRAIGHT AFTER CUTTING OFF MY RIGHT HAND!

I IMAGINED EVERY POSSIBLE SCENARIO AND PREPARED FOR THEM ALL!

BUT I, DEATHMAGLA, HAD ALREADY PREPARED FOR THE WORST!

THIS IS HOW A TRUE MASTER OF INGENUITY PREPARES FOR BATTLE.

THIS ISN'T SUPPOSED TO BE THE FINAL BOSS!

WH-WHAT IS GOING ON HERE!?

BUT THERE'S NO WAY TO BEAT THIS GUY ...!!

MAYBE HE CAN PULL OFF YET ANOTHER MIRACULOUS TURNAROUND ...?

BUT...

MAYBE THIS OVER-CAUTIOUS HERO...!!

I CAN'T BELIEVE WHAT I'M HEARING...

I'M SUR-PRISED.

THIS WAS A REAL SURPRISE.

...WHAT THE HELL?

IS LOSING REALLY OUR ONLY OPTION!?

GYU (HUG)

"THIS IS HOW A TRUE MASTER OF INGENUITY PREPARES FOR BATTLE"?

I REALLY CAN'T BELIEVE IT.

YOU "IMAGINED EVERY POSSIBLE SCENARIO AND PREPARED FOR THEM ALL"?

NO... THERE IS ONE THING.

JUST ONE THING THAT COULD HEAL MASH'S HEART...!!

I'M PERFECTLY PREPARED.

KIN (CLINK)

I AM WORRIED.

COMMON SENSE TELLS ME THERE'S NO WAY TO BEAT THIS THING.

DO
(BAM)

IS THAT ...!?

THE BLACK FLAMES ARE TURNING RED...!

BIRI

BIRI
(BZZ)

ZU
(FWSH)

ビリ
ズ
ズ
ズ
ビリ
ズ

OSCILLATORY WAVE!!

IT COULD *SUDDENLY* BE EATEN BY INSECTS AS WELL.

BI *BI* *BI* (BZZ) *BI* *BI* *BI* *BI*

THERE ARE *COUNTLESS POSSIBILITIES.*

MY SWORD COULD *SUDDENLY MELT* OR *RUST.*

INSECTS AREN'T GOING TO EAT YOUR SWORD!!

BOKKO (PUNCH)

BOKKO

BECAUSE I REMEMBERED SEIYA MOUNTING CERCEUS AND USING HIM AS A PUNCHING BAG!

DEATH-MAGLA IS STARTLED.

BUT I HAD A FEELING SEIYA MIGHT HAVE KNOWN OSCILLATORY WAVE.

SO HE REALLY WASN'T BULLYING CERCEUS! HE WAS PRACTICING UNARMED COMBAT!

I FEEL SO RELIEVED...

...ABOUT SO MANY THINGS NOW!

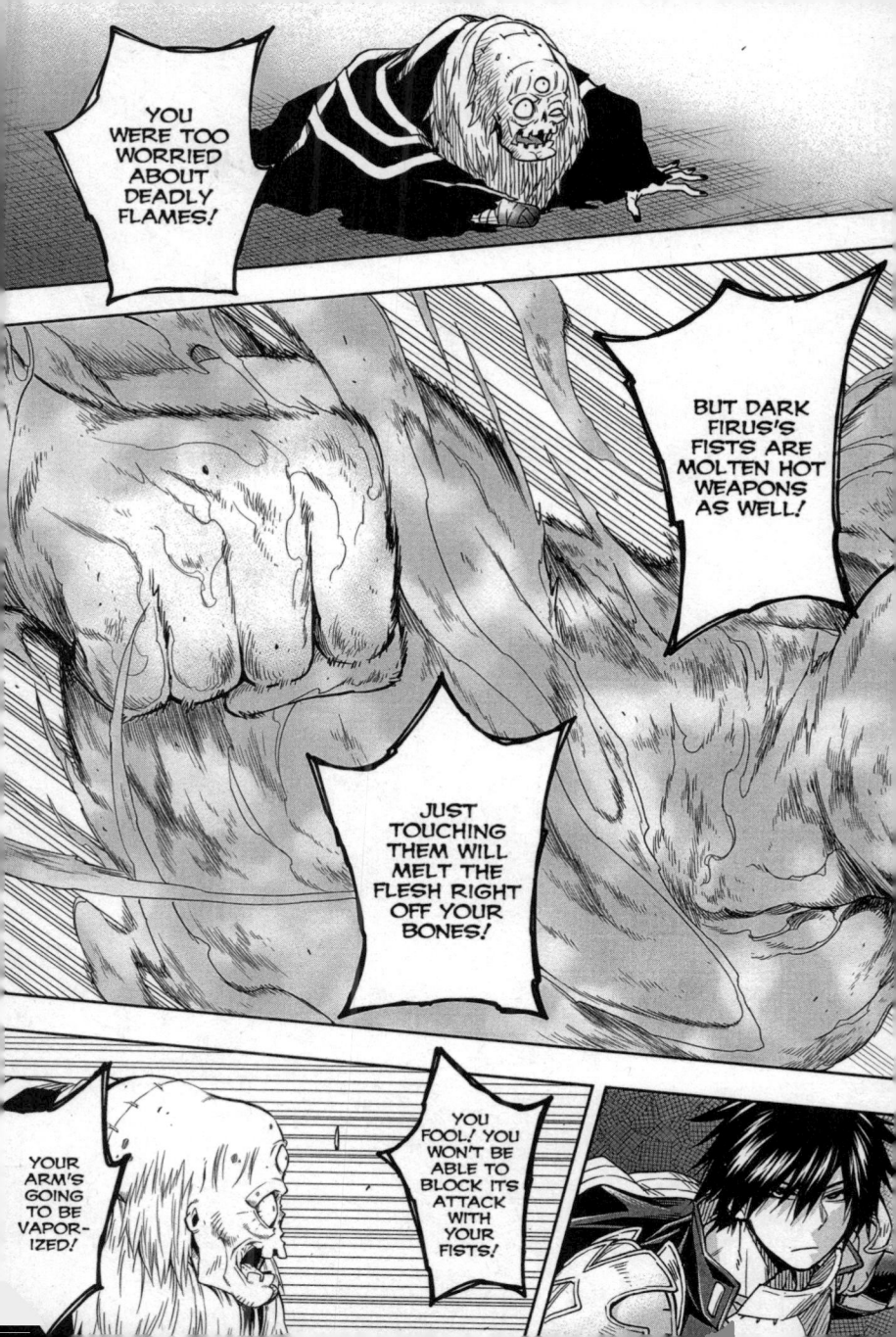

GO
(BAM)

GOOOOOOOO
(ROOOOAR)

HE ISN'T WRONG.

IT BREAKS THE LAWS OF MAGIC THEORY.

SO HOW IS THIS POSSIBLE!?

THAT BANGLE...!

BAKI
(CRACKLE)

BIKI
(POP)

NO ...!

NO...!

NO...!

NO...!

HE CAN'T POSSESS BOTH!

THAT CAN'T BE! FIRE MAGIC AND ICE MAGIC ARE OPPOSING ELEMENTS!!

BUT NONE OF THE WEAPON OR ITEM SHOPS AROUND HERE HAD SUCH A RARE...!

OH!

A MAGIC BANGLE! NOW IT ALL MAKES SENSE!! HE DOESN'T HAVE TO BE ABLE TO USE ICE MAGIC IF HE HAS THAT, SINCE IT FUNDAMENTALLY DOES THE SAME THING!

IS THAT AN ITEM THAT GRANTS ICE MAGIC!?

W-WAIT...

YOU DID, DIDN'T YOU, SEIYA!?

KOKU (NOD)

SYNTHESIS!? DID YOU USE SYNTHESIS TO CRAFT THAT!?

GOCHAA (CLUTTER)

ごちゃあ

BUT WHAT IN THE WORLD DID YOU COMBINE TO MAKE THAT...?

...ICE... + I USED A NORMAL BRACE-LET... WELL...

BUT IF A FEW HAIRS CAN HELP GET US OUT OF THIS PINCH, HE CAN HAVE ALL HE WANTS!

I HAVE MIXED FEELINGS ABOUT THIS!

HE USED MY HAIR AGAIN ...!!

...AND, OF COURSE, SOME OF YOUR HAIR.

GOSO (RUSTLE)

THIS ISN'T THE ONLY ONE I CREATED EITHER.

BYA
(FWOOSH)

WOW! IT'S LIKE A MAGIC TRICK.

SU
(SST)

OF COURSE, I MADE SPARES AND SPARES FOR THE SPARES AS WELL.

A DARK BANGLE AND SO ON.

A HOLY BANGLE.

A LIGHTNING BANGLE.

ANYWAY— YOU CAN DO IT, SEIYA!

PHYSICAL ATTACKS WILL WORK ON IT NOW!

AND THIS WAS ALL THANKS TO THE NUMEROUS STRANDS OF HAIR LYING AROUND YOUR ROOM.

JUST HOW MUCH HAIR DID I LOSE!?

AM I GOING BALD!?

IM-POSSI-BLE...!

DON'T TELL ME HIS ATTACK POWER EXCEEDS DARK FIRUS'S DEFENSE AS WELL!?

AM I ... LOSING TOO MUCH HAIR...?

i found a few dozen hairs lying on the floor in my room after just five minutes, making them the perfect item for Synthesis. I've already lost four hundred thousand hairs!? I am legit worried about my future.

HE WAS SUPPOSED TO HAVE ZERO CHANCE OF WINNING...!!

WHY...?

WHAT THE HELL IS GOING ON...?

HOW...?

HOW DID HE DEFEAT THAT MONSTER...!?

NO.

NO.

NO
...

ズル
ズル
ZURU
ZURU (SCOOT)

NO...!

I BET YOU'RE FEELING STUPID NOW FOR TELLING US HOW TO WIN!

THAT'S ONE-IN-A-BILLION TALENT RIGHT THERE!

BISHI (POINT)

ビシ

YOU SEE THAT!?

YOU'RE THE PERFECT HERO, AFTER ALL!

YEAH, I'M SURE YOU WOULD HAVE!

I WOULD HAVE FIGURED IT OUT SOON ENOUGH, REGARDLESS.

SORTA CUTE VERSIONS OF THE DEMON GENERALS I DREW WHILE WORKING ON THE STORYBOARDS.

DEATHMAGLA

GREATER DEMON

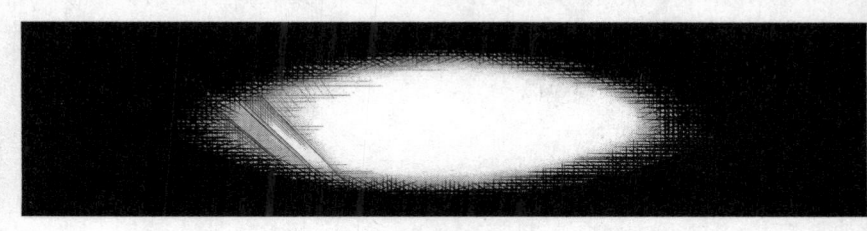

THE INN IN SEIMUL.

...!

WHERE AM I?

HA
(START)

PACHIN
(POP)

KOKURI

KOKUKI
(BOB)

CHAPTER 11
BAG CARRIERS

NAH, I'M FINE.

I'M SORRY, MASH. DID I HURT YOU?

I REALLY... DON'T FEEL ANY PAIN AT ALL...

IT'S STRANGE, THOUGH...

YOU WERE RIDDLED WITH WOUNDS.

DID YOU HEAL ME?

IT TOOK ME OVER AN HOUR TO HEAL YOU.

BAN (BAM)

...I'M SORRY. I OWE YOU ONE.

OH...

UM...

THANK YOU... FOR SAVING ME.

BOSO (MUMBLE)

SO THE MUSH-ROOM'S FINALLY AWAKE.

WHAT !?

SEIYA? LET THEM REST A LITTLE LONGER.

MORE IMPORTANTLY, I HOPE YOU TWO ARE READY. IT'S TIME TO GO.

UM... "IT'S TIME TO GO"...?

MASH JUST WOKE UP A FEW SECONDS AGO.

SO...

SO...

MASH...

YOU WERE RIGHT.

IT...IT REALLY BECAME CLEAR TO ME THEN.

YOU TRULY ARE ON ANOTHER LEVEL THAN US.

IT LOOKS LIKE THE TRAUMA FROM BEING TORTURED BY DEATHMAGLA AND DARK FIRUS IS TOO DEEP.

GU (SQUEEZE)

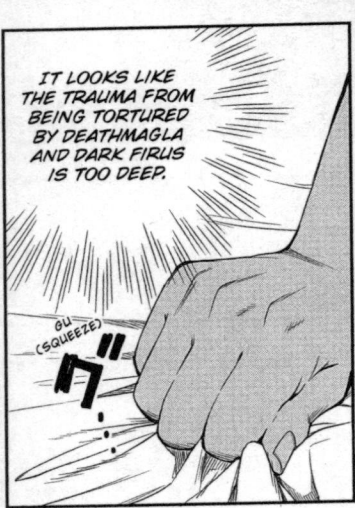

WE WOULD JUST GET IN THE WAY.

SO...!

...BUT STILL DECIDED HE DIDN'T WANT TO COME WITH US...

THERE'S NOTHING I COULD SAY TO CHANGE HIS MIND EVEN IF HE DID OVERCOME THE TRAUMA...

BUT THE TWO DRAGON DESCENDANTS WILL BE JOINING AS PLANNED, SO I GUESS ALL'S WELL THAT ENDS WELL.

ER...THIS ISN'T YOUR TYPICAL HERO PARTY...

ELULU! SHOW SOME RESPECT! CALL HIM MASTER!

HEE HEE! ♪ THANKS, SEIYA!

HA HA...GO AHEAD... I DON'T MIND...

I AM A GODDESS, YOU KNOW...

SQUEAK! SQUEAK!

RISTIE

NO GOOD?

RISU: JAPANESE FOR "SQUIRREL"

THANK YOU TOO, RISTIE!

"RISTIE"? YOU MEAN ME?

"DRAGONS' DEN"?

IS THERE SOMETHING SPECIAL THERE?

OH! YOU'RE TALKING ABOUT THE DRAGONS' DEN, RIGHT!?

ANYWAY...! MASTER, THERE'S ACTUALLY SOMEWHERE I'D LIKE TO TAKE YOU!

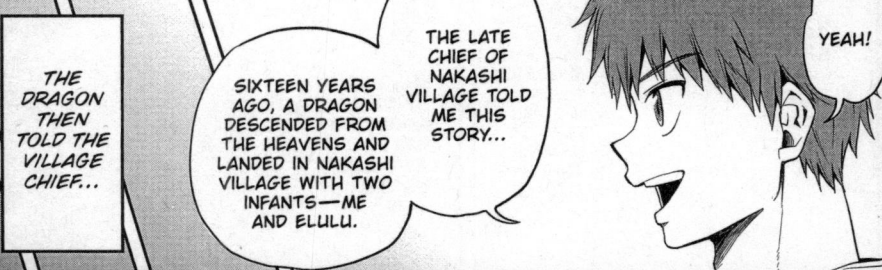

THE DRAGON THEN TOLD THE VILLAGE CHIEF...

SIXTEEN YEARS AGO, A DRAGON DESCENDED FROM THE HEAVENS AND LANDED IN NAKASHI VILLAGE WITH TWO INFANTS—ME AND ELULU.

THE LATE CHIEF OF NAKASHI VILLAGE TOLD ME THIS STORY...

YEAH!

When the Hero appears, go to the Dragons' Den and break the seal. There, the ultimate weapon to vanquish evil awaits.

SO WHAT DO YOU SAY!?

These children, rich with the blood of the dragon, shall join the Hero who has received divine revelation and protect Gaeabrande from evil.

...

WE HAVE TO GO GET IT!

SEIYA! DID YOU HEAR THAT!? THE "ULTIMATE WEAPON"!!

I HAVE TO MAKE SURE I'M PREPARED TO FIGHT DRAGONS JUST IN CASE.

NO. I NEED TO TRAIN IN THE SPIRIT WORLD FIRST.

I FEEL KIND OF BAD FOR HIM...

BUT I JUST SYNTHE-SIZED A PLATINUM SWORD-PLUS...

YEAH! THERE AREN'T ANY BAD DRAGONS!

M—

MASTER, WAIT! DO YOU PLAN ON WIPING OUT MY PEOPLE !?

ER...DON'T WORRY ABOUT THAT RIGHT NOW. LET'S JUST GO CHECK OUT THIS DEN!

AND YOU'RE COMING WITH ME.

ANYWAY, I'M GOING TO THE SPIRIT WORLD.

I CAN'T BE SURE UNTIL I SEE FOR MYSELF.

THIS SANCTUARY IS AMAZING...!

IT'S SO BIG! EVERYTHING LOOKS LIKE A WORK OF ART.

WOW!

HEY, RISTIE...! THIS IS WHERE ALL THE DEITIES LIVE, RIGHT!?

LOOK AT THE FLOWERS IN THAT VASE! I'VE NEVER SEEN ANYTHING LIKE THEM!

I'M GONNA GO—

MUNZU (GRAB)

ELULU! LOOK AT THE GUY OVER THERE WITH A HALO OVER HIS HEAD! IS THAT AN ANGEL!?

RISTARTE, LONG TIME NO SEE.

HESTIACA
Goddess of Fire

MY...!

MY NAME IS ELULU! IT IS A PLEASURE TO MEET YOU!

UNLIKE CERCEUS, HESTIACA IS A LOVELY, SWEET GODDESS!

IT'S SO NICE TO SEE YOU AGAIN!

GREAT.

ELULU'S IN SAFE HANDS WITH HESTIACA.

NOW LET'S FIND MY NEXT TRAINING PARTNER.

WHAT BEAUTIFUL RED HAIR YOU HAVE. HEE-HEE... WE'RE TWINS.

THERE'S NO NEED TO BE SO NERVOUS. I WON'T BITE.

HM...

A GOD STRONGER THAN CERCEUS?

I CAN'T THINK OF ANYONE...

BUT A STRONG DEITY WHO WOULD SPAR WITH SEIYA?

THE SPIRIT WORLD'S A BIG PLACE, SO I'M SURE THERE ARE PLENTY IF YOU LOOK FOR THEM...

I-I'M SO SORRY!

AH!

DON (BUMP)

MAYBE I SHOULD GO ASK ARIA FOR HELP...

HM...

GUI (GRAB)

EEK!?

THE HERO IS OVERPOWERED BUT OVERLY CAUTIOUS 2 END

The Hero Is Overpowered but Overly Cautious 2

THE HERO is OVERPOWERED BUT OVERLY CAUTIOUS 2

ORIGINAL STORY: **LIGHT TUCHIHI**
CHARACTER DESIGN: **SAORI TOYOTA**
ART: **KOYUKI**

Translation: **MATT RUTSOHN** ✳ Lettering: **BARRI SHRAGER**

THE HERO IS OVERPOWERED BUT OVERLY CAUTIOUS Volume 2
© Koyuki 2019
© Light Tuchihi, Saori Toyota 2019

First published in Japan in 2019 by KADOKAWA CORPORATION, Tokyo.
English translation rights arranged with KADOKAWA CORPORATION,
Tokyo through TUTTLE-MORI AGENCY, INC., Tokyo.

English translation © 2020 by Yen Press, LLC

Yen Press
150 West 30th Street, 19th Floor
New York, NY 10001

Visit us at yenpress.com
facebook.com/yenpress
twitter.com/yenpress
yenpress.tumblr.com
instagram.com/yenpress

First Yen Press Edition: July 2020

Yen Press is an imprint of Yen Press, LLC.
The Yen Press name and logo are trademarks of Yen Press, LLC.

The publisher is not responsible for websites (or their content)
that are not owned by the publisher.

Library of Congress Control Number: 2019953328

ISBNs: 978-1-9753-1408-8 (paperback)
978-1-9753-1409-5 (ebook)

10 9 8 7 6 5 4 3 2 1

BVG

Printed in the United States of America